I0630392

WOLF'S BLIND

BOOK SIX OF THE NICK LUPO SERIES

W.D. GAGLIANI

Copyright © 2015 by W.D. Gagliani
ISBN 978-1-63789-156-8
Macabre Ink is an imprint of Crossroad Press Publishing
All rights reserved. No part of this book may be used or reproduced in any manner
whatsoever without written permission except in the case of
brief quotations embodied in critical articles and reviews
For information address Crossroad Press at 141 Brayden Dr., Hertford, NC 27944
www.crossroadpress.com

First Crossroad Press Edition - 2025

Praise for *Wolf's Cut* and the Nick Lupo series

"Gagliani has cemented his place in werewolf legend with a muscular and smart series that deserves a much bigger audience..."

- HorrorWorld

"*Wolf's Edge* is an exciting page-turner full of suspense, mystery, and thrills. Don't miss it!"

- The Horror Zine

"Gagliani has brought bite back to the werewolf novel..."

- James Argendeli,
CNN Headline News Book Lizard

"In *Wolf's Bluff* Gagliani once more proves that werewolves are scary as hell. The book is fast, vicious and thoroughly satisfying."

- Jonathan Maberry,
Bram Stoker Award-winning author of
The Wolfman, Patient Zero, Rot & Ruin,
and *The Dragon Factory*

Dedication

Once again, as always, I'd like to dedicate this book to my Mom and Janis, who make it possible with their love and support, and in memory of my Dad, who lived some of the adventures that have found their way into my scribblings.

Acknowledgments

Great thanks are in order to: co-conspirator and collaborator David Benton—the Alpha of Beta-readers who also suggested the title, editors extraordinaire Geoff Brown (Cohesion Press) and Jonathan Maberry, Tony D'Amato of The Gun Store (Las Vegas), all my many friends and colleagues (you know who you are), and Don D'Auria (whose patience is now beyond legendary). Also the hard-working crew of the Oak Creek Starbucks at 8880 South Howell, who furnish me with a friendly office away from the office.

I'd like to again acknowledge the stories my grandmother and parents told me of their childhood in Italy 1943–44, under German occupation and Allied bombing, as well as the war's aftermath. Some of those stories, experiences and locations have made their way into this novel, as well as the previous two, *Wolf's Edge* and *Wolf's Cut*, albeit in greatly altered, fictionalized form.

This time out I also would like to acknowledge the timeless work of Edgar Froese and *Tangerine Dream*…I've been a fan of all their eras, styles, soundtracks and "projects" since about 1977, especially their Virgin and Blue periods. I've just reached 71 recordings in my collection. This novel was written mostly under the influence of *Tangerine Dream*'s synthesizer explorations. When I wrote this note, I didn't expect it to end this way, but as of January 20, 2015, I must add with deep sadness: Rest in peace, Edgar Froese, and thank you for decades of music. Travel well—you already know the soundtrack by heart…you wrote it. And the legendary Chris Squire of Yes, who left us much too soon. He was the heartbeat of Yes and so my musical world shrank once again. Onward through the night, and into the heart of the sunrise…

Author's Note

The real Eagle River is located in Vilas County of northern Wisconsin. The real Milwaukee is located in the far southeast corner of the state on the shores of the great Lake Michigan. As always, I have altered these places as needed (geographically, socially, and with regard to local city and police department organization) in order to suit my purposes. All characters in these alternate versions of Eagle River and Milwaukee are either fictional or used fictitiously and in no way resemble their real-world counterparts. However, some things will always be true. If you drive up into the North Woods from Milwaukee, especially after dusk, you might notice lean shadows keeping pace with you just outside your view inside the tree line. And later, if you look up you might see the moon's silvery sheen filtering through the swaying treetops. Don't roll down your windows—and never, ever stop the car on a dark, lonely road...

blind (*traditional definition*): unable to see; sightless, *Also*: unable or unwilling to perceive or understand

From Wikipedia: blind (in *Poker*): a forced bet placed into the pot by one or more players before the deal begins, in a way that simulates bets made during play. Also, kill blind is a special blind bet made by a player who triggers the kill in a *kill game*

blind (in *hunting*): a cover device for hunters, designed to reduce the chance of detection

Prologue

Berlin Underground
The Führer Bunker, April 1945

The SS guard showed him into a waiting room deep below street level, so far down that the almost constant shelling was barely audible through the several meters of concrete. The reinforced staircase had taken them below the corner of Wilhemstraße and Voßstraße not far from the partially destroyed Reich Chancellery, and into the main underground complex.

Occasionally a small amount of dust was shaken from the corner molding above him, but otherwise he might have been in any doctor's waiting room. It was comfortable, but sterile. He waited patiently on the black leather armchair.

He had all the time in the world. Or so he liked to think.

A hardy, handsome man with leonine salt and pepper hair and a serpentine burn scar on his left cheek, his fingers lightly stroked the "Spezial-SS" flashes on his collar, the lightning bolts woven through a silver wolf's head, a rare insignia but one feared by those who knew enough to be afraid. He straightened his immaculate black uniform and absently flicked imaginary dust off his coveted *Totenkopf*—death's head—sleeve diamond insignia.

The bombardment was inaudible except for an occasional blast that might have been a thunderclap.

When the inner door finally opened and a beautiful but frightened Aryan secretary herded him inside, he expected to see the same Führer he had seen the last time he had visited the *Wolfsschanze*, the Wolf's Lair in Eastern Prussia. But that had been over a year ago, and the Führer he saw now sitting behind a desk that dwarfed him was harried, sleep deprived, and more than a little glassy-eyed.

Benzedrine, he thought. *Not the first hit today, either.*

In fact, the inhaler was on the blotter next to a stack of black files, right where the Führer could reach it whenever he needed it.

Obergruppenführer Helmut vonStumpfahren, forced away from his own underground headquarters of the SS Special Units Division below the destroyed length of what had once been a beautiful Berlin thoroughfare, fidgeted in front of the utilitarian desk, a far cry from the elaborate one he had sat across not so long before.

Indeed, Adolf Hitler seemed a pale imitation of himself of himself.

VonStumpfahren was certain he knew why he was here. And he itched to leave as quickly as possible, for the Götterdämmerung Projekt—although it had reached amazing heights—would no longer be completed, at least not in any way anyone had predicted. But he knew the ashes would give birth to another project, Hydra. He spied the Götterdämmerung code name stamped on the top file of the stack sitting before the Führer, who finally looked up as if he hadn't heard the general's arrival.

"Your reports are of great interest to me, General," said Adolf Hitler, tapping the top file folder. "I knew when it began that you would bring our plan to successful heights."

VonStumpfahren nodded his thanks. He should have stood and saluted, probably, but this Führer was weary and seemed uninterested in the same formalities he would have embraced only a year before. The General sensed what was coming. He watched the great man's eyes.

"Now we must use it to prolong the life of our beloved Reich, General. You have learned much, according to your report. The experiments have worked. The path is clear ahead of us."

VonStumpfahren took a risk. "But Herr Führer, is it not too late? The Soviet devils are at the gates—beyond the gates, really." A nearby shellburst knocked dust off the ceiling as if to reinforce his point.

Hitler waved an impatient hand at him. "Of course, of course, all is lost *here*. But there are other places, other battles. The war is long. Your Werwolf Division is still producing results, is it not?"

Yes, but it's a losing proposition, he thought.

He said, "Most assuredly, Herr Führer!"

What he also didn't say was that his own plans were shifting by the day. Plan *Hydra* was about to begin, and he wasn't sharing this with the Führer. He understood that the Führer's plans and his might intersect, but VonStumpfahren's reward would be financial as well, not merely political or philosophical. He had decided that politics and philosophy didn't pay for the lifestyle he had adopted.

"I have watched some of the film of Schlosser's secret work that was shared with me over the last few months." Hitler's eyes gleamed, though it was impossible to tell whether it was excitement, or drugs, or...insanity.

And then Adolf Hitler said: "You will make me into a *werwolf* now."

Part One

Chapter One

Lupo

He'd been sitting in the dark, feeling every ache in his body. The last few days had been tough and he wasn't as young as he used to be.

In his hands he held an H&K MP5A3 submachine gun with the stock retracted.

His elbows rested on the desk and he felt the blotter under them, wondering how recently his father had done the same, rested his arms on the desk and perhaps lowered his weary head.

Lupo had hoped Ghost Sam would keep him company, but the Indian was nowhere to be seen or heard.

Maybe he's had enough.

Lupo was grateful, more grateful than his generally unreligious attitude usually allowed.

He was grateful that Jessie was home safe.

He thought of the raids he and his friends had managed to pull off, those hellfire raids. He'd turned Reaper missiles meant for him on his enemies. The few mobsters who'd survived were likely on the run now. He would have to clean it up. Time had been bought, but good people had paid the price.

Charlie Black Bear, his ally from a while back, had paid the ultimate price. Lupo hoped there was something to that afterlife fantasy, because the big guy deserved to be at peace with his family in some version of paradise.

But Lupo himself doubted it.

His mind wandered. The darkness was conducive to introspection and analysis. Who had warned the occupants of the drone command house, and where had they gone to ground? The thought that the group that called itself *Wolfclaw*—they had a limited imagination after all!—was still out there, still active, and still seeking to fulfill its nefarious agenda…it was almost more than Lupo could handle.

The padlock rattled gently in its hasp.

He stiffened, his heart suddenly pumping faster.

His muscles tensed and he grasped the MP5 more tightly, finger brushing the trigger. Only a tiny amount of pressure needed. A full 30-round magazine. He aimed the suppressor directly at the door.

Goddamn it, now he would know who had been dusting—and using—his father's files. Who'd been pulling strings, making Lupo dance from afar.

The door opened on its oiled hinges. There was a square of light from the hallway, a dark figure standing in it momentarily then stepping inside. The door swung closed behind the figure and the light disappeared, then Lupo heard the sound of fingers scrabbling for the switch.

There was the hiss of inhaled breath as the overhead lamp went on and revealed Lupo and his leveled submachine gun.

"Surprise," Lupo said. His finger was squarely on the trigger.

A rugged, elderly man stood inside the doorway, startled but not terribly surprised at all. He wore khaki pants and a heavy sweater under a blue North Face vest.

"I wondered when you would find me," the elderly man said.

Lupo detected a slight accent. He said nothing.

They stared at each other for an endless minute. Then the older man spoke again, quietly.

"My name is Corrado, and I knew your father and grandfather."

Lupo felt his head spin. The gun in his hands was suddenly beyond heavy. The muzzle sagged downward as if strength had seeped from his wrists into the desk.

Besides the impossibility of the moment, something else flared in Lupo's head like a lightning migraine. The wood-holstered blade tucked in Lupo's boot seemed to grow hot next to his skin, almost as if its magic had been reversed.

If this was indeed the partisan Corrado, he had to be ninety-one or ninety-two.

But he looked barely fifty-five or sixty.

Lupo gripped the MP5 harder and brought it to bear, but even as he did he knew it was the wrong choice.

The overhead light winked out, and Lupo squeezed the trigger.

Click.

Again: *Click.*

The empty metallic sound was like an explosion in the artificial quiet of the insulated unit.

Lupo expelled his breath explosively. *What the fuck?*

In the darkness, Corrado sighed. "I suspected you would shoot first and—what do they say?—ask the questions later. I took a precaution and removed the firing pin."

"You bastard—"

The overhead light went on again.

Corrado said, "You will want to check the firing pin on the, how do you say, the *throw-down* piece in your ankle holster, too. I knew you would not use your service gun to try to take me."

"Fuck!" Lupo instinctively reached down and felt his baby P290RS Sig, which he'd carried as back-up to the off-book H&K submachine gun. *Nice to know the fuckin' guy's predicted my every thought.* It was still there, but useless.

Of course, he had his dagger. He could still…

But no, the moment had passed. The moment in which he might have lost his explosive Lupo temper and gone for the blade.

This Corrado had outplayed him somehow.

How the fuck did he manage to sabotage my weapons?

Now he had to sweep his place. He could kick himself—maybe Corrado had bought his way in when the damage was being repaired after the raid? That was one angle he hadn't protected against.

"Yes, well maybe now we can talk instead of kill each other, no? Can you keep yourself from drawing that blade in your boot, at least until we are finished? Yes, I can sense it, which is not supposed to be. Many things are not supposed to be, yet they are. You, for instance. Me, as well. As old as it is, that blade still carries my DNA, this I would bet." He stopped, tried a slight smile. "Can we dispense with death for a few moments and talk about your father?"

Lupo swallowed but his throat rebelled. He set the useless submachine gun down on the table with disgust. How had he allowed that to happen?

The guy had been in his house! But then, since the shootout in his place, he'd had work done on his walls and windows. Perfect opportunity for someone to gain entry and…commit sabotage. He wondered briefly if the rest of his arsenal had been compromised.

Definitely a rookie mistake not to have checked.

But then, a voice in his head whose sound he had squelched, suddenly found the volume it needed and began to nag him. *How did you think you were going to hide the aftermath of a shooting in the middle of a storage facility?* There were cameras mounted at various locations. How would he have managed to outplay the requests for digital video that would show him and DiSanto arriving, and this Corrado later, and then the removal of the victim's remains?

All in all, Lupo reluctantly admitted to himself finally, he had gone off on an emotional vendetta he could barely have explained, let alone forgiven. He'd had to do so many things against his will, against his ethics, against his own code—hell, against his own morality. He'd covered up so much, dragged so many with him into the dark…he'd known it was all wrong. He hadn't told DiSanto what he planned here tonight, hadn't shared the contents of the gym bag he'd carried.

Now, faced with this smooth and charming opponent and too many unanswered questions, he felt lost. He considered forcing a Change and letting his Creature out to slug it out with this new player, but the question of the man's age held him back.

He has to be a werewolf.

And if he was, wouldn't he have been Frank Lupo's sworn enemy?

Lupo's head spun. His father was becoming a greater enigma than he had ever imagined.

"These files?" he said, cocking his head at a row of cabinets. "You and my father?"

Corrado nodded grimly.

"Yes, but not in the last few years. Then only myself."

"After my father got sick?"

"Before. He was weary. He was...disillusioned. He was ashamed of what we—*he*—had done, in a way. Not because of the monsters. But because of how it had hardened him against his own family." He gestured at a stack of storage boxes. "May I sit, or will you attack me?"

The man's salt and pepper hair was movie-star perfect, as was his chiseled jaw—definitely the jaw of a younger man. His eye color was difficult to discern in the poor lighting. That was a clue...

"Sit," Lupo said, not making any moves. Corrado hadn't lived so long without developing advanced survival skills, after all.

Suddenly Lupo wished Ghost Sam would show up, but it was just him and Corrado and his father's ghost, as manifested in the handwritten files.

Goddamn it, I'm Hamlet.

Rabbioso

"Fuck you!" The words were mashed by the broken teeth and blood in the guy's mouth.

Joe Rabbioso chuckled. The guy was tied up like a sausage to an uncomfortable chair, beaten, ribs cracked and broken, couple fingers twisted at odd angles. And still he refused to tell them what he'd been doing, cozying up to Marina.

"Are you sleeping with her?" Rabbioso waited for the words to stop echoing in the meat freezer, then smacked the guy across the face again, because the guy started to say "Fuck you!" again. "Are you? Because you're either fucking her or trying to get something out of her, you asshole, and when I warned you to stay away you gave me the finger. Let's see you use that finger now, you miserable piece of shit." His voice had become a hissing whisper.

The guy was spitting out blood and crud, coughing. Maybe he'd choke to death before Rabbioso got what he wanted. Maybe not.

Let's see.

A couple of the boys had picked up the scumbag at Sonny's (real original naming, that one!) and scraped him off the bar late last night. Marina had just left. They'd been on the two of them since Rabbioso had issued their orders—*when she's gone, bring him to me.* They had done so, with maybe a little too much enthusiasm—the guy had some rib damage and bruises blowing up on his face by the time Rabbioso left his usual restaurant and met them here, behind the butcher shop.

Another cliché, eh, Gus?

The old Don, who hadn't been so old, had lived his life like a never-ending string of mob movie clichés (except for the porn addiction, that was something new but appropriate to the Vegas Vibe), and Rabbioso had started to change that since he had taken over the Bastone family, but even he had to admit that having a butcher shop you could take a scumbag to, after hours, and pop him into a walk-in freezer...and maybe out the back door in slop buckets...even he had to admit that sometimes that hit the sweet spot for a new boss who hadn't quite garnered the respect he deserved.

Rabbioso had been forced to defend his takeover bid with tooth and claw, literally. He had caused a couple pretenders to the crown to disappear, though they had tasted good. He had gone old school with a couple and hired out hits like in the movies, a little cloak and dagger to keep the traditionalists happy. Gus had surrounded himself with traditionalists, but they sometimes had their uses.

And then there was Marina.

She was the old Don's freewheeling daughter. Ha! *Freewheeling* was putting it mildly. Rabbioso had brashly married her in a fit of...of what? Bad ideas? Totally masochistic tendencies? Why the hell had he thought he could control her? He knew her father the Don never had been able to, and now that the idiot Don Bastone had been reduced to a frail old-before-his-time invalid by that fuckin' cop Lupo, now he sure as hell couldn't control her. Rabbioso thought he could manage to muzzle her, at least for a while, with that mumbo-jumbo at the altar, but he'd been wrong. Very wrong.

And he'd been annoyed enough that now he was handling some of his own wetwork. Well, sometimes it paid to keep his hand in, and it helped with the younger guys who respected an up and coming head of family who could still kick some ass on his own.

Marina had hopped a plane heading back home to Milwaukee right after meeting this guy. She'd barely told him she was planning to do that, but it turned out she'd had a ticket for a week. Having to deal with her and her moods made him angry, although when she was in the mood the sex they shared was mind-blowingly kinky and satisfying. Gave him a boner just thinking about her mouth on his cock, her tongue in his ass, her body splayed backwards and upside-down on his, and...all that other stuff. People thought that *Fifty Shades* crap was kinky—they had no fuckin' idea.

Yeah, dealing with her made him angry, especially when she wasn't within reach to keep the underlings from forgetting that, as her husband, he was now the Don, like it or stuff it.

He *was* angry. He was fucking pissed off.

And he was in the mood to prove it.

Rabbioso punched the guy right in the classically beautiful Italian nose, his big diamond ring tearing up the guy's skin and bone and turning the center of his face into a gushing mass of hamburger.

The guy screamed, and Rabbioso stopped him with another fist in the mouth.

Careful now, or he won't be able to talk.

He only needs to say a few words.

No, fuck *you*, thought Rabbioso.

He was running out of kindness and patience, and the wolf inside was getting hungry.

As he beat the guy to a pulp, he finalized the fun idea that had been rolling around in his head the last few days of his healing period. He was still thinking about it when he heard the words he wanted to hear whimpered from the ruined pie-hole, then shed his clothes and pissed on the bastard before forcing a change. The guy's eyes widened in shocked terror, even distracting him from the pain he felt everywhere, but he remembered how to scream, all right, when the wolf in the room suddenly went for his belly and ripped it open like a Christmas package.

The wolf's growls blended with the ragged screaming and reached such a crescendo that even Rabbioso's closest lieutenants, who were relegated to guard duty in the hall, cringed and mouthed prayers they didn't normally believe in.

Lupo

They faced each other across the desk.

A communist desk, they would have joked at the precinct. It was one of those Sixties manufacture drab, battleship-gray metal desks that weighed a ton. *They were sure enough sixty-year-old government issue, but ours — not the Commies'*, Lupo thought. So how had that flip occurred? How had an accepted symbol of the enemy's aesthetics turned out to be designed and built by the so-called free ones, the capitalists? Wasn't there some kind of irony at play?

Lupo thought about that.

Irony abounded in his life, that was certain. He hadn't had the best relationship with his father, true, but he'd thought of his old man as a dull and boring example of the older generation, a stern and taciturn man whose worldview rarely matched that of his son.

So Nick Lupo had spent a large part of his adult life avoiding his father, partly because for some reason his father had kept a silver-loaded Beretta shotgun in the house. Nick had given that gun a wide berth and his father hadn't been pleased that his son was so uninterested. But Frank Lupo was a more complex man than Nick could have imagined, and only after his death had his mother told him much of the history the elder Lupo had always skirted. That, and a letter from his grandmother that revealed more secret history. Some of it very painful, indeed.

But this?

No, he'd never expected to learn his father had not only hunted Nazi werewolves during World War II, but that he'd continued pursuing them after the war. That even as Nick had grown older and become a cursed werewolf, his father had secretly been involved in something greater than himself, something that tied him to his youth and the war.

There had been some travel young Nick had never understood. And more.

These files.

This jury-rigged office in a storage unit, intended to be kept a secret for over a decade, maybe twenty years—and probably designed to be rolled out in a van in very little time if necessary.

And Corrado.

Who as a young partisan commander had known Frank Lupo when he was barely out of his childhood.

Corrado. Who sat across from him now, handsome and much younger-looking than he should be.

Lupo knew what this meant. But the question was—had Frank Lupo known? From Nick Lupo's earliest days as a monster, he had understood—perhaps subconsciously—that his father hated monsters. Young Nick had had no idea his father was aware of the existence of werewolves, but even now he remembered vividly the night Frank Lupo and the neighborhood men had hunted down the monster who had been Andy Corrazza, the neighbor boy whose bite had cursed Nick. Only much later had he realized that the neighborhood men had *all* been aware of the truth behind the legends.

"So now what?" Corrado finally spoke in his slightly accented English. "You want we stare each other to death?"

"There are other options," Lupo said. He felt the Creature inside itching to break free and challenge this unknown intruder. He sensed the silver blade in his boot almost lusting to feel the night air and taste Corrado's blood. He stared at the older man and saw a reflection of his own father.

"Yes, there are many options as you say, but one is we can just talk. Man to man."

"Monster to monster," Lupo muttered.

"It is what *you* see, but it does not have to be this way."

"All right." Lupo sighed. *Let it play out.* "Did my father know?"

Corrado smiled thinly. "Know what? About the wolves? Oh, yes, he learned the worst way possible. But you already know that he knew."

"Yeah, he killed his own father. With this blade in my boot."

"Or its twin, yes. And he became a fearsome werewolf hunter, and later a hunter of men too. Perhaps it was his destiny."

Lupo's tone was steel itself. "And what was *your* destiny?"

Corrado shrugged, a thoroughly Italian shrug. "I'm still learning that. At the time, first we fought for our country and for our families. The Germans were a scourge on us, and—how do you say?—we had a grudge. They had created a small army of werewolves, too late to change the war, but they used them against us..."

"And anyone else?"

Corrado cocked his head, obviously pissed at being interrupted. *Good,* Lupo thought. "The Werwolf Division is known to have existed," said Corrado, after a theatrical sigh. "But most do not know—they would not believe—that at its center were real *uomini-lupi,* the werewolves. I am sure some Russians on that front probably saw them and were forced to learn fast, or they died. Some Americans, most of them died. Is this what you mean?"

Lupo nodded. He'd been curious. "Go on."

"Okay." Corrado continued, "You know about the German scientific approach to everything, right? Well, they went ahead and decided to scientifically create not only the werewolves, but also to, to build in a strength, a resistance to silver—the one thing that can really stop a werewolf. This was a top-secret operation that took place at several concentration camps, using inmates as test subjects, as prey, as reward..." He stopped, his eyes hardened. "These were the worst of humanity, you understand. These men were the representation of evil."

Lupo nodded grudgingly. He had pieced together some of the information, but Corrado—well, he had lived it. Maybe it was best he hadn't just killed the bastard.

"All right, I get it," Lupo said. "I know enough about the Germans and their connection to Wolfpaw, descendants of some of the Werwolf guys, yada yada. But what about all this?"

"I am getting to this," said Corrado with a sigh. "You young people, always in a hurry. Yes, your father and I did not stop the hunting of werewolves when the war was over. You are aware that your father traveled quite a bit after the war?"

"Yeah, he was at sea a lot."

"It began accidentally, but it became a way to catch and kill more escaping Nazi werewolves. Nazis were fleeing to South America in droves using what are called *ratlines*, indirect routes to other countries. One of these went from Germany to either Rome or Genova, the seaport as you are aware, and then from there to South America. By God, even the Vatican helped the bastards escape, or at least some factions in the Vatican. My old friend Father Tranelli, who knew your father very well, he was mortified that fellow priests and cardinals helped them escape, and he knew from first-hand…well, he was the reason my brigade had the sacred blades, which were removed from the secret Vatican repository, and which you now have."

Lupo was fidgeting. "All right, this is all very interesting, but what does it have to do with me now?"

"Again, be patient. Every road leads to Rome, eh? In this case, Genova, your parents' hometown. And mine." Corrado stopped to think. "I will edit the story, somewhat. On one of those ratlines, a route to Buenos Aires by freighter, went a young man named Franco Lupo and a priest named Tranelli. It was not meant to be, but young Franco was very persuasive…"

"I'll bet," Lupo said with a snort.

"Yes, your father was a hard, stubborn man, and he had been that way all his life. He had seen too much, done too much by the time he was in his teen years, and he hated the Nazis — and the Nazi werewolves even more. Much happened on that voyage, three weeks at sea, much that would change your father. But the important fact right now is that eventually he learned some things that would have changed the world, if they had been exposed. But we were young, you see, and we were mostly alone. We did some damage, but we could not…"

Corrado's eyes blurred with sudden tears. "We could not do it all, and we already dealt with things people would not believe or understand. We—we did the best we could."

"Why did anyone not help you expose these ratlines? Why did you have to go it alone?"

"In Argentina, Juan Perón himself welcomed Nazis to their new land! He recruited them, in a way, gave them what do you call it, the *welcome mat*. The government itself wanted these monsters, so how could a couple ragtag partisans who had never been outside their villages stop them? In the end we only made a small dent, and created a mess for them, but it was not much, like the speed-bump, no?"

Lupo glanced around the jury-rigged office and its many cartons of files. If this was a *dent*, then he could barely imagine how much had slipped by.

"Go ahead," he said. "I might as well hear you out."

"Yes, you might as well," said Corrado wistfully.

Chapter Two

Franco Lupo

On the Freighter Zeniča, crossing the Atlantic Ocean
December 1945

The *thrum thrum thrum* of the venerable engines had become a living heartbeat, a continuous vibration he felt through the freighter's steel decks and bulkheads and, indeed, through every piece of furniture bolted or otherwise affixed to the cabin he called home from the moment they sailed from the port of Genova.

The landmark medieval lighthouse, rebuilt in 1543, had slid by quietly as Franco watched from the ship's railing, bundled in his new bulky coat which once belonged to an escaping German officer of the Waffen SS.

An officer who had been a werewolf, making good his escape from Europe.

He'd watched the square lighthouse obelisk and felt nothing. His father was dead. His mother was safe, but he could not return home. He should have shed a tear, but he was too hardened now to feel sadness. Soon the tugs had the steamship far out enough on the Mediterranean that the hawsers had been withdrawn, salutes exchanged, and the ship was on its own.

Night had fallen quickly then, and soon the twinkling lights of the northern Italian coast reminded him that the blackout was over. Tonight, as for the last few months, there would be no danger of bombers homing in on factories. Allied planes now landed safely at local airports as occupying forces flew in to bolster the wedge that would soon face the Soviet juggernaut now massing in Eastern Europe.

At least, that was what the newspapers said. Franco barely paid attention, for the sole focus of his self-imposed mission had led him to this ship, to inject himself into a routine transaction that somehow involved diamonds, ocean passage for Nazis, forged papers, and a destination to a far South American shore. The previous recipient of the transaction had begun to decay in a steamer trunk stored in Franco and the priest's adjoining cabin.

Have to do something about that soon.

Franco was very pragmatic for a compactly-built lad of fifteen, and his eyes had seen more than most people's, even given the ravages of the last half-dozen years of war, surrender, occupation, and pitched fighting visited upon the Italian populace.

He watched as the inordinately gay lights of other ships began to disappear.

Soon the dark violet-black of the steely ocean water was joined by the slowly dropping line of the darkening horizon and the two became indistinguishable to the untrained eye. At that point only the shrinking lights to his right indicated where land ended and the dark vastness began.

Franco's knees shook slightly at the thought that below him the unseen chasm was growing in depth with every mile the heavy oil-burning engines put between the ship and the dwindling coastline. He rarely felt fear, but the depths below him were a vast and dark unknown that somehow affected him.

He heard a rustle beside him and his hand brushed the wooden grip of the Beretta M1934 pistol under his coat. But it was only the old Jesuit, Father Tranelli, shivering under his own commandeered foul-weather jacket.

"They'll serve some kind of dinner for passengers and crew soon," said the priest softly. "We should eat, pretend we belong." He was still holding his head where Franco had laid him out with the heavy pistol earlier. There had been a little blood, but Franco had cleaned him up and the bruise was almost invisible on his scalp, half-hidden by his thinning, unruly white hair.

"We had better watch what we say," Franco said. "We don't know who else is aboard. *What* else is aboard." With Corrado not here, Franco had easily slipped into the role and taken charge of the operation.

Tranelli shuddered visibly, made the sign of the cross, and spit out into the darkness.

Chapter Three

DiSanto

He was driving around aimlessly, a feeling in his belly that he couldn't define—and that he couldn't deny, either.

There had been that meeting with Stephen Barton, the Homeland Security guy everybody hated. DiSanto got along well with him. He guessed he got along well with just about everyone, which maybe said he was bland. But he just wasn't an in-your-face kind of guy. Not like Lupo, whose temper had a short fuse.

Of course, now that DiSanto knew Lupo's secret—had known for a while, actually—he could guess where some of that barely checked anger came from.

And he thought *he* had problems.

He had learned first-hand that being a werewolf was a messy problem at best, most often canceling out any of the benefits. Lupo told him he'd hated his *condition* from day one, whereas DiSanto thought he could work with it. Kind of like a super-power, wasn't it, and the problems be damned.

He made a turn that he would have said was random, but as soon as he made it he knew where he was going.

Damn it.

It was like being a prisoner.

Except he was feeling like a prisoner everywhere. At home, his wife had changed and now looked upon him with suspicion and—was it *dislike*? Was it really? If it wasn't for his kids, he'd stop trying to repair the broken limb that had been their marriage.

Then there was work. He was a good cop, maybe even a great homicide detective, and partnering with Lupo had been the best thing ever in his career. They complemented each other's strengths perfectly. But since the DHS task force had come along to follow up on the bus shooter investigation, which was going on in multiple cities where the shooter had done his deed, ever since then there'd been a wedge placed between him and Nick. Barton had taken him for the task force, while Lupo had wanted out because of his troubles and now he was *really* on the outside.

Thing was, DiSanto was committed to the shooter investigation. He wanted to catch the lunatic and stop him as much as anyone, but he had begun to suspect something else was going on there. The DHS might have been the sensible agency to deal with this potential terrorist, but more and more it seemed the work of a wandering lone wolf, not a cell, and ever since the first day they'd arrived, Barton's interest seemed to lie elsewhere. But where?

"Nick Lupo, that's where." He pounded the wheel lightly. His temper didn't usually peak with destruction.

Yeah, Barton seemed to be keeping one eye on his weak-tit task force and the other on none other than Nick Lupo, who seemed oblivious.

And now that Ryeland had just introduced everyone to the new IA head, Lieutenant Roman, DiSanto thought *he* had some sort of agenda featuring Lupo. But it was separate from whatever Barton was doing, like two different orbits. Ryeland, bless his New Orleans origins and subsequent outsider status, didn't seem to be aware of it. Or maybe DiSanto had just become a paranoid wacko himself, seeing conspiracies everywhere.

So he felt like a prisoner at work, just unsure as to who would torment him more.

Here, on the street, he knew where his torment came from.

It came from *her*.

If he hadn't realized it earlier, he knew now that he was heading for the trendy Third Ward—where he and Lupo often grabbed some lunch or dinner—because *she* lived there. At least, she lived there when she wasn't muckraking, stirring up trouble, investigating, instigating, or even anchoring the local evening news, which she still sometimes did as a guest fill-in with unnatural star-power.

Heather Wilson lived part-time in the Third Ward, and he might as well admit that he was going to drive past her building to see if he could catch a sighting.

Or?

"No or," he muttered. "No goddamned or."

But he knew better. He knew what his loins said, and his loins were calling him a liar right now. Just the thought of her statuesque Amazonian frame, lean and muscular like a wild animal, and that fine face, with its perpetual pout and sarcastic eyebrow movement...just the thought of how she looked made him hard. In fact, he was so hard that he shifted in his seat right then, wishing he could relieve the pressure.

What am I doing here?

Don't be a fool, you know *what you're doing here.*

He wanted to see her. And more.

Yes, and more.

His wife's face was prominent in his memory, but as often was the case she had an angry smirk written on her features as she criticized and insulted him for some slight, real or imagined, some infraction of a rule written only in her mind. Her features had caused him to fall in love with her, but they seemed to twist with hate so much these days that he often thanked his lucky stars for the worst shifts, the double shifts, and the overnight investigations or stake-outs. These days he felt like a prisoner both at home and away, and his wife was his jailer.

And so Heather Wilson's face and body pushed his wife out of his mind's eye and he turned down Heather's street, his groin a painful knot of deliciously dangerous tension.

Yes, she was like Lupo. *A werewolf.*

It made her all the more exotic.

He was beginning to understand Nick's problems a little better. There was one guy who'd had more than his share of crap to put up with, and not all of it was his fault, either. But DiSanto could see where his own problems were largely of his own making.

Christ, Nick, how do I get myself out of all these prisons?

Lupo

Lupo said nothing for a long while.

"You are still angry."

"What do you think?"

Corrado sighed. "I understand, but this is not, eh, a normal thing, right? We have been forced to do things that are not good, when you look at them, but they *must* be done. We have taken approaches that are not approved by everyone, but they *must* be done. You can be angry, but this is not all about you, Nick Lupo. This is about elements that can hurt everyone and everything you love, and the whole world."

"Sounds good, but…"

"Listen, you did not know there were other werewolves at one time. But logic should have told you there could be. After all, you were one. And just because you did not know *they* existed, let me tell you, they most certainly knew about you."

"What about my father?" Lupo was impatient with this soft-spoken but very dangerous man.

"Yes, what about him? He was a fireball, an avenger, an executioner. But he loved you very much."

"Yet he never said anything to me."

"Yet he did not. He protected you. He had no idea you had been dragged into his world. You see, he had walked away years before."

"Why?"

Corrado smiled bitterly. "Because of me."

"What did you do?"

The old man's voice wavered. "It was a betrayal of sorts, though I did not think so at the time. But it came later. For a long time we hunted Nazis, and then we hunted Communists, too."

"Communist werewolves? Christ!"

"There were never as many, and they paled in comparison to the numbers that came from Germany and Austria. And the Nazis had their experiments, to make them impervious to silver."

"And are they?"

Corrado nodded. "Some are very close. Some less so. But there is a strain…you should know, you are one of them."

"What?" Lupo looked at him sharply. "Me?"

"Yes, but it's not easy to explain."

"Try."

"All right. The Nazi experiments yielded some success. Wolfpaw was born in those early days. Then one day a shaman from these parts showed up in Europe, someone you have heard of…"

"Joseph Badger? Are you kidding?"

"No, it was he. He found a way to bridge the Nazi strain and the one that came from here, and also from the distant past. Through Badger, your friend Sam Waters was involved, and his son. And you know the rest."

"How did Badger run across the Vatican blades?"

"My friend, that is a story for another day. Joseph was terrified at what he had wrought, you see, but he was also a savior in a way, because he had to bring the strain to you."

"He *had* to?"

"In a manner of speaking. I think there was destiny. Remember your grandfather and what happened to him. Your father may have unintentionally obstructed the way things were meant to be, when he killed Giovanni Lupo. I came to respect Giovanni as a brave soldier, but when he was wounded by a German werewolf and became one himself, there were only two ways it could end. Either he could pass it down to his line, or it could be interrupted. Franco killed him and interrupted it. Your father was a forceful man. He was both a loose cannon, yes, but also a brave and fearless fighter. He killed many monsters. You see here some of the fruits of his work, and mine. We were a team."

Lupo lowered his voice. "Did he ever find out about me?"

"I think he may have suspected. He became withdrawn, did he not?"

Lupo nodded.

"He would have blamed himself. And he would have been conflicted, no? His whole life he killed werewolves—monsters. How could he not kill you, and yet how could he? He had already faced that dilemma."

"And he had killed his own father..." Lupo shook his head. "I just don't understand..."

"It was an act of love. He set his father free from the, the being of a monster, do you see what I mean?"

Lupo shrugged. "Dead is free, but only in a way."

"Indeed."

"So what else do you have to say?"

"Give me a chance. We wanted to keep you out of it all, but we have learned that the, what do you say, *the big picture* is beyond even our comprehension."

"We?"

"Yes. When the time is right, you will see."

"This all sounds ominous..."

"It should. Wolfpaw was but a spire of the iceberg."

"Tip?"

Corrado made an annoyed gesture. "Yes, *tip*. And Wolfclaw was behind them here, entrenched within your military, and the logical outcome was that they would attempt to complete their own agenda."

"The drone program?"

The elder man nodded. "They jumped the gun."

Lupo thought of DiSanto and his penchant for using every cliché available to him. "So who dimed them out?"

"*Dimed?* I don't know this term."

"Made a call, threw them under the bus, like that. Someone got them out of the drone house before we got there. Most of them, anyway."

"Yes, there is another shadow behind the shadows. It is always like this." He looked at his watch. "So you see, you—no, *we* both—are part of something much larger than what you have here." He gestured at the files that surrounded them. "One thing you must remember, they have made layers, like a cake, yes? No matter how you...*scrape* at one layer, there is always another. But we cannot do this all at once. We will meet later. Your abilities are unique, and now you know much that you did not even recently, so we want to bring you into our group."

"When?"

"Soon. I will be in touch."

Lupo wondered why he let the old man leave, why he accepted what he was told. But the files told much of the story, and he knew deep within that what he'd heard was the truth.

Still, trusting the old man after what he had done...that wasn't very likely. Lupo shook his head. *No sir, not trusting at all.*

Corrado

He watched Nick Lupo fade wraith-like into one of the dark pockets between storage buildings.

During the war, he would have believed he was watching some sort of German beast, Lupo the man's muscular frame hiding something fearsome and monstrous that needed to be killed. But then Corrado Garzanti had himself become one of *them*, and his whole world had changed.

Perspective was a bitch. It really tended to kill simple ideology. For some years his ideology had lain dormant. But then he had reconnected with Franco Lupo despite the bad things between them, and then his affliction had become an asset even though he sometimes thought he should just kill himself and be done with it.

Now he was wired into a whole new mindset, let alone ideology.

He waited a minute before taking the cell out of his pocket and bringing it up to his ear. *Love all this tech stuff,* he thought. *Wish we had had it in the war.*

"Did you hear it all?"

There was a voice at the other end. The line had been open. The voice spoke now.

"I can fill in the parts you did not catch," Corrado said, gesturing even though the other could not see him. "Later."

He listened.

"Yes, I know. We are at a dangerous point. But it's too late to be...subtle. Is that the word? I cannot pronounce it well. Yes, too late to be subtle."

He listened again.

"It can be done, of course. Do you think—?"

He nodded as if that gesture could be seen, too.

"I agree."

He looked at where Lupo had disappeared as if there might be some magic answer.

Lupo

He hadn't slept most of the night. After working on his neutered guns, he had turned in, trying to avoid the acid taste in his mouth from being so easily checkmated. Now whenever fatigue started to claim him, his brain returned to the storage locker and Corrado.

And what he had learned about his father.

The Nazi werewolf hunter.

As in: My father was a hunter of Nazi werewolves.

He'd learned some of the information from the old letter his mother had given him before her death, the one written by one of his grandmothers, but actually speaking to a man who knew so much about the Lupo family during and after the war—well, that was indeed eye-opening. And it was keeping his eyes open now, damn it. He couldn't help but think of Corrado as a strange link to his own past. All in all, he was glad he'd been unable to follow his gut and just kill the man. Too much to learn, too many mysteries, too many characters he knew nothing about.

Lupo tossed and turned, his thoughts dark.

Every sound in his apartment, or out in the hall, or in the walls and somehow transmitted to him through his trashed pillow made him itch to bring the H&K submachine gun closer. He had replaced the firing pin after meeting with Corrado. Thing was, if he was still in the crosshairs they could kill him any time—a drone strike on his building would do it. They could spin a web of lies about it afterwards: gas leak, furnace explosion, smoking in bed (even though he didn't smoke), anything at all. They'd done it before. They had commandeered military drones away from the official pilots based in Nevada and used them for their own purposes on occasion, careful to not overdo their reliance on the lethal hardware. The drone's command software included targeting based on the fortuitous marriage of spy satellite and face recognition technologies, which allowed almost anyone to be personally targeted.

Outrunning drones was possible, but not easy. Not easy at all. And getting harder by the day. He'd learned the hard way. He knew he'd just been lucky. And luck wasn't anything to count on for consistency.

He wasn't afraid of them, whether they were Wolfpaw or whatever name they chose to call themselves now, but he didn't want innocent people in his building hurt because of him. Maybe they were still called ODESSA, like in the Frederick Forsyth novel he had read as a kid, *The ODESSA File*. Pretty good movie, too, with Jon Voight. His father had seen it but made no comment, even though the legendary Simon Wiesenthal himself was a consultant.

What must have gone through his head when he saw the movie about Nazis escaping from Europe? When ODESSA wasn't even close to being a figment of someone's imagination, because most of the research had been accurate?

Did Frank Lupo burn with hate for Nazis or werewolves?

It was clear why he had hated the Nazis, but his own father—Nick's grandfather—had become a werewolf. And Frank Lupo had killed his own father in cold blood.

Was that why he had a Beretta shotgun always loaded with silver shot and slugs?

Would he have killed me *too, if he had found out I was turned into a werewolf by our neighbor, Andy?*

Lupo thrashed on his bed. He couldn't turn off his brain.

If Jessie had been there, she would have known how to keep him from thinking too much.

Although Jessie was becoming a part of his many problems now. Not intentionally, not maliciously, but her impassioned request for his bite reminded him of all those cheesy horror movies about vampires tortured by the choice of whether they should turn their lovers or not.

Why are they always vampires, he thought. *Why not a goddamn werewolf once in a while?*

Christ, I'm rambling through a catalog of my complaints and fears when I should really be sleeping.

What was Corrado doing right now? Lupo wondered how much he could trust the old man. No matter how slick-tongued he was—the man had made a living deceiving pretty much everyone around him, and those he didn't merely deceive he killed.

Lupo had no doubts about Corrado's efficiency as a werewolf killer. He could see it in the hooded eyes, the set of the jaw. He could only imagine how efficient he had been as a young partisan commander, ruthlessly killing Germans by slitting their throats or stabbing them from behind. But what kind of mental tug of war went on in his head?

The sad thing, Lupo realized, was that Corrado's tug of war probably didn't look much different from his own.

Christ.

So now should he suddenly believe everything Corrado had to say? How in the hell was someone who had been barely out of his teens during the war now involved in whatever high stakes game these cult-like secret groups were playing? How much was Corrado *not* telling him? And not for the first time he wondered how connected the old man might be, and connected to whom.

He was still tossing and turning, which was the way he often chewed at cases until answers popped into his head, primarily when he stood in the shower under a hot spray after a night of little sleep.

He still couldn't figure out how Corrado had been able to find his firearms in order to sabotage their firing pins. Lupo had gone to great pains to devise ways to hide them, such as hinged flaps hidden under bookcase shelves.

With sleep still eluding him, he padded into his living room after pouring himself a generous shot of B&B. He licked his lips at the thought of the sweet golden liquid and the way it would burn pleasantly down his throat. It was a go-to in the chilly North Woods air, but he enjoyed it anytime, anywhere.

He glanced through a shelf of movies on DVD. He was streaming a fair amount of his entertainment now, but he still had a good-sized collection of titles, some of which had belonged to Sam Waters. Like the complete Bond series. Lupo passed over those now—too many memories.

My problem is I'm too sentimental, he thought. *At least, too sentimental for a werewolf.*

He sipped the golden brandy and Benedictine concoction and let it pleasantly warm his belly. It might help him settle down and sleep. Half-heartedly, he searched through his streaming choices on the large television, but nothing caught his eye.

Fuck, I can't even have insomnia the right way...

He had the sound turned way down, preferring the company of his own thoughts, so he was able to hear a soft rustle out in the hall.

Almost no one else could have heard it through the armored door, which he had installed after the recent raid on his place, but his hearing was much better developed than non-werewolves. It was one advantage of his condition he had learned to use.

Silently, he made his way to a set of bookcases and reached under a shelf, flicking a latch that opened one of his hidden flaps, which dropped down and put a compact Sig Sauer into his hand. He'd replaced the firing pin in this gun, too—Corrado had been thorough during his exploratory visit.

He kept the pistol decocked with a round in the breech, ready to fire, so now he carefully padded toward the door. He'd had the door made especially for his purposes, without any gaps between it and the casing and jambs which meant it wouldn't reveal his shadow to whoever lurked out in the corridor.

It might be a neighbor, though whoever it was he had stopped making the rustling sound.

Lupo undid his locks as quietly as he could, then pulled the door open in one quick move. He leapt into the hall, pistol extended in front of him as he checked both directions.

There was no one there.

But there *had* been someone there, Lupo would have bet on it.

He considered forcing a change so he could bring to bear the Creature's olfactory senses, but it was too dangerous to give the wolf this much freedom in a building hallway when anyone could come up the stairs or off the elevator, or open a door. He tried to taste the air, to see if he could pick out the intruder's scent, but it was hopeless. He'd had limited success getting full use of the Creature's nostrils when not wearing his wolf shape.

He tucked the gun into his waistband and retreated into his place.

Was he just overreacting, or had someone lurked outside his door?

Goddamn it, what the fuck is going down?

He really could feel it in the air—something was gathering, preparing to strike. A new plot, a new group, a new enemy. An extension of the old enemies. Could he ever get out? Could he ever kill the snake's head, or would he forever chop off chunks of the body just to watch them regenerate as his own foot had done?

He flung his hands up in a sort of Italian shrug of surrender, a gesture typical of his family's heritage, and muttered a Genoese curse. He couldn't pronounce it as well as his father, but it amused him.

He froze, his hands still extended outward.

He stared past his right hand and noticed something he hadn't seen before. Either a spider, or some kind of a black fleck in the corner of the cornice molding, just below his ceiling. It didn't move, so maybe it wasn't a spider. He went closer and then he could see it didn't have legs, so not a spider.

What the fuck?

Lupo pulled one of his dining chairs closer, a solid old mission style piece that would hold his weight. He positioned it under the fleck, which still didn't move, and popped lightly up onto the seat. His face only inches from the fleck, understanding washed over him. And rage.

Fuckin' thing was a pinhole. *Wanna bet there's a camera behind it?*

From his perch he examined the other corners he could see. Diagonally across from him was another fleck.

The bastard Corrado had video-bugged him, literally.

In a rage he made his fingers into claws and pulled off the corner, which was just loose enough, stripping a section of the cornice right off the painted drywall. With a tug he ripped the whole section from the wall and tossed it to the floor. The camera was tiny, but he saw the reflection of his lights on the lens.

He flipped off whoever was watching or recording, feeling the heat of his rage.

Still fuming, muttering to himself, he grabbed a hefty MagLite from a closet and went on a hunt through his place. He found five more flecks, and behind each one was a camera. A long screwdriver smashed each of the lenses, then reached in and pried out the electronics. He snipped the wires, although he was sure they were all sending to a hidden wireless transmitter. At some point he would bust through and yank that, as well.

Rage washed over him yet again as he thought of the times he and Jessie had had sex in various rooms. *And positions.*

Jesus fuckin' Christ.

He had a bone to pick with that fucker, Corrado. Another bone.

He wondered if it had been Corrado out in the hall, or one of his henchmen. Or if it had been someone else. Another player in this game?

He was starting to lose track of all the players. As soon as he neutralized danger from one direction, something arose from another. He'd have to warn Jessie—maybe Corrado had bugged her place, too. It wasn't unlikely, if the old man wanted to keep an eye on him, literally.

Lupo stalked the halls of his place. It wasn't so much that he felt violated, as people do when they've had a break-in, though he certainly did...no, it was that he felt weak and easily outplayed, outmaneuvered. *Predictable.*

And he began to see that the game board was expanding. Whenever he thought he knew the boundaries, the limits, the way it all fit together, that was when something would show him he was wrong, he really didn't understand anything.

Finally the emotional and physical fatigue slowed down his anger enough that he thought he should try to rest.

After shutting down the TV and lights, he lay the Sig on his nightstand and flopped onto the bed, ready to fight the demons of insomnia.

Surprisingly, he slept. In his sleep, he thought he saw the lurking visitor. But by the time he awoke the image was gone from his memory.

Colgrave

Whenever she ran into Nick Lupo she felt a strange tug between cool and warm that left her puzzled and exhausted. Ever since she'd witnessed what he was, never mind the existence of more of them, she had a hard time reconciling between how attractive he was and how utterly frightening at the same time.

It was a complicated feeling, but then she'd always had complicated feelings. Her father's abuse had scarred her, but the scars hadn't become obvious to her until she'd been in a position to help others. She had developed a reputation for being a by the book cop, but no one really knew how off the books she had sometimes been during her career, and how not at all by the book she was willing to go when the situation called for it.

But clearly Nick Lupo far outstripped anyone or anything she had been involved with.

Well, maybe not that thing with the Serb's gang that Rich Brant had dragged her into…That had even caused nightmares, some of which lingered still. But even those nightmares paled in comparison to those she was having these days and nights. Lupo starred in most of them, as both monster and hero. She took comfort in knowing he wasn't the worst of what she had seen.

Now when she saw Lupo she experienced that bizarre blend. She felt her eyes narrow and her lips tighten in an almost angry set, but she also felt tingles down below, and it was the tingles that worried her.

So when Nick Lupo knocked on her office door, the whole gamut of feelings splashed through her chest and she had no idea whether she smiled, grimaced, or gave him a blank look.

"Do you have a minute?" he said, leaning in.

She hadn't spotted him coming her way. If she had, maybe she would have closed her door. But then again, no, she knew she wouldn't have.

"Yeah, come in."

His bulk seemed to dwarf the doorway, but it was only an illusion. There was a physical quality about him that belied his generally low-key persona. He looked like he could be a bully, but he wasn't. Although when pushed, he had a temper that could erupt like a volcano from his old country.

Right now, Nick Lupo looked weary and fatigued. Like a man who couldn't sleep.

She waved him to one of her chairs. He closed the door, then took a pile of folders from the chair and placed them on a corner of her cluttered desk. Finally he sank into the chair, dwarfing it.

"What's up, Lupo?" She shivered a little, saying his name. She knew what it meant, in his old-country language, and she knew once the images she'd seen came back to her they wouldn't stop coming.

And yet…

And yet now she wanted to talk to him. She'd avoided it since the *incident*.

She had barely managed to paper over the mess they'd made, by lending her Organized Crime task force stamp to the confrontation up in Eagle River, even though she hadn't been there. Her report, combined with Lupo's and those of a couple of malleable members of the tribe's elders council, had done the trick for Ryeland, but just barely.

So now that her career seemed to have been saved, she did want to talk to him. But she felt fear—in some cases knowledge can be a terrible thing, and she rather wished she didn't know some of what she did.

DiSanto didn't seem to have a problem with Lupo, or the knowledge that his partner was an impossible creature. *Monster!* a little voice in her head shouted, but she quelled it. No, DiSanto had seemed rather lackadaisical about it all at the drone house, as they referred to the mysterious structure they'd destroyed in their paramilitary raid. Although DiSanto wasn't looking too good these days either. In fact, if she thought about it Lupo's partner *had* been looking a little ragged himself after they'd returned. Were they working on something, some other off-book deal? She shrugged off the thought.

Lupo was weighing his words before answering, like a man who'd learned to be careful. She paid close attention to him.

"So, how are you dealing with…you know? All the stuff you witnessed?" Lupo leaned forward in the chair. He seemed forever poised to act, but she sensed that it wasn't always the best thought-out action. *The law of unintended consequences?*

She barked a laugh. Couldn't help it, really.

She said, "This is the first chance you've had to ask me?"

"I'm letting things set."

"Like an omelet? You sure did break some eggs—I'll say that much. It's a wonder I'm not locked up screaming in some gothic sanatorium."

He chuckled. "Don't go all Irish on me, Colgrave."

"I should go all medieval on you," she said, but didn't smile.

"Yeah, well, it wouldn't be any worse than some of what I've had to live through all my life. So have at it. But when you're done, please let's get on to what we're doing here."

"What are we doing here? I thought whatever we did was the end of things. The Bastone family hierarchy took a hit, the drone people—whoever the fuck they were—are gone, and all is right with the world. Well, not *all*…"

"That's the point, Colgrave. My sources tell me the Bastone family is regrouping. I didn't stop their chief enforcer, our infamous Joseph Rabbioso, from getting away. Wounded, but word has it he's healed up."

"How could that be? From what you said, he was—" She stopped, eyes widening. "Oh, shit, you mean he's—?"

"Yeah." Lupo nodded.

She sighed. "What else?"

"We don't really know much about the drone people, and you guys did a number on the house, so there aren't many records. We got one body identified, thanks to Wilson—"

"The reporter woman we, uh, that we rescued?"

"Yeah. Body was Lansing. He was a high-ranking general— on the Joint Chiefs of Staff."

"Holy shit."

"Yeah."

"So now what?"

Lupo frowned. "So now we have to figure out if this hydra has any more snakes growing." He tilted his head at the door. "But we also have to keep this Homeland Security asshole

Barton off our backs, and this new Internal Affairs guy, Roman, out of my ass. I think he's planning to crawl up there and ream me out with a camera like a living colonoscopy."

"Because of Griff Killian's disappearance?"

"Exactly."

"And *do* you know something about it, Lupo?"

He didn't like it. He made a face. "I might," he said, after a long pause.

"Oh, *Christ*," she said.

"But I didn't kill him," Lupo added.

"Holy fuck, but so you know he's dead…"

"Yeah, and I also know how that looks. But they wanted it to look that way. I just barely managed to get out of that trap…"

Now it was Colgrave leaning forward, intense, sweating. "Do you realize what you're saying?"

"Oh yeah, I realize it. And there's a lot you don't know." Lupo sighed. "A lot, lot."

"Does DiSanto know all of it?"

"He's my partner. I had to let him in. But there are some things even he doesn't know."

"So where does that leave me?" she asked, twisting her lips in a grimace. "Was I ever going to hear any of it?"

"I'm here now, aren't I?" Lupo sighed again. "I figured you needed to hear it from me."

"It's about time." Colgrave caught herself heating up and lowered her voice.

"I know."

"I'm having fucking nightmares, Lupo. Pinpoint headaches. I'm not getting any sleep, and when I do it's like…like…" She ran out of words.

He nodded. "I get that. But you clearly didn't want to talk. I waited until I thought you were ready."

"How did DiSanto take it? When you first told him?"

"We showed him. He took it about as well as he could have. Someone else we knew took it like a punch in the gut. Sat down on his ass like the world had tilted on him."

"Was that the sheriff? What was his name?"

Lupo's face was sadder than she expected. He said, "Yeah, Tom Arnow. He was our first outsider, and he wasn't very receptive. DiSanto was raised on all that comic book, horror movie stuff. I guess he was just better prepared to handle it. You could drop him in the middle of a *True Blood* episode and he'd be able to fit right in. Not Tom." He shook his head, then paused. "What about you?"

"I feel a little like, what did you say, the world has tilted on me. Yeah. But I've been through enough bad shit, I guess, that ultimately I can sort it out."

"Okay," he said. "The main thing, it's dangerous to know me, to know about all these things that have happened. It'll make you a target at some point. Right now, like I said, I suspect that Barton is here not only for the bus shooter task force. Every time I walk past him he gives me the stink-eye. I've caught wind of something going on, but nobody seems to know what. This guy Roman is creepy as hell, and I'm sensing he's going to shake things up. I don't know what Ryeland was thinking, but he might not have had any say...watch out for him."

"You gonna tell me everything?" Colgrave interrupted, fixing him with her intense stare. He wasn't going to walk out of her office without having given her something. No way.

"I got a little time, then I'm heading up north for a day or two. DiSanto's more in with the task force than I am, anyway. It's like they decided to split us up. Isn't that what you do to schoolboys who are just too rowdy together? Anyway, I've got some thinking to do. Some of this stuff goes deep into my family history, and—"

"I have a meeting in a while. Should be my last one to paper over that clusterfuck we were in on up in Eagle River. They want to know what else I have on the Bastone family attempted takeover of the tribal casino."

"Shit, I thought that was done."

"Not quite, but fortunately I have got some stuff, because they *were* moving in—they terrified the board and worse. We have enough testimony and statements to make it all stick pretty well."

"But now they're on the run, right? I mean, we don't have to worry about Bastone." Lupo looked pensive.

"Bastone didn't die, more's the pity. He's in a private hospital and probably will never fully recover. A bunch of his thugs are ashes. Others ran."

"Like that Rabbioso guy."

"I'll put a BOLO out on him, but it sounds like he's a slippery one. Turns out he had some military and contractor background."

Lupo was stunned, and didn't seem to be faking it. "What? No kidding?"

"He's one of…you said he's one of the wolves, right?"

He looked away, as if revisiting the scene of the gunfight. "Oh, yeah, that he is."

"Well, there you go. Some loose ends."

He sighed a long sigh. "Always the loose ends."

Colgrave checked her watch. "Meeting coming up, but I have some time now."

"Me, too."

"So, talk," she said.

And he did.

Marla Anders

The sounds of Christmas played almost subliminally from her office PC's speakers. It was the first *Narada* Christmas album, and even though it wasn't anywhere close to Christmas, she couldn't help it—she wanted the music on rotation year-round.

Maybe it was an atheist's way to marry the religious and the secular in a package that offered positivity and hope rather than anarchy and desperation.

Whatever.

I have to stop analyzing myself.

She flipped the pages of her day planner, spread out on the only flat surface of her desk (after brushing some crumbs out of the way). She wasn't one to use her computer calendar. She didn't trust the police department computer system, figuring they were recording her keystrokes, looking at her browser histories, reading her email, and generally peering psychotically into her business because they considered her business theirs. She couldn't prove it without a lawsuit—and that was probably not enough—so she simply tried her best to bypass the ways they employed to spy on her.

There was probably a bug or a camera in her office, but if there was she hadn't found it yet.

Paranoid much?

Or was she?

She expected her views would diverge from the police hierarchy's more often than they would not, so she had no trouble believing they might monitor her sessions in some way.

She shrugged and continued to flip pages. Marked a page in the planner, then another.

She had several open dates, but hadn't been able to pin down Detective Nick Lupo long enough to get him to sit across from her again.

And she really wanted him to.

He frightened her in some way she couldn't have explained or put into words at all. There was an aura of danger around him, of course. She'd heard the swirling rumors of misdeeds and investigations, and also those of heroics and above and beyond the line of duty acts. The commendations as well as the occasional wrist-slapping. The gas leak that had blown up both his apartment and part of his neighborhood.

Bad news seemed to follow him like one of those proverbial dark clouds.

Yet he was fascinating, and if she had to admit it, there was something very compelling about him. His intense gaze, his serious demeanor sometimes poorly papered over by a crazy and cynical sense of humor. Of course, all the detectives were cynical and dealt almost exclusively in sarcasm, but he was different. He seemed to bear burdens no one could possibly understand.

She was certain he was seeing something, something that should have made her question everything she had ever believed in. Hell, that wasn't new—she often found herself questioning some tidbit of supposed fact. Because she herself knew some things, had seen some things…

But there was more.

Not only was she sure he was seeing something, but she knew she was herself seeing something again, like the old days, and that it had to do with Nick Lupo.

Frustration grabbed hold of her and she smacked the pen down on her desk, from where it promptly bounced off and landed somewhere on the carpet.

"Shit!"

She got up and went searching. The pen was near the door, which she had closed. She cursed again, then went over and bent to retrieve the incidental javelin. As she did, she looked through the slightly open blinds spread across the window near her doorway—down the hall she saw Nick Lupo walk into Sergeant Colgrave's office.

A strange shiver of...*something*...slithered up and down her spine. She wasn't sure what it was, but the thought of Colgrave buddy-buddy with Lupo bothered her in a way the same thought with Rich DiSanto, Lupo's partner, did not.

She wasn't jealous, though.

Ridiculous.

She barely knew the guy. She was a recent hire, a transplant from Cleveland, even though her family had been from nearby. Had inherited him and his problems from the previous psychologist attached to the Milwaukee PD, the guy who had disappeared. What was his name? *Marco-something.* His disappearance was still an open case, getting colder by the day.

She had to wonder about that.

Was anything about Lupo clear *and* completely aboveboard?

She wondered when knowing him was going to complicate her life. At the same time, she wondered when she could sit down with him, face to face. It was a strange dilemma to be in. Her gut told her to run from him, but something about him made her want to be on his side. He seemed to elicit love him or hate him vibes from people.

So what does that mean about how I feel?

She shrugged it off. What about this whole ghost thing? What did it mean?

Her playlist, the whole New Age Christmas album, suddenly stopped in mid-song and restarted.

She jumped.

That was...*weird.*

Then it stopped again and restarted but within a different track.

It wasn't a CD. It was a playlist in her iTunes, and it really wasn't supposed to behave that way.

Then it stopped and restarted within yet another track.

She stared at her PC. Another *message* or a glitch?

She opened her laptop, avoiding the PC altogether, and sent Lupo another email he would probably ignore.

Why? Why was the weirdness starting again, just when she thought it was in her past?

She knew instinctively it had to do with her grandfather, and his whole world—which wasn't *her* world, not really, but it had occasionally intruded on hers. It had been a while, but now that she was here, her antenna was up and receiving, and she had no idea why. It had to do with the new job, and with Nick Lupo. No way to know why, but she thought if she could dig into her past and Lupo's, there would be some sort of connection. That had to be it, didn't it?

All she could do was wonder when it would all be made clear to her.

Part of her wanted to know, but the other part was frightened.

She remembered more than she wanted to.

Much more.

Chapter Four

Lupo

After he had awakened that morning he found he couldn't stop thinking of Jessie and the issue that had grown between them since they'd survived the apocalyptic pitched battle at the Bastone compound.

Make me a werewolf, she'd said while in his arms, shortly after both had survived having been close to dying.

They had retreated to her cottage on Circle Moon Drive after the circus that had been the aftermath of the battle, in which Lupo had managed—not that he was sure *how* it had worked, it had been a fluke—to turn the Wolfclaw drones against the Bastone family thugs had abated for the time being. There would be more questions later, and more lies to tell, but for the moment they had turned to each other...

He saw it as if it were a movie clip, as if he could enter both their heads simultaneously, and now he relived it in that very same way.

She slowly peeled off most of his ruined clothes and when his bruised and battered body was revealed to her she had lowered her face and gently kissed all the places he had suffered one of those bruises or wounds. Her lips caressed his skin and left behind heat whenever she moved on to a new place he'd tried to wreck himself while handling both enemy groups and, at the end, attacking those who would do her harm. She had much to thank him for, and she set about showing him her gratitude, though her own experience had brought her close to torture and death or worse...

She pushed him toward the sofa and even though the air was chilled and normally they would have started a fire in the great old brick fireplace, she set about providing the heat they needed with her flesh and her love. He was exhausted and when his legs touched the sofa he let himself be maneuvered into sitting, lying back into the well-worn leather as she edged closer, sinking to her knees and resting her head on his lap as his hands stroked her hair. They were a mess, but at that moment nothing else mattered and she slowly unbuttoned what was left of her top and slipped it off so her skin could touch his. She felt him respond to her closeness and warmth and she leaned back enough to have room to grab hold of his loosened pants and pull them away from him and down past his ankles. His hands still on her hair, she kissed him through his briefs, enjoying the rough manly smell of the sweat and adrenaline cocktail that had squeezed from his pores.

When his manhood began to rise along with his pent-up desire, stoked by the close call of that day's deadly encounter, Jessie reached under the white cotton and gently but firmly grasped his thickening shaft. He shifted on the sofa and she felt his excitement. His cock straightened in her grip and she started to pump it with one hand, while bringing her face closer to its length. She leaned in and kissed the hardening tip, then licked it tentatively while one hand continued to massage it and the other reached into his briefs and cupped his testicles.

When he groaned, she looked up and saw that his eyes were closed. With a lustful smile, she slowly engulfed the tip of his cock with her wide open lips. She let a string of saliva drool onto his hot flesh and began to suck him slowly down her throat. His hands tightened on her head, mashing her ears and attempting to control her tempo, but she ignored him and followed her own drummer, swirling her tongue below and around his glans, eliciting more groans and a tighter grip. Her lips slid down his slick hardness to its base and she felt him growing even larger inside her throat before sliding most of the way back off him, leaving behind the wet heat-cold of her saliva. When she looked up her eyes locked onto his, and she swallowed him again, her hands tenderly massaging his balls as she worked her lips up and down his length. His fingers were threaded through her hair, guiding her as she pleasured him with her lips and tongue, taking him down her throat until she could feel him beginning to burst. Then she pulled away and smiled when he stared at her in mock horror. But by then she was standing and dropping her ruined jeans around her ankles and kicking them away, and before she could even rip her panties off he had lifted her onto him, sneaking past the thin cotton fabric and finding the center of her pleasure, entering her with one solid thrust. It was her turn to groan as he filled her and began to stroke upward, and she moved with him, both of them rocking on the sofa and making their own heat born of friction and lust, love and need, and a sense of survival to be celebrated, for they had both come close to death.

She positioned her feet on the sofa around him and lifted herself up, almost leaving his flesh behind, but then levered herself down again, continuing the pumping motion as he grasped her body to him and met her with his willing flesh, reaching way up into her so that she felt his girth filling her. Her lower lips grasped him tightly, holding him inside her as he pumped more furiously to fulfill them both. Their lips met first, and then their tongues as she tasted the metallic tang of his residual adrenaline and he tasted both her lust and himself on her tongue. She cried out her pleasure into his mouth as he increased the speed of his thrusting, his shaft spearing her swollen flesh while her nether lips swallowed him whole. When she felt him ready to burst, his shaft hardening even more and the tension becoming almost intolerable, she unstraddled him in one deft move that would hurt her sore body later, and simultaneously knelt between his thighs and swallowed him with her hungry lips, feeling his hot seed spilling in jets against her throat and palate, swallowing rapidly to keep him to herself and sliding up and down to milk his last drops of precious fluid. The she licked him clean, drying his flesh with her tongue as his grunts quieted down and she felt him begin to shrink in her mouth.

He pulled her up onto him again and kissed her deeply then, and they shared their slaked desire until their bodies had ceased to vibrate.

"We really have to face certain death and torture more often," she said, as she nestled her head into his neck. His scent was pleasantly musky, and she thought she caught a scant trace of the wolf, the Creature inside him, which was always not so far below the surface. Especially when they made love, or—more accurately—had animal sex.

"Yeah," he chuckled. "We don't do this enough. And by this I mean get blown up, shot at, mauled, and almost r..." His voice faltered.

"You can say it," she whispered. "Raped. I was almost raped by those two thugs. If it wasn't for you, I would have been..."

His face was a sudden blend of sadness and rage. "It makes me crazy that because of me you get dragged into these...things. If it wasn't for me, you'd be a lot better off." He still held her closely, but she could sense he was pulling away.

That Catholic guilt. She often taunted him about it because he'd been raised Catholic, but his parents hadn't been very religious, and at eighteen he had distanced himself from the trappings of his nominal religion. His usual retort was that there wasn't anything wrong in feeling guilt if you had done something to feel guilty about. She always let it go then, because he seemed about to switch from guilt to anger. Nick Lupo was a conflicted soul, if not a religious one. And his triggers were sometimes raw and not so deeply buried.

"Stop saying that," she said gently, trying to get them back to where she wanted them to be. "If it wasn't for you we wouldn't have *just shared — what we just did."* She made a sound with her throat when she said it.

"Did you just purr?" he asked. *"Did you?"* He pushed her head away just far enough to look at her closely, and they both laughed.

"I think I did," she said. *"And I think I have every right, Mr. Lupo. If you treated every material witness like this..."*

"Yes?"

"You'd have more people wanting to give statements, I'll say that."

"LOL," he said, and it was so unexpected that she burst out laughing.

Maybe the moment had been defused. The moment that could have turned dark.

Did she want to go there now? Did she want to revisit what she'd asked him earlier?

And she went there, though she knew it would probably not end well.

"Why can't we discuss you making me a werewolf?" she blurted out. *"If I was, maybe I wouldn't be the weak link that always causes you trouble at the worst times."*

He was quiet a seemingly long time. *"Let me remind you that after that time with the Martin Stewart gang of idiots, it was you who saved me. And it wasn't the first or only time."*

She had a stubborn streak. She knew it, and she forged ahead anyway. *"But that doesn't change the fact that we would be in better position to, to fight these bastards —"* She spit out the word. *"The bastards who want you either dead or strapped to a dissecting table in some madman's lab."* Her voice began to rise. *"Don't you see that you wouldn't have to worry about me as much, and I could be on the same level as them and you, and it would be better for both of us and everyone we know, like your partner. And that cop, Danni Colgrave. And remember what happened to Tom?"*

He winced. She didn't know everything about Tom Arnow. This was dangerous ground.

And the best way to step off the land mine was to blow up prematurely.

So he did. "No, Jess, no! I'm not going to bite you in order to make you a werewolf! I'm not going to take the chance I'll kill you instead, and I'm not going to make you a target for every silver-loaded gunman in the country. I'm not going to—"

"Don't you think a regular bullet would kill me just as dead?" she shouted, falling out of their embrace to lean over him, her control lost, her afterglow dissipated.

"Don't you think I would be better off doing what you do, rather than either sitting at home worrying, or gambling for no goddamn reason, or...or getting myself raped by people who are after you, not me at all?"

And then they'd traded barbs until they had separated and let their night degenerate into grunted responses and cold shoulders. The heat of their tryst had escaped through the walls, and the chill in the air represented nothing if not the sudden feelings between them.

Lupo replayed the whole thing in his head, assuming he'd pegged her thoughts, her motives. He guessed they were the same, both stubborn, both seeing their own point of view as the safe one. He had been determined to talk to either Anders, the psychologist, or Colgrave, his fellow cop. He shrugged off the feeling that it might be a small betrayal, because he needed to talk to somebody, and DiSanto wasn't around. And if he was, he would have just uttered some atrocious cliché.

He had seen the door to Anders's office closed. Maybe she was in session. Whereas Danni Colgrave's door had been open. Even though he had the urge to talk to Anders, and not only because she was attractive (if a little odd), he chose Colgrave. Who was also attractive, if you were keeping score.

In fact, she reminded him of Jessie—but he hadn't really noticed before. A rawer, sharp-elbowed version of Jessie, maybe, but cut from the same cloth—as DiSanto would have said.

And now Colgrave knew his secret, though not absolutely all its elements. But she knew the ramifications, and the implications. She had been more patient than he had expected, however. He could hardly believe it, after she'd seen what happened at the northern Minnesota drone house, where she and DiSanto had rescued Heather Wilson. They'd blown it up after finding it bizarrely empty of most of the Wolfclaw organization, but she'd been strangely willing to go off the books on his behalf. At least for now. He hoped she wouldn't change her mind after thinking about it, and especially after what he had told her.

Hell, Lupo himself still couldn't put it all in focus. And it made his head hurt when he tried. He had become so reactive, so unable to go out there and shake things up the way he was used to on the street.

He had walked right past the empty office Ryeland had given Barton, the Homeland Security guy who was investigating the bus shootings after the horrific last one in downtown Milwaukee. His door was closed, too, and Lupo had wondered again what the guy was really up to.

And that new Internal Affairs head, the mysterious Lieutenant Roman.

No wonder he sensed the sharks circling. He was leaking a whole lot of blood in the water. There wasn't a lot out there to dig up about Roman, or Barton for that matter. How they'd stayed mostly off the grid he had no idea.

He had shrugged slightly, made sure he played up his false limp a little, and headed for Colgrave's office. And he had found himself telling her everything, even some things he had intended not to. It felt good to get some of the shit off his chest, to have someone else to spill it to. Could he trust her? He thought so. Not sure why, but he did. There was something unconventional about her, and it made her a viable...*collaborator*, maybe?

Barton didn't really want him on his task force, but he looked at Lupo like a fisherman sizes up the fishing hole...like, what could he get out of there? But why? Lupo wasn't going to ask—you didn't mess with DHS guys, even if you wanted to, because they could get secret paper and crawl up your ass and spend a lifetime there gathering evidence, and then you could disappear. He didn't doubt that black prisons still existed, despite all the chatter to the contrary—they would *always* exist, because bad stuff always had to be done by someone.

Not that Lupo didn't think he could handle Barton, but if things got to that point he might as well go on the lam and never come back.

He spent some time pushing paper, working on reports both old school and on-line, filing some overdue shit Ryeland had been on him to do, all the while feeling the itch to get out of town.

Sometimes the Creature inside just wanted to roam, to hunt, to romp.

He redoubled his efforts on the routine stuff. Not being on the bus shooter task force meant he could just work on his own cases, and right now pretty much everything seemed to be stalled. With DiSanto distracted, he didn't have a clear way to do anything at all—unless the phone rang and he caught a murder. Fortunately violent crime was down in Milwaukee, if you didn't count Wolfpaw assholes and their buddies doing their sinister thing.

Ah, crap, why think about it? They'd knocked the drone-stealing house out of its foundation and the mob was in full retreat when it came to the casino.

He pushed paper almost gleefully, which was surely a sign of the coming apocalypse.

He saw a bunch of cops and feds head to Colgrave's Organized Crime wrap-up and silently wished her well. *Better you than me*, he thought.

Later, he bothered to check and saw yet another email from Marla Anders, asking him to stop in and see her. Sent right when he was in the middle of spilling some of his guts to Colgrave. She'd been trying for days, but he had managed to evade her sorties. How could he explain that he wasn't traumatized by this stuff? But then again, maybe he should pretend that he was affected—like his limp, which he so often forgot to do.

He thought about it for a while, but the Creature inside him was starting to bounce off whatever passed for walls in there, and Lupo sensed he shouldn't tease it too much.

Anders would have to wait.

He was heading north.

Chapter Five

Franco Lupo

On the Freighter Zeniča, crossing the Atlantic Ocean
December 1945

They were all seated at the two tables that were both referred to as the captain's table in the officers' dining mess hall, the captain himself and the ship's dozen junior officers. The seven passengers didn't represent the entire roster of civilians making this crossing to South America—they heard in the early chatter among guests that there were at least three other passengers who had in true hermit fashion elected to take their meals in their cabins. The galley staff weren't thrilled about it, having to serve the meals while negotiating several pitching companionways whenever the weather turned stormy.

The captain was ill-tempered and glared at everyone from the head of Table One. Half the officers were seated at each large table, and the serving staff—mostly made up of other sailors—was forced to continue moving food in and out of the double cabin from the galley itself, where they prepared and heated up hearty Yugoslav and Czech peasant fare which was representative of most of the crew and that suffered only from occasional lack of fresh ingredients. Otherwise the shipping lines were coming back strong after war's end, and food was actually more plentiful aboard ship than in most cities.

Franco had learned to mask his nerves in public, so even though he wanted to bolt from the social situation—something he had little experience with—the priest had talked him into joining the dinner crowd.

"How else are we going to figure out who is doing what, and which are cursed wolves?" Tranelli had said. "We can only try to guess, and if we don't watch them we'll never know. Besides, we're both underfed."

Franco agreed and the priest gave him quick lessons on table etiquette. "You must fit in," the Jesuit explained, "or you'll be tagged a fraud no matter what your passport says."

How many of the diners at the tables were werewolves? How many were simply escaping Nazi concentration camp guards? How many were war criminals? These thoughts had taken hold of Franco, and he had not been able to let go of them. He stared at each in turn, but it was not obvious. Perhaps the only two had been those he and the priest had replaced.

Franco sat fidgeting next to Father Tranelli, who didn't let the tense situation faze his appetite. Franco himself had never seen so much food in one place. Even when living with Corrado Garzanti's partisan brigade, there had barely been enough food on the table at any one time to as much as dent his hunger. His body had grown lean, almost gaunt, during those days. It had been helpful, training himself to require less food, because the retreating Germans were less likely to barter with Italians who might or might not knife them in the back. Indeed, Corrado's men had accounted for a fair number of hungry Wehrmacht soldiers who abandoned caution at the dangled bait of a fresh egg, or fresh meat. Their bodies were routinely rolled down hillsides so they could litter the twisty roads that led out of the coast city, a grim message to the occupiers that their day was done.

Unfortunately, Corrado's men had also taken a terrible toll when the wolves came out at night and ambushed partisan patrols. They, in turn, left mutilated, butchered human carcasses throughout the countryside, their bellies slit open and entrails consumed by ravenous jaws. Many were left at crossroads to invoke the old legends and strike fear in the minds of the partisans. It was whispered that the German Army had created werewolves in a last-ditch effort to shrug off the Allied invaders and turn the war around. The number of victims grew and villagers withdrew their support of the partisans, refusing to provide them even the lean food supplies they had sacrificed from their own tables.

The situation had grown dire and it appeared the German forces, reinforced by the hell-spawn monsters, would succeed in holding off the Allied advance by cutting the throat of the partisan brigades who had been clearing the way.

But then the tide had changed again. Slowly, partisans began to win battles against the Nazi werewolves, and it was all because of Father Tranelli.

Well, not so much the Jesuit himself, but what he had given Corrado's brigade.

Now Franco watched surreptitiously as the Jesuit drank more than his share of the cheap table wine and brutal *slivovitz*, the Eastern European plum brandy. Franco worried about the drinking, which made the old priest much too talkative—and he was now engaged in a theological debate with the ship's first officer, who sat on his other side. The table had settled on Italian as the language of conversation because most of the passengers and officers spoke it well enough. The other table had settled on French and German, so Franco had to abandon the hopes of eavesdropping. His own table was interesting enough, with the captain and most of his ranking officers seated there. He sensed some secretive glares in his direction—after all, he was so young, he must be from a rich family.

If they only knew!

Franco was still biologically a teenager, but the last two years had hardened him and fashioned him into a formidable fighter, one who appeared much older than his years. His eyes had seen much, and reflected the knowledge of the darkness he had faced. One of the Vatican daggers was hidden in his boot, its silver blade shielded by the strange wooden scabbard so werewolves could not sense its presence.

He had used that dagger to murder his own father.

As a boy, Franco had shed many tears in the early days. But then he had directed the sadness and anger and guilt and turned the blade into a weapon of revenge, and Nazi werewolves had fallen under its wicked edge. It was a legacy his father left—even though he had been infected by a German werewolf, he had accounted for many more before being unmasked and banished. One way to identify the wolves at this table, Franco mused, might be to unsheathe the blade and wait for a reaction, but what if they were *all* wolves? No, the priest was right. It was better to tackle them one at a time. And unprepared.

"But you must admit, my dear Kamil, that the war was a catastrophe for many countries, not only mine!" Tranelli said loudly.

"Yes, but your country was one of the instigators!"

"You would dare compare the gentle Italian with the warlike Hun?"

Franco kicked the priest under the table.

His mother used to kick him like that when she wanted to warn him that his father was in a foul mood. At first he had reacted too obviously, which inevitably led to an argument between his parents. Eventually he learned to do it subtly, and now he did the same to the priest. And hoped the priest would not give it away.

The last thing he wanted was to draw attention to them. His passport had been a gift from Corrado, a hasty forgery done when Franco had horned his way into Corrado's group again. Now he hoped that it wouldn't be too closely scrutinized—on Italian soil, it would have passed most cursory examinations. But now that it would be shown abroad, there was much to fear. Customs police from any number of countries might well deduce its bearer was himself an escaping Nazi, an irony that wasn't lost on Franco. To this point only the Captain had seen the passport, when Franco had identified himself as a passenger, but theoretically there would be customs police at the far end of the voyage, though he had been told no one knew for sure how many formalities would be followed in South America. Plus a palm-greasing could avoid close scrutiny of the passport—a lot of that went on. The *Zenič̌a's* captain was an unknown. He was clearly involved in the smuggling operation that helped escaping Nazis, but how much he knew about their nature was anybody's guess.

Franco was a hothead. He would easily have killed the captain and worried about leading the ship's crew later, if at all. Tranelli had stayed his hand.

"If you kill the captain," the priest had whispered once they'd returned to Franco's cabin that first day, "you can't be sure the crew will simply continue to perform their tasks. They might mutiny, if they don't like the first officer. And the officers could very well investigate and, if they determine you are the culprit, clap you in irons until they can turn you over to the authorities." He coughed—he was coughing a lot more as of late, Franco thought—and continued, "My boy, you have to be patient. We know the werewolves are fleeing Europe in various ways, on numerous routes. This is only one, but we can shut it down if we follow the trail."

"Like detectives?" Franco said, smirking. He was a man of action, not investigation.

Show me a werewolf and I'll gut him like a fish and feed him his own intestines.

He suspected this was why Corrado had stuck him with the priest, to keep an eye on him and to keep him muzzled.

But sometimes the priest was the one who needed muzzling!

Right now, Tranelli's debate opponent said, "The 'gentle Italian' caused his share of havoc, my priestly friend. The 'gentle Italian' did not find genocide outside his capabilities, certainly not in Ethiopia…"

"You are confusing Mussolini and his gang of cutthroats with the majority of the Italian people…"

"No, you are confusing a nation of war instigators with a nation of peaceful souls like my Switzerland…"

Franco kicked the priest again, the table masking the movement.

Did the Jesuit mean to get them killed?

"Let us agree to disagree, then," said Tranelli, deftly moving his leg out of range. "Can you pour me another finger or two of that robust red?"

Franco sighed in relief. Maybe drinking would occupy the priest well enough to keep him out of trouble.

"And you, young gentleman, what takes you to the far southern shores?"

It was the Second officer, a rather unsavory individual with a bushy beard and pig-like eyes. He referred to Franco now, having been cheated out of a scene by the priest and his other tormentor.

Franco glanced at the captain from the corner of his eye. He seemed to have turned his head to better catch the conversation. *Suspicious?*

"I am on the way to inspect my father's business interests," said Franco, giving himself the needed self-importance (they would expect it). Inside, he shook with fear. What if they exposed him, right here, as a fraud? What would happen to them, to him and the priest? He attempted to put it out of his mind. "Before the war he bought a ranch in the south."

They'd agreed it sounded plausible enough, and he could be forgiven for knowing very little, as a city boy. He could claim he was there to learn the business.

"Well, boy, you're lucky to be leaving that mess back there," growled the captain.

Franco knew well that the captain was aware he was no innocent, not with the package and cash exchange they'd conducted while in harbor, but they'd gambled that he was only interested in his own financial angle. How much of a stake did he have in the smuggling operation? If they'd guessed wrong, they would be in trouble.

Franco was young, but he understood the possibility that their chain-wrapped bodies could go overboard late one night and no one would ever be the wiser. So soon after the chaos of the war, people disappeared with frightening ease.

"It's how the bastards are able to operate," Corrado had once told him. "The entire world is so fucked that people are disposable and go missing all the time. *Quei bastardi tedeschi hanno fatto la festa a millioni!*" Those German bastards wiped out millions. What was one more, he seemed to be saying.

"Yes," Franco answered the captain—*what was his name, Marek Nepovim?*—but he hesitated, for it was best not to express how big a mess his life had become. Best to act as if he'd been privileged as they suspected. "Yes, but my father says we were able to salvage our family business by moving some of it to South America…"

"A lot like those Nazis, eh?" said Kamil with a guffaw, spittle flying from his mouth, somewhere inside his beard. "I heard Perón himself is opening the doors to take them in."

Tranelli's eyes widened at Franco. *Don't take the bait.*

It didn't work. "I don't know about that, but plenty of Italians would have gladly danced on Hitler's grave," he said, much too quickly. "Unlike plenty of Yugoslavs who were only too happy to suck his dick."

The dinner talk quieted. Everyone at the table wanted to see how the gruff Kamil would respond to this young snot-nose.

They were dining on cabbage rolls drowned in thick gravy that also smothered mounds of dumplings. But forks and spoons halted the general din of the meal as passengers and officers waited to see what would happen.

The captain glowered at him, while Kamil seemed pensive rather than incensed.

Another ship's officer, Milos Havlik, nudged Kamil. "The young one has a mouth, better watch out!"

Kamil lost his pensive look, his eyes narrowing as he stared at Franco.

"At least, that is what my father says," Franco said innocently.

There was a pause as everyone seemed to hold his breath. Then everyone broke out into laughter and raised their glasses, the icy atmosphere broken at least temporarily. More wine and *slivovitz* was poured, and glasses clinked. Only Kamil continued glowering at the smart-mouth boy.

Franco heaved a sigh. Here he'd been worried about the priest getting them killed, and then he had gone ahead and opened his own big mouth. He wasn't accustomed to this kind of gathering and conversation. Now he let the rest of this conversation get away from him, and sat back to eat the fattening food. It was good, if greasy, and seemed to help ease his crippling aggregate hunger from the last few years. In fact, he ate enough for three, shoveling food onto his plate and into his mouth like a starving animal. His time with the partisans had featured much thin soup, boiled potatoes, and the occasional chunk of horse meat. This was a banquet by comparison, and he ate his fill as if there were to be no food the next day. The priest made a face at him, indicating he shouldn't make such a pig of himself.

After the remainder of the dinner, which was much quieter after the outbursts, some of the officers began to drink heavily as soon as the captain took his leave, a surly look on his face. Tranelli gazed longingly at the various open bottles and licked dry lips, but allowed himself to be led toward the door.

As they were leaving the mess hall, Franco heard the men get around to a topic that interested him, but it was too late.

"What about the woman passenger, the rich bitch?" Havlik said, smacking his lips lewdly. "Anyone see her out of her cabin yet?"

"She refused the captain's invitation, more's the pity. *Snob.*"

"But is she nice-looking?" someone asked.

"Is she? She's like a movie actress! Yeah, she's attractive all right and she's got quite a rack. I'd fuck her in a minute. Those long legs of hers would be up on my shoulders and I'd—"

Someone shushed the speaker, pointing at Father Tranelli and Franco, who had just reached the door. Franco hesitated, but the priest pushed him bodily. Reluctantly, Franco and Tranelli ignored the rest of the whispering and stepped out into the corridor. They heard raucous laughter from inside, where the men were clearly still celebrating the woman's copious traits.

"Damn it, we should have stayed," Franco whispered. "I have wondered about her, too."

"You saw her?" The priest's eyes widened.

"Just a glimpse."

"A rich Nazi? A general's wife, that kind of thing?" The priest made a face.

"I don't know. Maybe listening to them would have helped us."

"They wouldn't have talked freely with us there, you saw that."

Franco frowned. It was only the first dinner. Would she refuse to dine with the rest of them every evening?

He wasn't sure why he was so curious about her, but the alluring glimpse she'd given him had awakened something inside him, an interest he hadn't known was there. He wasn't sure what, but something was happening in his loins. His father had once joked that Franco would know when he was suddenly interested in girls, and now he wondered if that day had come. All he knew was that he tingled at the thought of that woman, even though it had been only a quick glimpse.

They headed back to their adjoining cabins.

A midnight excursion came to mind, but Franco doubted Tranelli would approve. Which was why he waited for the priest to adjourn to his own bunk. After pointedly saying good night and faking a yawn, Franco lay atop his narrow bunk and pretended to fall asleep.

The ship's engines provided a soothing droning rhythm that threatened to put him to sleep. But his senses were fully awake, and excitement flowed through his nerves. He fidgeted until he thought he would explode. Soon it was time. Tranelli snored audibly in the other cabin. Franco dressed quickly and wandered into the dimly-lit corridor, the Vatican dagger tucked into his belt under the coat.

Even though there was no one on either side of the long corridor, the sense of dread was palpable.

Chapter Six

Rabbioso

Climbing rapidly from McCarran inside the belly of the mostly full Airbus, he watched the lights of the Strip twinkle magically below until the plane banked and the window turned dark.

His seat mate, a florid businessman in some kind of paper industry, made a half-hearted attempt to engage him in banal conversation, but Rabbioso's natural glare took the fun out of it for the guy.

When the cart came around, jostling elbows and legs, he bought an outrageously expensive drink from a surly attendant (credit or debit card only) and tuned out a few more half-hearted attempts by the businessman to engage him, until finally he stared at the guy and growled just loud enough to awaken his Paleolithic brain and shut up out of pure fear. Muttering, the guy settled back facing partly away to sleep, leaving Rabbioso to his own thoughts.

Thankfully. *Have to look into picking up a private plane. Or chartering. Anything's better than this.*

He tried to get back on track.

What was Marina up to? He realized he didn't much care, but he needed her to be on his arm to quell the rest of the family's suspicions about him. It wasn't often an enforcer made a power play and took over a family, but this had been different. The whole upper hierarchy of the Bastone family had perished or been paralyzed—*literally*—in that fucking raid by the pretty doctor's cop buddy and his henchman.

Rabbioso still didn't understand exactly what had happened. One minute they'd been at the new compound, the empty house full of muscle, and the idiot Don Gus Bastone about to put the hammer on the doctor chick...and next they were all in the middle of a fucking war.

He remembered the electric insect sound he'd heard after the doc had escaped and before the place had gone up.

Gas leak, they said later in the news.

Fuck, yeah, and I'm Santa's little helper.

Somehow the fuckers had called down a goddamn drone strike on the compound and it had ended up burned to the ground.

He wasn't really interested in the details, but he did want revenge against the cop who seemed to have orchestrated the whole thing and managed to keep it out of the papers. And then the bastard cop turned out be a wolf, and their fight over the doc had left him damn near dead and in pain worse than anything he'd ever experienced. If he thought about it, the rage would consume him. And he'd always had the reputation of being a cool-headed customer. Only hot-heads brought down their own houses.

But that fuckin' Nick Lupo—he chuckled at that—had to learn you didn't fuck with Joe Rabbioso, or the Bastone Family. Soon it would be the Rabbioso family, and he had plans for when that would come about.

After that, Marina would become superfluous.

He glanced at his seat-partner, glad to note the guy's curiosity had dissipated and he now feigned sleep. That was the way to deal with people—intimidate the hell out of them.

He waited until the more attractive flight attendant was nearby then waved her over and bought another drink. Let the airline make a few dollars off of him, what did he care? The old Don was still paying the tabs, even if he didn't know shit about anything.

It was a good position to be in, even if he'd gone through hell to get there. And now he was itching for what was about to come.

And before he knew it the Airbus was on approach and dropping fast.

Oh yes, he was itching to play some games.

Lupo

He mostly hated driving, but the ride up north was always a liberation, a dropping of the bullshit by degrees, enhanced by the improving scenery as the surrounding trees slowly transitioned from deciduous to coniferous. Helping his mood was always his stash of playlists, one of them now cranking from his new Mustang's sound system.

Right now he was avoiding the Alan Parsons Project only because it reminded him too much of the rift that was slowly dividing him from Jessie. He had sequenced some of his favorite early Tangerine Dream albums so they flowed into his favorite later period albums. *Goblins Club* was on at the moment, and he was already looking forward to the newer version of "Stratosfear" that would follow when the album *Tyranny of Beauty* began. After that *Live Miles*, *Ricochet*, and *Cyclone* would weave in and out of his favorite period of their output.

He missed his old Maxima and its souped-up engine and greater comfort, but he had to admit he rather liked cornering with the pony car, and the sound was definitely an improvement.

Maybe he'd start enjoying the driving after all.

He was trying to purge his mind of all the crazy thoughts he'd been having since the shoot-out with the Bastone family had intersected the Wolfclaw attack. He still had nightmares about those moments, when the high-pitched monstrous insect sounds of the small but deadly drones signaled their arrival and the imminent deployment of the Reaper missiles. The two had occurred concurrently and he had taken advantage, improvising based on a shaky concept. He had no idea how he had managed to make that bit of magic work...but somehow it had.

Fuck, it was a thing of beauty.

Except it had given him those goddamn nightmares. He could relate to Danni Colgrave's admission that she also wasn't sleeping very well, although in her case it was the werewolves she'd seen that now made her sleep elusive—that and having killed a bunch of them with bursts of silver slugs. Plus all the other grisly shit she'd seen at the drone house.

He shook his head and slowed as he entered New London, his sort-of halfway point. He could avoid it now that newer highways had superseded the old two-lane state roads, but he still liked to slow down, gas up, stretch his legs. Grab a stale filling station sandwich and a tub of iced tea for the road.

He pulled into the large station in the center of town and glanced around. It was still the same place, and it recalled happier times. Even though he was heading up to Eagle River, his so-called "happy place," he wasn't feeling it yet. Too much on his mind.

And he was doing a stealth run. He hadn't told Jess he was coming, and hadn't decided whether he was going to see her.

Damn it, are we doomed? The two of us? When I'm sneaking in and not even telling the woman I love?

He just wanted to think.

He wanted to be away from Ryeland and Barton and Roman. From DiSanto, too, and whatever was burning him up. Something was wrong there, but DiSanto was being mum about it. The bus shooter had been quiet since the Route 15 massacre. Lupo should have wanted to work on that task force, but he got a strange vibe from Barton, whom they still called Hart-Bart behind his back due to confusion about his name when he'd arrived.

All that, and he also wanted to put some distance between him and Colgrave, who was looking at him funny these days. He hadn't expected that...

Turned on? Geez.

And he'd been ducking Marla Anders even though his orders included mandatory sessions with the psychologist. She was trying to force him into a corner, he figured, with some agenda of her own. He had a long list of emails from her he hadn't bothered to read, and he had managed to spot her from afar and abort any errands at work that would have taken him past her usual haunts.

And he hadn't seen Heather, so he assumed she was still healing from the torture she had suffered, although she seemed to be bouncing back faster every time—as if her body was learning something, or simply repairing itself faster. He wondered if he might be the same. But in any case he wanted to be away from her, too.

Especially her.

She routinely played with his feelings, and with the lust the Creature within him automatically felt for the beautiful but amoral muck-raking reporter.

The only place to find some solitude, some quiet woods where he could let the Creature out on the hunt, was in Vilas County. And he would be there soon. But he had to go in silent mode, or he would be back to facing one of his looming problems. Not that he wanted to think of Jessie in that way, but it was happening and he was powerless to stop it.

He gassed up, paid for the fuel, a vat of iced tea and a turkey/cheese/limp lettuce sandwich, and headed back to his car.

In the next gas lane was an idling black Expedition with tinted windows.

If werewolves had a spider-sense, he mused, his was suddenly going off the meter.

He forced himself to appear nonchalant, but watched the windows from the corner of his eye as he fussed with his purchases, leaning into the passenger seat and setting down the food.

They weren't getting gas, getting out to visit the can, or buying junk food. Whoever was in the truck was just…sitting there.

He reached below the dashboard on the passenger side and plucked out the MP5 submachine gun he had clipped there, pulling back the bolt as he held it below window level. He wasn't going to start anything, but if the Expedition's doors opened, he was going to have a word with them. And he sensed if they opened the doors or opened a window all hell would break loose.

Or not?

Fuck this, am I just paranoid?

Then again, this wouldn't be the first time —

The black SUV's engine suddenly growled and the vehicle tore away from the pumps, turned right past Lupo and squealed off the lot with barely a rolling stop. Traffic was thin, so the truck headed in the opposite direction without having to slow. It roared away in a cloud of exhaust fumes.

Lupo sighed in relief. It was nothing, after all.

Just a typical road-hog jerk trying to give everyone a good look at how dangerous he was. People like that all over the North Woods, and he'd run into some of them. People who'd run you off the road with their heavy-duty Dodge Ram 3500s if you looked at them funny while they passed you in a no-passing zone, belching smoke and ruining the quiet of the woods with their barely muffled V-8 engines.

Yeah, another one of those.

He carefully decocked the MP5 and replaced it, then got back into his seat.

And waited.

He wasn't quite convinced the guy hadn't been taking a long look at him. The suspicious vehicle itself was just the kind Wolfpaw had loved. Big, bad, black.

Lupo gave it a few more minutes, sipping his iced tea, then started up and headed for a nearby park where he could pull in and have his sandwich in peace. He remembered some years before running into a motorcycle gang there, but they'd made him as a pig and left him alone, spitting gravel after they decided to scram.

The middle of the state was chock-full of strange little pockets of anti-authority, some of which were biker gangs connected to larger bands such as the Mongols, the Outlaws, and even Hell's Angels. Here, after all were the origins of the Posse Comitatus, as well as the KKK itself. There were places in middle or northern Wisconsin where you might as well have been in New Jersey's Pine Barrens, or in a bayou somewhere in the deep South. He'd always loved it there, but sometimes he also felt especially happy to be armed.

This was just a strange but meaningless encounter, he told himself. It had to be.

He chewed the slightly soggy sandwich thoughtfully, keeping an eye on his mirrors.

"You know what you're doing?" It was Ghost Sam, sitting slouched in the passenger seat. "These aren't really very comfortable seats," he added, even though he was nearly invisible.

Lupo snorted. "Like you can tell." *You're a ghost*, he wanted to add, but he didn't.

"You'd be surprised what I'm allowed to experience." The old man sighed. "Listen, we have to talk. I understand you're not in a good place with Jessie right now, but you have to pay attention to the other things that are going on around you. There's a bigger picture, you know? You've become aware of some parts of it, but there are others and I can only help you in some ways."

"Why not? Is there a rule book?" Lupo said around a mouthful of sandwich. He slurped up some tea.

"Maybe there is, I don't know. What I do know is that the big picture is bigger and goes back farther than you can imagine."

"What am I supposed to do about that?"

"I don't know," said Sam, "and that's what scares me the most."

Lupo chewed silently.

"You can't get distracted by some things that don't matter."

"Does Corrado matter?"

"I think so."

"Does Barton?"

"I believe so…"

"Does Roman?"

"Be careful there...you might want to—"

"Wait," Lupo said. "What do you know?"

"There may be someone else who can help with the Roman situation, but I—I'm having trouble with that. It seems I'm limited from giving you direct help on some things. I'm trying to recruit someone else who can help you, but you have to be open to it, or this help will be meaningless. And bad things are—" The ghost was fading, and so was his voice.

"Wait, what doesn't matter? What should I be careful of? Who's going to help?"

But Ghost Sam was gone. The seat was empty.

Too many goddamn riddles.

He finished the sandwich, but he actually felt lonely now. A few minutes later he was on his way north again, hoping Ghost Sam would pop back in, but he didn't.

By the time his playlist hit the latest Steve Hackett album, he'd all but forgotten the Expedition and its strange behavior. And he'd put Ghost Sam's ominous warning out of his head.

He pointed the Mustang toward a corner of the rez relatively far away from the hospital, and Jessie, and hummed along with his music, the Creature inside him already feeling the loosening bonds of his urban prison.

The woods called to the Creature. Its hungers were starting to awaken.

Chapter Seven

Rabbioso

At the Dane County Regional Airport, he collected his bag and made his way to the end of the terminal that housed most of the privately owned hangars. There he quickly located the helipad (actually just a wide concrete apron with several yellow crosses painted on it), on which stood the AgustaWestland AW109E Power.

Rabbioso approached the royal blue, two and a half-million dollar aircraft. The long, lean chopper sat with its rotors already spinning. At the controls was Matteo LaMano, who looked awfully young inside the flight suit and helmet. But Matty's father had been Manny "The Hand" LaMano, one of the best-trusted lieutenants of Gus Bastone's old man, and the only member of the old guard Rabbioso had held over. Now that half the better guys had been slaughtered in the compound firefight—*a real fuckin' massacre*—Rabb had gone back to some of the older guys and elevated them in his new hierarchy.

The only great thing Gus had done, between viewings of whatever kinky porn trend he'd been into at the moment, was sending Manny's son Matty to flight school and buying this fucking great Italian-manufactured helicopter, of which they'd just recently taken delivery. It had been Gus's bright idea, the solution for traveling quickly from the Madison airport to his new Eagle River compound, but they hadn't had the time to get it all squared away before Lupo had blundered through the family like a fucking chainsaw.

Rabbioso had just purchased a new property—which would become a "compound" soon enough—but he was royally pissed off that he'd had to do it with Marina's okay and signature.

Still an outsider.

Well, fuck that, and fuck her.

He nodded to Matty as he climbed into the chopper's luxurious interior, a long case in one hand. One of his men, Alonzo Brujo—a rare Hispanic among his more traditional colleagues—followed him, also carrying a long composite case. Rabbioso had begun styling himself as an Indiana Jones type man of action recently, mostly leaving behind his more Vegas-inspired mobster look of bowling and Hawaiian shirts for calfskin boots, sheepskin coats and leather flight jackets, and black jeans for ops such as this one.

"Take us up, Matty," he said once he'd fixed his headset into position.

"You got it, boss." Matty was young, but he'd been raised old-school in the old ways, by a father who'd beaten into him how the system worked, who was in charge, and why. He knew his place, despite his ability to handle the bright blue flying machine. He flicked his controls and the two Pratt & Whitney engines purred, speeding them upward vertically like an elevator, banking around in a tight turn that took them northeast over rolling glacial hills within minutes, leaving the Midwestern charm of Madison behind.

Inside the main cabin, Rabbioso and Brujo set about opening their cases, breaking out the weaponry Brujo had brought along. The cases held two black SIG556xi tactical rifles with expensive FLIR infrared sights already mounted.

Brujo was grinning.

"What?" said Rabbioso.

"Man, I fuckin' love Cabela's."

"You bought these at *Cabela's*?"

"Well, yeah. This is Wisconsin, everybody's packin'. Those deer don't stand no chance, man. Where you want me to get shit like this, a back alley in Minocqua?"

Rabbioso bit down on his first response. "I assumed we would send some weapons overland."

"Overland meanin' by car? Boss, all that transporting state to state is fuckin' hairy these days."

"We've done it before." Rabbioso took a breath. "Okay, okay, forget it, help me get this stuff ready."

He was miffed. Didn't seem normal to off a cop with totally legal hardware.

Of course, he wasn't exactly planning to *off* him with this. Still…

"Rifles are sighted in and ready to go, boss."

"Got the special ammo?"

Brujo grinned again. "Nothin' but the best for this pig, huh?" He dug into his jacket pocket and took out several 5.56mm 30-round magazines for the Sigs. "Guy liked makin' them with the silver and all."

Rabbioso nodded. Once again, he was tempted to bring some of his top people—like Brujo—into the fold. But no, he'd wait for the right moment. And when was that, really? Not now, just as they were about to go up against a werewolf. There would be time enough for that. This was between him and Lupo.

"These babies'll punch through anything," Brujo was saying.

"Yeah, I'm counting on that."

Soon they were approaching the new family compound, and Rabbioso wondered how soon he would get to play with the new hardware. When they landed, Brujo handed him a phone.

He thought: *The eagle has landed.*

Jessie

It was earlier than she expected, but getting dark already.

She finished her rounds at the reservation hospital, where she was chief administrator and almost always on-call as physician, and felt the pull of the flashing neon lights across the parking lots, but this time she fought it. She fought it and won, because she found herself instead walking to the hospital cafeteria for a snack, not using her hunger as an excuse to head for the casino.

The building itself had become a nightmarish memory. Too much death, too many good people, too much crime... The casino had been a curse after all, just as Sam Waters had predicted. Sam's vote against its construction had been part of what had driven so much of the calamity that had befallen their lives, so much of the evil, the crime, the death. She wondered what Nick was doing right then. Something routine and boring, she hoped. She feared for his life, she really did, but an anger simmered below her fear and the love, an anger that sometimes bubbled up in a splash of acid she could taste in her throat.

Nick Lupo, homicide cop and werewolf.. How many people could say that and mean it?

But the days when some sense of wonder came along with the words were long gone. Now there was anger and weariness, and the bitter taste of jealousy.

Where's Heather Wilson right now?

She really didn't want to know, but she couldn't help let that thought bubble up to the surface, too.

That bitch.

Entering the cafeteria, she chose a corner table and dropped off her clipboard and iPad, then headed for the only open counter. The food choice was dismal by now, and the casino certainly seemed more attractive right then, but her need had passed. The therapy was working. What she needed was therapy to combat jealousy.

The tired attendant recommended the lasagne, and she nodded, but uncertainly. After a short wait, what she got was a far cry from what Nick would have produced during one of his late-night kitchen extravaganzas. It looked like something out of a dented box on a sale shelf from the worst grocery store in town, but she added dry garlic toast and a wilted iceberg salad with dressing in a plastic tub, and a bottle of water. *Talk about a downer.*

She sat and nibbled at it, thinking of Nick and where they were going. Where their relationship was headed.

Make me a werewolf, she had said. It had surprised even her.

He'd been hurt, tired, vulnerable. He'd nodded, hadn't he, and they had embraced. But then he had reneged on the promise.

"It's not a promise," he said, when they argued about it. "I was exhausted. I didn't think it through. I just nodded. I don't want to subject you to a life like mine."

Damn him!

What did he know about her life? Maybe her life was shit as it was, and being like him would be the perfect way to fix things.

And that goddamn bitch Heather wouldn't have an advantage anymore.

Lupo

Lupo pulled up to the cottage and felt the usual contradicting emotions. The small cabin was filled with fond memories of Sam, a place where they had managed to become close despite their differences—nights spent watching *good bad and medium* James Bond movies, making funny comments while drinking their way through a dog-eared 'New York' bartender's guide.

Sam Waters had unexpectedly left his beloved secluded cottage to Lupo. It had shocked Lupo to no end that a man who had once been ready to kill him, to empty a few silver-loaded shotgun shells into him, had thought so much of him by the time of his death to write him into his will. The place was just inside the more remote portion of the rez and could barely be found, though it had been found one time by some very bad guys, who had tainted the place with the slaughter of Tom Arnow's family.

Afterwards, Lupo had cleaned most of the bloody gore himself, using the brutal tragedy to initiate some updates from Sam's very rustic décor to include a modern kitchen, a larger pantry, more comfortable beds in the alcove off the main room and in the master bedroom/loft, and soft leather furniture and even a 55-inch Samsung LED television.

Sam would have loved Thunderball *and* For Your Eyes Only *on that screen.*

He pulled his Mustang into the new detached garage that he'd also recently built to replace the dilapidated old structure, then hiked across the gravel and weed driveway to the house itself.

After talking to the old man who had been his father's friend, or at least collaborator—*Corrado? Could it really be him?*— he had felt penned in. The city was on pins and needles, as were the cops. DiSanto had been sucked back into the DHS-run investigation of the bus shooter case that had everyone frightened, but the new Homicide head had kept Lupo out. That guy from Homeland Security, Barton? (Other cops called him Hart-Bart behind his back, but Lupo knew his name was Stephen H. Barton.) In his experience, the man was a better cop than most DHS agents. But Barton seemed to be inexplicably interested equally in Lupo himself as much as the bus shooter, who had gone quiet after his last dramatic outburst which had left so many dead and wounded.

Whenever Lupo felt penned in, he headed for the North Woods. Eagle River wasn't as pristine a paradise as it had been when Lupo had first started coming some twenty years before. Trees fell by the acre to so-called progress, and so Lupo had begun to cherish the small legacy Sam had left him.

Lupo had bypassed telling Jessie he was heading north.

He told himself it was just because she was working hard — not only running the hospital, as she had been, but also serving on the elders' council. They'd convinced her to take a seat after what had happened to Davison and Bill Hawk and although she had always opposed the casino and hotel project, she now found herself inextricably involved in its affairs, even if she wasn't running it.

Lupo shook his head, thinking about the speed with which all this had happened.

They'd barely managed to hold off the attacks of the Wolfpaw backing group, the secretive Wolfclaw—*couldn't they ever get off a theme?*—and the goddamn Bastone family, who wanted a large slice of the tribe's casino profits. It had taken a stroke of luck for Lupo to manage to cancel out two opponents by using Wolfclaw's drones equipped with Reaper missiles. It hadn't been a sure thing. If he'd been as much a gambler as Jessie had become, Lupo would have bet the house against himself on that one.

And the drone command house…who had warned them to clear out before the raid DiSanto and Danni Colgrave conducted there?

And where was Heather right now? Had she managed to heal from her terrible wounds?

There were so many questions still swirling in his mind. He reached the back door and took hold of the knob.

Overhead, he heard a flight of Canadian geese. *Late*, he thought, without looking up. They usually vacated earlier in the season.

When the door swung open under his hand, the explosion took out the cabin's entire rear wall and hurled him across the wooden back porch.

Debris washed over him, a deadly wave of projectiles.

If his eardrums hadn't been bleeding, the last sound he might have heard would have been that of frightened geese somewhere above, scattering across the gray sky.

Chapter Eight

Jessie

Her meal finished, such as it was, she dragged herself to her old Pathfinder and sat in it while the food settled. The cafeteria's version of lasagne left a lot to be desired, and she was now quite educated on what a respectable lasagne should taste like, thanks to Nick Lupo's peevish irritation at what restaurants tended to offer.

"Damn the mozzarella," he would say, scraping it off. "It should be Parmigiano-Reggiano and *maybe* a little ricotta, and the rest of what people think should be cheese is really supposed to be a béchamel—flour, butter, and milk—not this gummy pizza cheese! Don't get me started..."

But if she did get him started, he'd also mention that the layers of pasta should be much thinner than what most places served, and there should be more of them. "It's a lot more delicate to have a dozen thin layers as opposed to three or four thick pasta layers stuffed with cheese and meat. The meat sauce should be a delicate ragu'—though my family always made it meatless and I got used to it that way."

Jessie smiled at the thought of Nick's outrage when it came to what he considered poor Italian food. It was one of the things she loved about him.

Yeah, *love*, she thought.

Even though he was so difficult at times, she really couldn't see being with anyone else. His passion for everything made him special, but sometimes it all translated into a deep sense of stubbornness that could be infuriating, too.

Take her request, for instance.

Although part of her was terrified at the thought of becoming a strange creature, a werewolf, something she once would have laughed at the notion of believing, now she really did think it would save their relationship. She already knew what he had to go through, and she had decided she was willing to make the necessary sacrifices…and the necessary adjustments to her lifestyle.

More meat in my diet, she thought, and mostly rare. But instead of hurting her health, it would be the basis of a whole new approach to diet. And rare steaks were one of the ways Nick kept his wolf side away from hunting humans.

Though deer and rabbits in the wild…well, they were sacrificed to the wolf on a regular basis, on hunts in and around the reservation and the nearby national forest. Could she live with that?

Yes, she had decided she could live with that, especially if her transformation checkmated the bitch Heather out of the equation.

But stubborn Nick Lupo had first agreed, then started to waffle on whether he would do it. As if he didn't want to share his 'gift,' she sometimes thought. But then she would remember how much hell it sometimes put him through, and she realized that in his mind, at least, he was watching out for her.

She sighed.

Didn't make it any easier.

She burped, surprising herself.

God, she thought. *Too much garlic in the so-called lasagne.*

That was another pet peeve of his. *There's always too much garlic!* he would have cried out in frustration.

It made her smile as she started the Pathfinder and put it in gear, then nosed it out of her administrative parking space and toward the street. She tried to avoid looking at the casino, with its rows of blinking lights and neon strips, but the glow was just too powerful. And the draw. She felt the urge to pull in gaining strength, but at the last second she turned right onto the road that would take her away from the temptation of the slot machines.

A black Expedition followed her onto the street.

That's funny, she thought.

She saw him in her mirror, but hadn't noticed the SUV in the hospital lot. She wasn't used to anyone leaving when she did, so it startled her a little. As did the fact that she didn't recognize it, when she had a tendency to know most of the vehicles on the rez.

Must have intended to pull into the casino lot but instead parked in the hospital's. The two surface lots were basically side-by-side, and the casino brought in plenty of non-rez cars. Hell, half the rez women worked in the casino, but couldn't afford to spend their money there as customers. Though even she had to admit the pay was rather awesome compared to pre-casino days. She'd learned a lot since they'd convinced her to sit on the board, and now they wanted her to run for the chair. Well, she was definitely ambivalent, but there was a lot of good she could do from within. She shook her head. So many decisions to make.

What about *this* now? Was it a problem?

She drove slowly. The Expedition followed a few car lengths behind her, matching her speed. Its windows were tinted completely black, so she couldn't see anyone.

Jesus, she thought. *Am I ever paranoid!*

Or was she?

Ever since Lupo had called up those demons from hell, otherwise known as Wolfpaw—in all its evil guises, and God knew there were many—nothing much would have surprised her.

She could play this game. Maybe not a few years ago, but now she definitely could.

She slowed and took a sudden right onto a wooded lane, no directional, turned off the ignition, and watched the mirror.

The Expedition sped up and roared past, apparently frustrated with her hogging of the road at such low speed.

Well, that's more normal for this area!

She pulled back out after a few minutes, figuring she really was paranoid. The road was clear ahead of her and she drove on, heading home but at the last second she decided to take a roundabout way, making a large loop but ending up at her Circle Moon Drive. It was a sort of private cul-de-sac in which her cottages were arrayed on the shore of the channel between Catfish and Cranberry Lakes, with much wooded acreage between them. She noted that Lupo's place was dark, and she felt a stab of loneliness. His rental of that cottage as his getaway had begun their relationship, but now she wondered if he planned to be in residence again anytime soon.

Wolfpaw had come crashing into their lives, with its army of sadistic warrior werewolves, and he hadn't been the same. The deaths of Sam Waters and Tom Arnow had hit him hard, harder than she'd suspected, and he seemed to carry the weight of the planet on his broad shoulders these days. Even when he was around, they were so rarely carefree. And last time they'd almost died at the hands of the werewolves and mobsters and, according to Nick, the drones some secret group had hijacked. She wasn't sure about any of that, or even how in hell they'd managed to cover up the truth afterward.

She sighed, and put on a nice tea from Portland she'd discovered recently, Boyd's. It was a dark, rich color and its flavor matched without bitterness. It was the best-tasting tea she'd ever had, and she lusted for a large mug doctored with a good slug of rum. Nick had taught her that. She had always used brandy, but he'd come along with his predilection for rum in both tea and hot cocoa, and she'd never looked back.

She put on the water in an old-fashioned tea pot.

When it started whistling she went to fetch her favorite mug, a large black Yes mug Nick had given her. One of his bands, a great classic Roger Dean design. She just liked it.

While the tea steeped, she puttered in her kitchen.

She barely had time for one short, hot sip of tea. The sound, when she heard it, came from out back.

Gravel shifting under a light foot.

She had good ears. That was somebody sneaking around out there.

Nick had rubbed off on her. Under the large, rustic table she had clipped a Remington 870 tactical shotgun with a pistol grip and short barrel. It was a devastating weapon in close quarters, Nick had explained, and it would be the best and most effective self-defense weapon she could brandish—plus it would frighten most in-the-know attackers.

Now with barely a thought she plucked the loaded Remington off its clip and gently opened the front door, which faced the water's edge at the bottom of a slight slope. She snuck out into the darkness and closed the door gingerly behind her.

There it was again, gravel disturbed behind the house. She made her way up the slope along the dark side of the cottage, shotgun held at the ready. There was a shell in the chamber—whenever Nick wasn't around she kept it that way. He'd told her there was no reason to have the gun if she couldn't use it at a moment's notice. She rounded the corner with caution, careful to avoid making the same mistake as her intruder, but she knew every dip in the terrain, every loose stone, every stray tree root, and her feet didn't betray her.

There he was, a light-colored blob against the darkness. The intruder was skulking around the back door now, looking as if he might be trying to break in.

But that wasn't the worst part. Her heart skipped and the breath caught in her throat.

He was naked.

That was why he seemed so light-colored.

Naked. That meant only one thing to her.

Werewolf.

She steeled herself for confrontation. If the guy was ready to shape-change right at her door, whoever he was he wasn't here to just have a spot of tea and conversation. No crumpets, no scones. He was here to kill.

She felt the beginnings of an unfamiliar rage building way down in her soul, or whatever organ passed for a soul. It was almost a blind rage, an uncontrollable urge to do the opposite of what she had done all her life. She felt no connection to any physician's oath right then. She felt no compassion, no mercy, no sense of ethical fair play. As it was, she still gave him a chance.

"Stop right there!" she said, raising her voice enough to startle him into complying.

Instead, he turned toward her with a deep growl in his throat.

She couldn't make out his features, but the sound of the growling frightened her deep down in the pit of her stomach.

"I mean it," she said, much more quietly. She hoped it was more menacing.

He wasn't buying it.

He must have thought he still had the element of surprise on his side. Maybe he hadn't been well-briefed. He advanced, a half-chuckle, half-growl emerging from deep in his throat. She could just make out his enormous erection, aimed at her like a weapon. He was turning toward her, and when he did his thing, she was ready.

At exactly the moment he blurred and turned into a muscular wolf, planting his rear paws to leap, she stepped back and let him have a full blast from the shotgun. *No regrets.*

She knew her way around guns and didn't miss.

He let out a half-scream, half-screech that she knew would haunt her nightmares.

Silver shot pellets.

The impact tossed him violently backward, bleeding from a dozen wounds throughout his torso. He flickered from wolf to human and back with incredible speed, screaming and trying to put himself out where the silver pellets caused fires to spring up. With human hands he beat at himself, temporarily causing the flames to do their work inside his body. His penis was flaccid now, no longer menacing.

Rolling around as if he could stop the burning silver that coursed through his system, he shrieked loud enough to obscure her voice as she asked him repeatedly, "Who do you work for?"

His growls were menacing, but his silver-poisoned body was no longer.

Or so she thought.

He was getting up. Painfully, but still he was working through the pain of the silver poison in his system to get himself back in position to attack his tormentor.

Jessie Hawkins had had it. She was no longer the country doctor with a Hallmark Channel heart of gold. She'd been battle-hardened more often than she could count. She felt almost as if she herself had transformed into some other kind of creature.

"Last chance!" she screamed, approaching him. "Tell me who you work for and what you want!"

She thought she heard him say it between the shrieking. *"Fuck you, bitch!"*

The rage born of so much stress rose up in her, overwhelmingly frightening, further blinding her.

She shot him again at point-blank range, and she could see bloody chunks of his flesh blown off by the silver shot, turning part of him into hamburger.

He was still rolling like a man on fire when she set the shotgun aside, drew the Vatican dagger, leaned in as if possessed by some kind of monster in her soul, and slit his throat as if she'd done it all her life.

Barely avoiding the great fountain of dark red—almost black—blood that reached out to her, she closed in again and, having lost all semblance of control, drove the dagger into her attacker's heart.

She felt him seize up as the silver blade further scorched his insides, and she knew he was gone when he went limp, even though she could see him fluttering between his two faces, monster and man.

Shaken, suddenly aware of what she had done, she stepped back and vomited up her crappy dinner.

After she was empty of everything except thin, reeking bile, she straightened and stumbled back to look at her would-be killer's remains.

She found his clothes hidden nearby. The SUV, his black Expedition, she found stashed down the road. He had a phone, with calls made to an out of state number with some kind of code name, calls made just today.

She collected evidence in her mind, but she was already certain she had assessed the situation correctly. Now she stared at his remains. Slowly the pragmatic took over from the emotional. What to do?

She dug her own phone from a pocket, swiped it on, and dialed from her Favorites.

"Please pick up, Nick," she said, through tears that were just beginning. "Please."

But there was only the curt voicemail prompt.

Chapter Nine

Franco Lupo

On the Freighter Zeniča, crossing the Atlantic Ocean
December 1945

The painted metal corridors were empty of late-night traffic. Most of the crew would be asleep in their quarters one or two levels below this one, from what Franco gathered having asked a few of the roughnecks about their jobs. There would be a shift officer on the bridge, probably peering into the radar screen or steering using the ship's wheel.

Franco stared at the door across from his, wondering what the woman was doing behind it, picturing...*things*. He let the hazy pictures play through his mind a few moments, then he moved away. He walked softly on bare feet, the cold floor beneath them made of painted metal, his hand on the railing mounted on one side of the corridor. The cabin doors made of polished double-layered utilitarian wood with brass fittings, but were almost an afterthought since every ten meters there was an open hatch that could be bolted closed to seal off a section of the corridor.

In case we're sinking. He pictured them trying to hold off rising ocean waters by sealing the hatches—but then he realized it could work the other way, that someone could seal them into the flooding section and they would drown as the ship tilted and finally slipped beneath the waves to die on the ocean floor.

He shook his head, dismissing the image.

The corridor hatch doors themselves were made of thick layers of metal plates with a cloudy porthole set into the upper third, their complex tumblers exposed. Turning a wheel would set all the tumblers simultaneously in their cylinders. Franco examined the first one closely.

Closing one of these might also be the difference between living and being slaughtered by some cursed man-wolf.

The monsters might be everywhere on the ship.

Should he head upward toward the bridge, or down below to where the crew's quarters were located?

Franco had no real idea what he was trying to do. He assumed he would learn something by exploring, whereas if he simply slept he would learn nothing.

Down then. The crew's quarters and their mess hall should be easy to find. In fact, the mess hall door was propped open and he heard the sounds of laughter and glasses clinking. The off-duty crewmen who sat at one of two long tables were engaged in a couple card games, bottles and glasses lined up next to them.

"Look," one of the crew said when he spotted Franco at the door. "It's the Italian boy. Come in, boy, play with us!" He smiled a gap-toothed smile and made a come-in gesture.

"What's wrong, couldn't sleep? Seasick?" One of the other card players asked. "Never been to sea, eh boy? Never seen land fall away? Feel the depth of the ocean under you?"

Several of the men chuckled.

"My grandfather was in the navy last war. I have been on ships and boats," he lied. "I can handle it. I am looking for some fun."

A glass appeared in front of him and someone poured clear liquid. "We know how to have fun. Do you have money?"

Chapter Ten

Shooter

He shivered in the stiff bedclothes, unable to warm up, waiting for the meds to start working. His mouth was desert dry and even the plastic cup of water from the bathroom tap hadn't quenched his thirst. He tried to tuck himself into the stained sheets and the two blankets, but the cold still cut through him. His shivering exhausted him and he knew he could barely get himself off the bed to use the toilet, if he had to. Maybe he'd just piss himself, he thought.

The meds, a clozapine and ziprasidone cocktail with a risperidone chaser, were shooting through his system, setting off explosions of white light behind his eyelids.

Jesus, I'm so cold. Jesus, I'm so cold. Jesus...

The visions had stopped now, due to the light bursts, and in a minute or two the shivering slowed and he felt almost as if he could stop huddling under the blankets.

And then all of a sudden he was sweating, heat radiating off his skin like a coil in an electric heater. He threw off the bedclothes, but he was trapped in them and he tried to squirm free and fight them, but all he did was trap himself more. The sweat seemed to leak from his pores like water from tiny faucets, soaking the sheets and mattress below him for the hundredth time, maybe the thousandth.

He groaned.

Jesus, so hot, Jesus, so hot, Jesus...

He wondered where they were right now. Were they surrounding the motel? Crawling through the scraggly bushes that lined the rear parking lot? Hiding behind the end of the strip mall his window overlooked?

He could hear them getting into position. He closed his eyes and he could see them, signaling, gesturing with hands that became paws. Claws. He could sense they were near.

Or maybe they were on the bus again.

Maybe they were on the bus heading for his other hideout.

He thrashed around, attempting to free himself so he could thwart them again. He ignored the sweat dribbling off his forehead and into his eyes, ignored the burning sensation, riding the fear that had suddenly overtaken him. He could see the table, where he had lined up his defenses. He kicked and punched the bonds that prevented him from crossing the floor, and even though he heard the tearing of cloth he was still tied up, bound like a hostage, and they were just outside his door, he could hear them breathing...

He could hear them breathing...

And he screamed, his mouth wide open and the taste of sweat-salt on his tongue and down his throat, and he vomited, barely able to turn his head in time for the gush, and then he was suddenly so cold that he sought the warmth of the ruined blankets again.

Jesus, so cold, I'm so cold, so cold, Jesus, so cold, Jesus...

Lupo

He regained partial consciousness when the roaring in his ears threatened to make his head explode.

Not only that, there was pain coursing through his blood.

Silver. He was laying on his stomach, pinpoint jabs of silvery-hot liquid pain calling in from every square inch of his body, it seemed. He tried to move, failed, and heard a faint groan. It was his groan, an involuntary response to the sharp, crippling pains that wracked his body from head to toe, seeming to flow like fire through his veins.

But that wasn't all.

The jumbo jet roaring inside his head and its ringing echo was circling in a hold pattern, rising and falling with the air currents.

He tried moving again, forcing himself to work past the irrational pain, and felt some sort of response. His arms worked, and he was able to bring up his right leg partially. His left leg wasn't answering the call. His head spun as the jet engines increased RPMs, ready for take-off. He groaned again, aware that the pain was more intense than just about anything he had ever felt, and also aware that it was starting to ratchet up as his nerve endings came on-line.

Jesus, somebody blew me up.

There had to be silver shrapnel in the bomb, enough to just about paralyze me...

It was a voice in his head, but it was almost drowned out by the jet. The screaming echo was settling down in his left ear from what he could tell. His left leg was ignoring him, while his right was starting to throb in a dozen places. His left hand screamed when he tried moving his fingers, but his right was able to move. He felt the deck planks and countless tiny bits of hot and spiky debris that all lay like a carpet under him. He tried to inhale though his nose, but wetness—*blood?*—resulted in a snort and he gasped as it slid down his throat.

Silver shrapnel should have killed me. But it didn't...

Now that he was certain he was still alive despite the obvious discomfort brought on by the multiple wounds and his head trauma, he was beginning to feel things, other things, and one of them was heat.

Not the same heat he still felt as the silver shrapnel did its worst inside his body's byways and highways.

No, there was also a fire not far away. A *real* fire. He cleared out his nose in a rush of blood and mucous and then he smelled it: scorched flesh and hair.

His *scorched flesh and hair*.

Fuck.

His cabin was burning.

He was burning from the inside, and about to be burned on the outside too.

But he couldn't move. And he couldn't see.

Head laying sideways away from the fire's increasing heat, he tried to gently open his eyes, but the shearing pain—a new, all-enveloping pain—made him scream as some grit, or maybe silver shrapnel debris, grated across his eyeballs under the lids like razor blades.

Jesus fuck!

He'd never felt so much sharp pain in his eyes. But if he didn't open them and get himself out of there, the whole cabin would go up and take him with it.

He wasn't ready to give in yet, not when he could tell a portion of his body was willing to respond despite the damage he'd suffered.

He tried again to open his eyes, felt the blades across his corneas and gritted his teeth past it, and then a new fear took him and he groaned as it became obvious to him that something else was wrong, something even worse.

His eyes *were* open.

But I can't fucking see.

Marla Anders

It was late, but she was wired and couldn't sleep anyway. She had been thinking of her grandfather, and suddenly she thought it was possible the phenomena that had been occurring around her—cryptic messages, simple mysterious warnings and the like—were aimed at her by her grandfather.

He had certainly believed in such phenomena.

Hell, he had lived his life around these beliefs.

Her grandfather had been a shaman for his tribe, and even though she had gone to school in the white man's world and distanced herself from her background in part by avoiding her mother's side of the family, she had certainly learned a lot from him when she had been impressionable, before she had decided his tribal life wasn't for her.

He had sought to make her in his image, and would have succeeded, but her father had put his foot down and even though it had nearly torn her family apart, she had stayed within the white man's boundary lines. That was how her grandfather had described it, and although she had been little when the split happened, she remembered it all too well.

But now, after some years of little phenomena surrounding her, and this latest wave of them manifesting ever since she had taken her new job, she was forced to question what was happening to her.

She rolled around her bed more than usual, although she was definitely a thrasher, and finally she decided to get up and either watch some mindless TV or take a dribble of brandy, the Wisconsin state booze.

She lifted her head from the foam form-fitting pillow and gasped.

There was someone in the bedroom with her!

The outline was sitting in the straight-back armchair she kept in the corner, a seat she liked to use for reading before bed sometimes.

She reached for her nightstand drawer, where she kept a loaded Smith & Wesson .38 Special revolver, an old cop's gun—in fact, her father's first service piece. She had it, the old checkered grip familiar in her hand, and she aimed it at the outline.

"Whoever you are, freeze right there!"

Just because she did head-shrinking for cops and listened to Christmas music, didn't mean she couldn't look out for herself. She was comfortable with the gun in her hand.

"I mean it, don't move!" Her other hand sought out her phone, but it was out of reach.

She realized it might have been silly, reiterating he shouldn't move. He hadn't moved at all. It was as if he were not really there, just a reflection or a shadow.

"Put your hands up!" she tried.

The outline did nothing.

"Who are you? What do you want?" Damn it, she was running out of questions. She would have to get up out of bed, but she was afraid becoming distracted with maneuvering her body and keeping him in her gun's sight would give him the opening he needed to…to do what?

"Talk up!" she called out, getting desperate. "You're about to get arrested."

Maybe the light.

Get a look at him first. Maybe blind him, get rid of his night vision.

She reached for the light switch right over her head. At least this one was close.

She felt around for the familiar toggle.

Finally.

Started to click it in the right direction…

As she did, thoughts gushed through her brain.

He could be armed. Holding a gun himself…

Too late to worry about that.

Click.

The light wasn't great, but it was enough to dispel the deepest shadows in the room. She gripped the Smith & Wesson harder, ready to shoot if her intruder's outline moved or otherwise threatened her in any way.

None of that happened.

No, she saw an image of an elderly man, but even as she stared at it, it seemed to fade in and out.

She was trembling by now, the gun shaking in her hand. If she fired, she'd probably miss. Her luck, she'd kill a neighbor on the other side of the apartment wall. She lowered the gun slightly. She could always raise it. The elderly man didn't seem to be much of a threat.

"Who are you?" Then, when he faded again, "*What* are you?"

And why did he look familiar? She suddenly realized she had seen a photograph of him, somewhere. And he looked benign…

"Who are you?" she whispered again. "What do you want with me?"

He had to be an apparition. She could see through him. And she thought he looked about as old as her grandfather had when she last saw him, many years before.

As if a wired connection were being made, she suddenly heard his voice in midsentence.

"Don't be afraid," he was saying. "This isn't—easy as it looks, but I need—send a message, and I'm afraid you're—who can receive it—pass it along to—don't know who else..."

"Christ's sake," she said, exasperated. "You're like a bad connection. You're here, you might as well communicate." She lowered the gun. He was more not there than there, how could he hurt her? She'd been open to ghostly appearances all her life. Her grandfather had prepared her.

The outline spoke clearly. "I knew your grandfather. Joseph Badger, a good man gone bad. My name is Sam Waters."

Joseph Badger. She hadn't really started thinking of her grandfather until recently. It couldn't be a coincidence, not with all those strange messages.

And then she knew where she'd seen the apparition's photograph.

In Nick Lupo's file.

And, for that matter, in a frame in his office, in a photo of him sitting on a wooden porch or deck outside some tiny cottage.

Chapter Eleven

Shooter

He didn't dare leave the dingy, run-down motel room he had taken in the southern suburb of Chicago.

Even though his cocktail seemed to be holding him together, keeping his body from betraying him too much, he knew if he went out *they* would find him. They would capture him, and what he'd seen would happen to him. And, worse, he would become one of them!

No, even if he got hungry he wouldn't go out. It was when he broke down and went out among the people that he soon started to see them, sometimes everywhere he looked. And then even the drugs couldn't keep him from the panic attack, the rage, and ultimately the revenge. He would find them, root them out, and kill them much as his buddies had been.

Christ, it wasn't hard to relive the day.

That fucking day.

It had been at least a hundred eighteen degrees in the sun, with a breeze that shifted sand around and drove the tiny, gritty particles into your clothing, your boots, your eyes, your mouth…there was sand everywhere, and your skin was chafed by the grit until you lost feeling in your outer layers of epidermis. You even stopped thinking of it as your skin, but instead as another layer of cloth.

The raging firefight that stretched into the endless battle of Fallujah, an ebbing and flowing action spanning summer through fall and thousands of "flags"—American troops—and contractors, had changed the shooter's life forever.

He was a Marine sniper, so his squad had nicknamed him Shooter—no different than a cowboy cook was referred to as Cookie, he used to say back when he had people to talk to—and he had a growing number of confirmed kills notched on his M40A5 rifle. He didn't shy away from the war's ugliest violence, having watched enemy heads explode while bracketed within his telescopic sights when his high-velocity rounds caught them just right.

But on this day, they'd been exhausted and were given a chance to stand down in somebody's abandoned clay hovel. It was probably a mansion to these people, but it was not much more than a shed with a tin roof as far as he was concerned. But shelter was shelter, and just getting out of the sun had the effect of making one feel human again.

They'd been fighting brief, intense actions since the previous month, when a group of contractors—mercenaries—had been ambushed and killed after a massacre of innocents. They'd been dismembered in public and hung on a bridge, a stark message to the occupying forces. The incident had led to an increase in search-and-destroy patrols, turning the dry desert town into a kill-zone where both sides did their worst every chance they got.

In the slightly cooler interior of the empty house, they'd had water and some of their inedible rations, sandy grit crunching between their teeth, while keeping their weapons close to hand. Barely a half hour into their nervous rest, they'd heard screaming outside. It came from beyond the wall that surrounded the home's small courtyard, a sort of lawn minus any living greenery. The screaming seared the young soldiers to their very souls. It was women and children, and it was blood-curdling.

"What the fuck is that?" said Karicke, a thin sunburned kid from somewhere near Chicago.

"Shut up," hissed their commanding officer, Sarge Lockett. He waved his hand to quiet the inquisitive mumbling. "I'll take a look," he whispered. "Shooter, with me."

It made sense, if they saw something happening the sergeant's Colt SMG and Shooter's sniper rifle would be sufficient to at least hold off an attacking force until the rest of the squad could rally and provide support.

They'd run at a crouch out the low doorway and crossed the courtyard, covering each other, becoming aware that the screaming on the other side of the wall was now mingling with the sound of growling, snarling dogs.

"The fuck...?" said Lockett, a large African-American from the Deep South. "Sounds like dogfighting shit." They were hunched over between a ragged hedge of scrawny, starving bushes and a couple malnourished date palms.

Shooter frowned. It sounded nothing like that to him. It sounded like dogs against humans, and dogs were winning.

A howl drowned out the screaming before fading into some kind of bizarre growling. The Marines looked at each other and Sarge gestured a careful look-see over the wall.

They raised their heads cautiously. Shooter's eyes focused quickly, one of the qualities that gave him his sniper's skill.

A line of men, women, and children were roped together and held at gunpoint by a dozen mercenaries. The contractors wore the distinctive wolf's paw patch on their black uniforms. Seeing those uniforms, Shooter always recalled his high school history class on World War II and the pictures he had seen of the German Schutzstaffel—the SS—and the dreaded Gestapo, the secret police. The mercenaries always looked like Nazis to him. The locals were screaming because the mercenaries had started to kill them one by one. Two or three bloody bundles of rags were all that remained of the first victims, and huge splashes of dark blood had splattered the mud walls behind them like gigantic surreal tags on a train car.

"Jesus—" he muttered, and Sarge elbowed him in the ribs and widened his eyes, making their hand-sign for *too many of them*. Shooter nodded and bit his tongue.

At first Shooter thought the Wolfpaw scum'd been shooting their prisoners in the head, but then his breath caught in his throat and he thought he was having a stroke, because the blood seemed to drain from his brain and he felt his knees weaken.

He wasn't used to feeling much of anything, not after all he'd done from behind a rifle sight.

But this, this was different.

This was way different.

No, this was completely inexplicable, completely alternate-universe unbelievable.

The Wolfpaw group leader and his hired guns held the screaming people at bay while one of their fellows squirmed out of his black tactical jumpsuit to reveal a nude, hairy body that was both muscular and lean. And with a gigantic erection Shooter could see from across the alley.

He could have sworn he heard the leader call out, "Go, Jacko, all yours!"

Before he could process this new and unexpected sight, or really register the import of the twisted, brutal aspects of the scene, it changed again when the naked man blurred and like a CGI effect was suddenly an enormous gray wolf. *Where the man had been now stood an impossibly large animal that had no right in any universe to be there.* The closest Afghani man screamed incoherently, his sanity seeming to leak out of his eyes and nose and mouth.

And then Shooter saw what now haunted his nightmares despite the drugs he ingested to help him forget...

The wolf's head approached the victim-to-be, lolling almost as if relaxed, but then its muscular jaws opened wide and closed down on the man's head, crushing it between rows of drooling fangs. Blood squirted out in all directions. Shooter had the fleeting thought of a large grape, crushed between his teeth and the juice squirting and running out...

The body fell, legs twitching, dragging down the next victim in the hellish chain gang.

It was a child, and the high keening wail would stay with Shooter the rest of his life, as the same wolf took seconds by repeating his actions and crushing the child's head, then ripping it off the blood-squirting neck, shaking it like a ball before tossing it to lie limply on the bloody dirt of the alley.

A different Wolfpaw asshole monster was already shedding his equipment and tac-suit, and turning into a different-looking wolf, killing the next screaming victim, the woman whose family had just been slaughtered.

Beside him, Sarge slipped off the ledge and fell in a heap inside their covering wall, but his moan was too loud and one of the Wolfpaw mercenaries turned just in time to see Shooter duck out of sight. It was enough.

"Flags!"

The group leader had seen them.

Dozens of 9mm rounds from Wolfpaw Colt SMGs sprayed the wall and the bushes behind it, showering Sarge and Shooter with sharp debris from both.

Shooter grabbed Sarge by the neck like a rag doll and pulled him across the courtyard, trying to handle both their weapons at the same time, but already the Wolfpaw gunmen were scrambling to pursue the witnesses. Only seconds later several large wolves leaped over the wall, skidded to a halt in the center of the barren courtyard, spotted their targets ducking into the doorway and leapt in that direction.

Shooter and Sarge flew into the dark house shouting, trying to rally the dazed Marines who had been sleeping and relaxing. Sarge barred the flimsy door but immediately it began to splinter under the wolves' attack, and then dozens of rounds perforated the door and the walls around it, piercing helmets, vests, armor, and flesh.

Screams loud in Shooter's ears were drowned out by the ragged bursts of automatic fire and the growling of wolves who wreaked havoc on the surprised Marines, biting off limbs and tearing out throats one by one, until there was only the moaning of a single Marine, whose throat was cut by a Wolfpaw gunman moments later.

None of the wolves had been affected by the gunfire.

Buried under Sarge's dead body, Shooter played dead as the wolves nosed around among the corpses of his buddies and tore flesh from the dead in a gruesome victory dance. Their grunts and growls were as obscene as their gluttony with the human flesh and bloody organs they ingested. He was too dazed to even think of praying that they didn't sniff out the fact that he was still alive. Maybe they were too inebriated by the taste and awful stench of dead flesh and spilled blood and feces, or maybe they were just too distracted by all the offerings on this most disgusting buffet. In any case, they did not find him.

Shooter heard the voice of the Wolfpaw officer issuing orders, then the sounds of gunmen and wolves leaving the charnel house and the tell-tale clicks of pins being flipped off grenades.

"I'm so sorry, Sarge," he muttered through a veil of tears and acrid sweat that covered his face. "I'm so sorry…"

Desperately he rolled his dead Sergeant's body over him as well as he could and cringed underneath it, crying tears of helpless rage and fear. And awaiting the explosions...

Chapter Twelve

Franco Lupo

On the Freighter Zeniča, crossing the Atlantic Ocean
December 1945

After an hour of playing *scopa* and other elementary card games, he had lost almost half the money in his pockets. They weren't cheating him, exactly, yet he was unable to make a move that didn't involve losing the hand.

There were smiles all around for the child—an unofficial mascot—and he gave as good as he got in the games, although the pot always seemed to elude him.

"Too bad we sailed at night," said the brutish machinist's mate Havlav. "You will miss seeing Gibraltar."

"Not that there's anything to see worth a shit," said another grease-stained motorman. "It's a rock. Like a wart on the ocean surface."

They were speaking a mixture of Italian, rough German, Czech and native Yugoslav or dialects, and hand-motions in deference to their visitor. They had taken to the boy quickly, gregariously, and he wondered if they would have felt the same if they knew he had a loaded Beretta in his pocket and no shyness in its use.

Franco had rarely been so subtle, but he forced himself to grin and bury his true intentions. But finally he blurted out, "Do you know if there are any Nazis aboard?"

He wanted to ask about werewolves specifically, but recognized the topic would not be well-received. But his blunt inquiry had an effect—several of the off-shift motormen, those whose job is to maintain the boilers and the screws that propel the vessel, looked at each other before shrugging or shaking their heads.

All right, they know the ship sometimes carries escaping Nazis. Do they benefit, or is their silence unwilling?

Franco pressed his questioning. "What about strange passengers? Are there any of those?"

Havlav laughed. "Some would say you and that priest are very strange," he said, making an obscene gesture.

The glare Franco turned on him killed the laugh before it could cross his features. "He is not like that."

"No one really knows what men have done with the excuse of war," another grease-stained off-duty crewman pointed out. "I have seen it."

"If I had seen what you describe, I would have cut off his balls."

Franco was satisfied when he saw that the effect of his statement was a kind of horror. He believed in telling people the truth.

"And if I saw certain Nazis, I would do the same."

"So you are a hunter of men, eh, boy?" the grease-stained mariner said, not quite joking.

"More a hunter of monsters."

"Yes, monsters, it's agreed. Scum of the earth, those Nazi bastards." Havlav mimed spitting.

"So no one has any information to share?" He stared at the few crewmen still around — the others had drifted off to their bunks, apparently.

"We just ferry cargo, we don't judge it," someone muttered.

"Perhaps you should," said Franco, emboldened by the spirits.

"Perhaps you—"

"Let him be." Havlav stared down the complainer.

Silence descended on the mess hall. A ship's clock on the bulkhead made the only sound, a loud ticking amplified by the metal wall.

The moment passed, and Franco ignored the complaint. The cards were dealt again, and soon a new rhythm had begun. He continued drinking as he played. He was not a natural, however, and he also continued losing until he declared he could lose no more.

"Watch out for Nazis," someone called out as he slid his stool from the table.

Leaving the mess hall, he tripped slightly in the doorway.

Wandering the long corridor, teetering slightly with the ship's rolling motion, Franco found his way back to the companionway and took the metal staircase up to his own deck. As he stepped out unsteadily, he heard a scrape behind and below, but he burped loudly and shuffled off the steps.

When someone came stealthily up the companionway, Franco was ready. He had silently doubled back a few meters and waited around the stairway corner. Although slight of body, he was all sinew and muscle, and his weight in a flying tackle was not inconsiderable. He took his follower off his feet and slammed him to the metal bulkhead, the Vatican dagger drawn and its blade poised on the man's neck.

"What do you want?" he shouted. The metal bulkheads returned his words as an echo. Franco's hand shook convincingly as he allowed his bared blade to nick the fat neck of Havlav, recently his friend down below. At the moment, Havlav was spluttering, albeit very carefully, since any great movement would slit his throat.

Franco dug the blade in and screamed in the motorman's face, "Why are you following me? What do you want?"

He registered the fact that the blade wasn't causing any sort of burning or sizzling on the man's neck. He wasn't a werewolf. But then, just *what* was he?

A thin line of blood appeared on Havlav's neck, parting the fat like a slab of bacon. If Franco sliced in one direction or the other, or bore down, the skin—and more—would part under the almost supernaturally sharp blade.

"You wanted to kill me?"

"No!" Havlav chanced speaking, his eyes filled with terror. "I wanted to warn you! There are others on board who will seek to kill you and the priest. You must believe me."

"Who are they?"

"I don't know. I have heard talk. Whispers. The crew, sometimes we hear things."

"Then you have heard enough to tell me."

"No, no. I do not, but I can, maybe, listen more…" His voice faded as he waited for Franco to decide his fate.

Franco stared into the older man's eyes—and deep into his soul, he thought. Havlav was a thug and a borderline criminal…but at this moment Franco sensed he was truthful.

"Very well," he said. "I will need your help." He thought nothing of enlisting someone even against his will. "Otherwise I can just kill you and throw you overboard." He was clearly not exaggerating.

Havlav nodded furiously. "I can help…"

"I need two lengths of chain. The heaviest you can still carry."

"Chains?"

"Bring them to my cabin an hour from now."

"What—why?"

"Are there guards on deck at night?"

"Guards?" Havlav seemed to be trying to define the term.

"Armed guards? Patrolling?"

"Ah," Havlav said, light shining in his eyes. Maybe it was the dagger's reflection. Franco was still holding it in the vicinity of his neck. "No, no guards, but there is duty officer or mate on bridge always. He may be able to see movement…"

"But he's not looking for it?"

Havlav said, "No, he will be looking to get warm and comfortable. He might scan the surface for icebergs, but this far south they are small."

Franco leaned on the dagger's blade once more and nicked Havlav's skin. "Bring the chains. One hour." He gave the cabin number and stalked away, leaving Havlav shivering.

Chapter Thirteen

Lupo

His head still ached and throbbed, but that wasn't the worst of it.

Despite the multitude of pins pricking his eyeballs and the blades slicing into them, and the pressure in his eye sockets, which were probably at least bruised if not cracked or outright broken, he *knew* he had opened his lids. He knew he was looking out at the ruined back wall of his cabin and the deck—now probably debris-strewn—that served as the cabin's rear porch. The fire was still raging, though it didn't seem to be spreading as fast now—thankfully, because he still hadn't been able to move from where he'd been tossed like the proverbial rag doll.

He knew he was looking at it, but couldn't see it.

Have to try and put out that fire before it spreads. Propane tank too close.

Fuck me, this could turn into a fucking forest fire.

Just one spark…

He tried speaking to himself internally in a calm voice. He wasn't sure why he also couldn't move his leg, or his left arm, really, but they'd been closer to the blast.

C4? Thermite? Plain old dynamite?

He was sure it wasn't a drone strike. He knew very well now how those fucking drones sounded as they approached, and he knew the growly *whoosh* the Reaper missiles made before they hit their target, and he hadn't heard that. He was sure he'd heard some geese overhead, just before the blast, barking like dogs in the sky. Unless some new kind of drone imitated that sound, there was no reason to think he'd been attacked by geese or goose-drones.

No, it was a plain old contact bomb. When the door opened...

When the door opened some kind of fuckin' bomb full of silver shrapnel just about wiped me off the face of the earth.

But it hadn't.

A mistake? A bad bomb-maker? Bad materials?

It didn't matter. Lupo groaned again as the thoughts flashed through his brain. In his mind he could see the damn door, but the sight was dredged up from his memory. He was facing the far side of the porch, so he should have seen that. His eyes *were* open, but he couldn't see.

No matter what else he felt, the liquid fire still in his veins, the fact that his eyes weren't working was somehow more terrifying to him.

And he couldn't quite move. Something was keeping him down on the ground—something that wasn't working. The multi-faceted pain had spread across all his nerve endings, some from the blast itself, some from the silver debris that had hit him, and—now, finally—from his own scorched skin.

Half his face was on fire!

Jesus Christ, my face...

It couldn't really be the case, but it felt that way. If he'd laid his head down sideways on a grill he figured it would have felt this way and he could imagine his skin, charred and blackened and flaking off or melting...

He imagined all that, but he still couldn't see it.

He knew one way to help fix his broken body, the one way he had been granted. All he had to do was force a change and, once in his wolf shape, he would immediately begin to heal. Since the silver shrapnel hadn't killed him outright, then he knew from experience—hell, Heather's experience, too—that it was possible to heal from just about whatever damage had been done.

Plus when they'd taken down Wolfpaw the first time, some of the stolen material the journalist Wineacre had given Heather had led him to believe that somehow he might have benefited from a stronger strain of the werewolf gene. It had been part of the reason he'd shown up on Wolfpaw's radar in the first place. Perhaps the shaman Joseph Badger's work, however esoteric it might have been, had tapped into the lycanthrope strain first developed in those Nazi labs. Perhaps that was why Nick Lupo was a stronger werewolf than average, somewhat resistant to the painful influence of silver. He'd managed to shoot handguns loaded with silver slugs and heal from the damage. Now he didn't think others could do that.

All this flashed through Lupo's mind in seconds, but it was useless to him since the silver still coursed through his veins, scorching him from the inside out. It was small comfort to know he could handle it better than another creature...the pain was still excruciating and he could feel convulsions starting to develop. To shake him.

He was alternating from extreme heat, like a spiking fever, which made sense, to some sort of super chill as if his blood was turning to ice in the scorched veins and making his extremities tingle as if about to succumb to frostbite.

The shaking surprised him, like a symptom of Parkinson's but somehow more frightening because its origin was a complete mystery.

The nearby flames seemed to be licking up the remaining portion of the cabin's back wall, but it was almost a silent fire and it was the crackling of the combustibles themselves that gave its presence away. That and the heat that still radiated outward.

He was still aware that the flames could reach him if he didn't try something soon.

Lupo half-dragged himself away from the fire and promptly rolled off the deck-cum-porch, bouncing down the sharp-edged three steps and landing on the weedy gravel with a grunt. And a new contusion on his face where the edge of a step or two left a furrow on his cheek and barely missed breaking his jaw.

Fuck!

Now he hurt even more, although this pain was more normal and manageable. He could understand the kind of pain that would end up leaving bumps and bruises. His problem was the silver and what it was doing to him, making his insides scream. He could still feel the fire's heat and he rolled farther away, barely able to propel himself given that he was still somewhat paralyzed on one side.

Okay, now he sensed he was far enough removed from the flames.

He tried to gather himself and managed to somehow push himself onto all fours, even though because of his paralysis his balance was off and felt as though he would tip over sideways any second. He hung his head like a dog in pain.

He had to do what he always did to cause the change and bring the Creature inside him, his wolf, to the fore. They would both ride in the wolf's head, so to speak, and though he couldn't communicate with the Creature directly, he had learned to direct the wolf's behavior more often than not, although sometimes the wolf seemed to prefer the Creature's orders over Lupo's.

With some difficulty he forced himself to focus, then he began to visualize himself as the wolf.

Normally this process would mysteriously—he would have said *magically*—resolve itself into a sudden, tingling change as his DNA realigned and he would hit the ground running on four paws, his body shifted into that of an oversized black wolf.

He visualized, squeezing his sightless eyes as he attempted to force his change in the only way he knew how. He visualized, but the image he managed to put together was blurred and hazy, and he did not feel the usual tingle and sexual arousal that paralleled the required DNA realignment…

Jesus. What the fuck?

He tried again, focusing harder in order to visualize the change. Sweat broke out of his pores and streamed down his forehead and into his useless eyes, burning like acid until he swore again and lay his head on the gravel so he could scratch himself. The burned patches on the skin of his face shrieked and so did he, but the sweat still burned and the image of the wolf still wouldn't come, no matter how hard he tried to conjure it.

Goddamn it, it's not working.

This had never happened to him.

But then, he'd never been blown up before. He had come close recently, when a secret Wolfpaw lab near Minocqua had been blown just as he and DiSanto were trying to negotiate the fence around it, but they'd been far enough from the blockhouse that the blast hadn't hurt them besides tossing them to the ground. And there hadn't been any special shrapnel…that was a difference.

Was it the silver in his system?

But no, he'd seen Heather manage to change when grievously wounded by silver, and she'd begun healing immediately, even if at a slower rate due to the severity of her wounds. But Heather was amazingly resilient—*maybe she was also a beneficiary of the Nazi gene?* Who had bitten her? Wasn't it that Wolfpaw weasel they called *Tef?* Had he been a descendant of someone who'd undergone the wartime experiments conducted by the Nazi doctor who had worked for some general named VonStumpfahren?

If it wasn't the silver, and if the explosion itself hadn't yet killed him, then why was Lupo unable to shift into his wolf body?

Then it came to him, a jab almost as excruciating as the many sharp pains from which he was already suffering.

It had to be because he was blind.

Fuck, I'm blind.

And the one thing I need to do to start healing is the one thing I can't do...

Shooter

He was still in the throes of his flashback, the narcotic cocktail roaring through his system but not diminishing the effects of the visions or the fever. The trashed motel room came in and out, and when it faded away...

He was there again, in the charnel house where his friends had been murdered by creatures that could not be. Monsters that could not exist in a God-fearing world.

He was there again, as if he had never left.

The grenades exploded, ripping and tearing apart the corpses of his squad, but the half-deaf Shooter was shocked to realize moments later that he was still untouched, as if selected by God himself. Covered in blood, offal, and bits of bone and brains, he stumbled to his feet and became a walking corpse. His rifle still in the steel-like grip of hands he couldn't feel, he made his way through the slaughterhouse to the far wall, where another, smaller doorway led to a narrow hallway staircase. His nose by now closed to the stench of violent death, he ducked then tripped and rolled down the uneven steps until he lay near a rear doorway.

Behind him, he heard the crash of ordnance piercing the walls, followed by multiple explosions.

RPGs.

He knew without a doubt that the Wolfpaw murderers were obliterating the evidence, which now would likely resemble an enemy RPG attack on an unsuspecting squad of Marines. No one would test the fragmented corpses. The rocket-propelled incendiary grenades would turn his dead friends into liquefied hamburger.

He crashed through the doorway and rolled into another narrow alley, this one narrower and apparently between buildings. The sounds of screaming and gunfire behind him led him to run stumbling in the other direction, taking a jagged right as soon as he could and finding another narrow corridor between walled courtyards. An abandoned neighborhood, most likely. Now dragging his heavy rifle after him, he continued to take alternating lefts and rights in order to escape the marauding mercenaries…

And whatever *they* were.

He knew what he had seen, what had chased and almost killed him. Hell, almost eaten him.

Still he refused to contemplate the nature of what he had witnessed, but deep inside a psychosis was taking root, though he was unaware of it.

He thought he heard snarling behind him and gathered his strength to run faster despite the broiling sun overhead, despite his dazed condition, and despite the heavy equipment he had never had the chance to drop.

Were the monstrous canines or wolves still giving chase, or had he escaped their notice after the massacre of his squad.

Lockett was dead, Karicke was dead, they were all dead.

All dead. *No, all murdered.*

They'd been murdered by those Wolfpaw monsters, he knew that, but who would believe him?

Who the fuck would believe him?

And how many more of the monsters existed?

Where they everywhere, all around him? Was every black uniform one of *them*?

He didn't realize it then, but his right eye had started to twitch.

And, just like that, his career as a sniper was over.

But his career in insanity had just begun, and it continued to worsen.

The psychological discharge came about six months later, when he could no longer function as a Marine, let alone a Marine sniper. They went easy on him, considering, choosing not to blame him for the death of his squadmates. But the military meat grinder turned and deposited him into the clutches of a Veterans' Administration hospital that was overwhelmed with battle scars, both actual and virtual, and his own had worsened so much that one by one his advocates folded up their tents and apologetically left him behind.

And by the time the next two years passed, Shooter had begun to see the masks of humanity slip—the monsters inside showed themselves to him on the sidewalks, in the stores, in parks, in the places where he was hired only to be fired within days. And on public transportation…they were all over the country's trains and buses. He couldn't afford to fly, not on his meager benefits, but he bet even planes overhead were filled with the filthy monsters.

Someday he would get to them. But for now, his mission had changed. It had become all about ridding public transportation of the bloodthirsty creatures, and he had become an expert at spotting them no matter what "normal" human mask they might be wearing—he could always see behind the grotesque masks to the real features behind the façade.

His first bus shooting liberated humans who didn't know enough to be grateful. They'd screamed and screamed, and he had been forced to convince them to keep quiet—and when they'd disobeyed he realized that the monsters even controlled the innocent people, who were therefore no longer innocent.

He began with the very next bus shooting to spare no one, to deal out death to monsters and potential victims alike. He started to see it as a cleansing—but he was unsure whom he cleansed more: the monsters, the victims, or himself.

And he moved from city to city, rooting out the monsters as they rode the city and county buses, killing them and anyone near them indiscriminately. After all, he knew that surviving the bite of one of them brought you back as a monster yourself—and he had made contingency plans should he suffer a bite.

He killed again, and again, and again.

The werewolves were everywhere.

Interlude

Berlin Underground
The Führer Bunker, April 1945

Three hours had passed, and by then VonStumpfahren had to find his own way into the bunker's secret doorway in the garden of the old Reich Chancellery and down the concrete-encased staircase. The beautiful secretary was gone, replaced by an old man in an ill-fitting uniform who showed him into the same waiting room he had recently used. By now several cracks had appeared in the ceiling and the sound of shelling didn't seem quite so muffled, or perhaps it was his imagination.

He gave the military salute as he entered, and the three men who awaited him stood stiffly at attention and returned it.

"You are to come with me, Herr Untersturmführer," he said to the young second lieutenant with the special collar flashes. To the other two, his armed escort: "You are to wait for my orders." The two noncommissioned officers clutched their black scorpion-shaped MP-40 machine pistols with the paratrooper stocks folded.

All three men clicked their heels. He noted that their boots were no longer shiny, and their uniforms had been patched. The shortages had hit everyone, and he felt the bittersweet sting of nostalgia for the days when the pageantry had seemed eternal.

He followed the old man into the inner sanctum, and the second lieutenant followed him without question. Inside the empty office with the huge desk, he ordered the officer (whose name was Beutner or something like that) to disrobe. While the young man did, VonStumpfahren clicked open his briefcase and removed a special set of four manacles connected by short chains.

If Untersturmführer Beutner was surprised, he did not show it. He stood naked now, his leanly muscled physique still a tribute to the Aryan ideal, his penis flaccid but classically shaped and more than acceptable, VonStumpfahren noted.

Under other circumstances...

He shook his head and set to the task of chaining the lieutenant, whose face still showed no surprise or questioning. But his penis was beginning to grow and harden as the general snapped the manacles closed and made sure they were locked. He stepped back and gazed admiringly at the young man, his eyes roving over every centimeter of the superior body.

The future of the Reich.

And so was Hydra.

The general sighed, stepped back and nodded at the elderly guard, who left the room. He heard voices from beyond the doorway, one of whom he had heard just that afternoon. The general then nodded at the lieutenant. "You know your orders already, Untersturmführer."

Hair began to sprout along the young Aryan's arms and shoulders, and his eyes started to swirl like kaleidoscopes flitting from color to color, and by the time Beutner's penis had become engorged and his body had begun to transform, the general backed out of the room. He shut the door behind him and waited.

The doors were solid in the bunker, several inches of steel-lined wood reinforced with additional bands of metal. Two, then three minutes passed. The sounds he heard were muffled, but audible enough that he could visualize what had happened. The lieutenant had been carefully briefed. The unusual circumstances and his glorious role in them had been outlined. Von Stumpfahren felt the floor beneath him shake slightly, and more dust sprinkled into the waiting room from the ceiling cracks.

Time is of the essence.

He could feel the stranglehold tightening as avenues of escape began to close. He checked his watch, a fine old Swiss timepiece with impeccable time. With luck, there were still hours available for him to finish all his tasks. He forced his upper-class calmness to overwhelm the urge to fidget. He kept away from the two SS men and their weapons, feeling some heat washing off them, but not enough to cause him undue distress.

Events were unfolding now, and there would only be the one chance.

Suddenly the door was thrown open and the elderly guard gestured wildly, his eyes wide and crazed.

"Inside!" the general ordered, and the two SS men preceded him into the office. At a glance, he saw the old man bent over the bloodied body of the Führer in one corner. Nearby, was the naked lieutenant, still manacled but only barely, with two bloody hands freed from the shredded metal handcuffs. Patches of coarse hair seemed to flow over his muscled body. His penis was still swollen.

"Guard," VonStumpfahren commanded, "check the prisoner."

"But, Herr General, the Führer—"

"Never mind the Führer, he is fine! Check the man who has done this and whose hands are free!"

"Jawohl!" The guard stumbled toward the blond Lieutenant Beutner and when he hunched over him, VonStumpfahren said, "Fire!"

The SS men emptied their MP-40 magazines into the two figures, the silver slugs sizzling as they ripped through the lieutenant's body. Suddenly there was silence as the last of the spent brass stopped rolling on the concrete floor. Both men were shot to bits, but the lieutenant's body seemed to be roasting from the inside, his skin sizzling and the smell of scorched flesh and blood permeated the air along with the haze of cordite.

"Quick, take them in these blankets and carry them up the stairs and into the garden." VonStumpfahren handed the stunned SS men two folded cloths. "Your Führer commands you."

They slung their Schmeissers onto their shoulders and set to the disgusting task, their faces screwed up in horror as the lieutenant's body continued to combust from the inside. The general had made sure ahead of time that the MP-40 magazines they'd been issued were filled with the special silver rounds. He followed now as they dragged and half-carried the bloody, ruined bodies up the staircase. Once outside, the Soviet shelling now impossibly close, the General gave them two cans of petrol and a lighter, the order obvious.

"For Germany," he said, "and for the Reich!"

They obeyed as they had been trained, and in seconds the bodies in their blankets were engulfed in fiercely-burning flames that shot sparks a dozen feet into the air. Nearby buildings shook as Russian shells seemed to creep closer.

Where the hell are the Americans? The general knew the plight of Berlin would be less dire with the easy-going Yanks. The

Soviets were sadistic devils who delighted in torture and rape like barbarians of old, their ancestors. He looked forward to personally killing a few before making good his escape, nevertheless he wished his beloved city could have been spared the destruction and death they would gleefully mete out.

The SS men stood away from the flames, watching the bodies burn. It was enhanced petrol, so they burned brightly and the remains were thoroughly consumed. The men, hardened as they were, held hands over their faces to avoid inhaling the horrific stench.

VonStumpfahren shot them both in the back of the head.

He reholstered his P-08 Parabellum and kicked the corpses onto the flames.

He descended the stairs to the bunker level again, fulfilling one last mission for his Führer. In less than a half hour he climbed out of the staircase and closed the hidden door.

Then he made his way through the ruined gardens, shells raining down all around the block—the Reich Chancellery was in their sights now—and found his command car miraculously still in one piece.

Hydra would begin as soon as he gave the word.

Part Two

Chapter Fourteen

Heather

She stretched languidly in the near-darkness. The last rays of the sun had set in the corner of the floor to ceiling windows that overlooked the squat converted warehouses of Milwaukee's Third Ward. She had left on mood lighting here and there, dimmed lights in recesses that provided a facsimile of lighting without brightening any of the room. Several dozen candles ringed the king-size bed in the center of the cavernous bedroom chamber of her secret double loft, their stuttering flames making flickering shadows on the dappled skin of her bed partner.

Drying sweat, clammy sheets, the heady scent of sex in the air, the burning of the wicks and the blending aromas of the candles… Heather Wilson could have purred.

Pain was a distant memory etched into the nether regions of her brain, but it didn't take much to transport her back to where her pain had been her whole life. Every movement, every position, every thought had been given over to the pain that coursed through her veins as she'd healed once again from wounds that had seemed like the edge of an abyss, an abyss that could have swallowed her whole—if she'd let it.

But Heather Wilson wasn't anything if not a survivor, and she'd nursed herself back to health...and faster than she'd expected.

She'd had some help, but it hadn't been much. They would have let her die, she knew, except for one of them and what he had told the others.

"Without her, we might not have gotten them," he had said.

Rich DiSanto was sweet, and she knew he was sweet on her. She smiled sarcastically in the dark, mocking his almost childlike crush and how easily she had manipulated him because of it. Although the fucking had been good, very good. Still, it had been nothing more than a chess move, at least on her part. She knew she needed an ally in *their* camp.

"What are you thinking?"

The voice was soft, but Heather could feel the steely edge in it. Hell, it was one thing she liked about it.

"Oh, I was just reminiscing about some friends," she said, letting her hand slip onto a lean but muscular thigh and following the smooth curve up to the perfect buttock that crowned it. "I was just thinking that sometimes it's best to leave some friends behind. You know, when new ones come along and take their place." Her fingers made circular patterns on the warm skin, and she enjoyed the candlelight's playful chasing of their shadows.

"That feels good. Haven't you had enough?"

The steely edge was replaced by gentle mocking and, for a second, Heather forgot who this was. "I never have enough, darling," she murmured. Her hands pried open the willing thighs and she climbed over and between them, positioning herself so she could look up into the dark eyes that held hers as her lips approached the beautiful vulva blooming before her. "Never enough," she muttered before getting to work.

The woman's sighs were stimulus enough, but her fragrant wetness drove Heather crazy with desire, and they rocked to their own rapidly increasing rhythm. Long, slender hands caressed Heather's head as she lavished attention on her lover until thighs squeezing her informed her the moment had arrived, and they rode it together, up and down its peaks and valleys.

When Heather was finished, she climbed up like a panther—*but she was more than that, wasn't she?*—soft, sweat-slick skin sliding on skin, and they kissed deeply and at length, nestling comfortably together. Then the other woman reached out and with her hands gently guided Heather where she wanted her, first straddling her breasts, then Heather's sex slowly approaching her open mouth and her reaching tongue. When Heather was positioned immediately above her lover's face, she squatted downward and felt the wiry tongue plunge upward, inside her. Tilting her head back, she growled her pleasure but was able to keep her *true* growl under control. The woman's long fingers spreading wide on her buttocks, she ground herself into the eager mouth below and focused on how the warm, wet tongue worshiped her inner and outer lips and sought out her bloated clitoris.

This woman knows her stuff, she thought, her eyes almost crossing from the pleasure.

"Oh, God," she said, her head tilting backward so her hair became a golden cascade. "Oh, yeah, right there..."

Too bad I might have to kill her.

Colgrave

The condominium association meeting frustrated her beyond belief, and she couldn't wait to pour herself a large drink.

No, wait, a hot chocolate laced with dark rum. That would warm her up—the chill she felt was as much the cool weather as it was what she felt from her fellow owners. She was a thorn in the board's side, she knew it. She wanted things done right, meetings run like real meetings, not free-for-all discussions and love-fests. She wanted problems tackled, not put on a list for future consideration. And when she called them on their many missteps, she felt their animosity—the board's because she was too rigid, and the other owners' because they loved their friends, the board members. Something about a church they all attended. Colgrave was a cop, single, an atheist, a hardnose—she wasn't into just sitting around counting your toes for fun.

So every damn meeting was an exercise in frustration. This one had ended with open hostility toward her. Some of the owners whined: *Why don't you just leave them alone? They don't get paid.*

That's no excuse for incompetence, cronyism, and near-bullying, she'd retorted.

It didn't matter. Deaf ears.

She put her key in the door and flicked on the lights. It was chilly inside, too, and she shucked her leather coat and swapped it for a thick sweater. Got some water going for instant hot chocolate and measured out a generous ounce and a half (maybe it was two) of Bacardi Select.

Shit, she couldn't get rid of the image of Nick Lupo standing in her doorway. Talking to her, keeping her happy as part of his team?

She stirred the thick chocolate-like liquid—she liked a *lot* of powder—and poured in the rum. Instantly, she felt warmer.

Maybe it was Nick Lupo's image in her mind…making her decidedly *warmer.* The big lug was sexy, mostly because he didn't seem to be aware of it. Maybe he wasn't aware of the musk or the sex pheromones or whatever it was that he gave off. Maybe it was because of what he was.

But thinking of Nick Lupo also brought back those other images, the ones that had affected her life more than anything she could ever have expected. Expected in a *normal* life, anyway.

She shook her head and sank into her favorite well-worn leather chair with the mug, keeping most of the lights off.

The fact was she dreaded going to sleep. She dreaded being awakened by the nightmares. She knew they lurked always behind her lids, beyond her view and control. She wanted to knock herself out with the rum, so she could snatch a couple hours of bad sleep out of a usually sleepless night.

What she'd seen in that strange house in the center of Minnesota's northern lake country was just too much. She had seen the men turning into monstrous wolves.

Impossible.

Impossibly.

Yet, she had seen it, and like Rich DiSanto, she had shot at them with the hot MP5s. It was like a fucking movie, except she'd lived through it and it was no movie. She'd seen the jaws full of fangs, the fur, the monstrous size of the wolves that had been human.

Then they'd rescued that Wilson woman, the TV journalist, who had seemed to be barely this side of death, but who had started to heal magically as soon as they had gotten her out of the clutches of the bastards—no, they were truly *monsters*—who had her.

The place, a sort of gargantuan homage to Frank Lloyd Wright's designs, had been decked out with high-tech control stations for the drones the bastards had highjacked right under the military's nose. She had seen it all herself, though she barely believed it.

Then they'd destroyed the house with explosive charges. *Fuckin' movie again.*

But what she'd seen there lived with her still, every night.

And what she now knew Nick Lupo to be—one of *them*—both bothered and excited her. And this confused her, which added to the fear. Colgrave had never been one to shrink from anything. She'd been fearless, some would have said reckless, in every one of her violent encounters—and she'd had more than most. But this was different, and it had put her in a kind of tailspin.

Now she forced herself to sit in the dark, with her cooling mug in hand, and waiting for sleep to take her...knowing something else would take her then, too.

Her eyes closed; soon the images came unbidden but inevitable. They coalesced into nightmares filled with monstrous teeth tearing human flesh. And spurting blood.

She fought the images but they won, and when dawn came she opened her eyes, grateful but exhausted.

Lupo

B*lind.*

He mouthed the word with a sense of fear he hadn't felt even when going up against heavily armed Alpha teams of mercenary werewolves, or the hit squad Wolfpaw had sent to his house. He hadn't felt any fear when raiding the mobsters' compound, being targeted by drones and their Reaper missiles.

Blind. Fucking blind.

Besides the paralysis and the pain that wracked his body, he couldn't see.

And he couldn't visualize his change, usually leading to the DNA realignment.

The Creature was locked up inside his damaged body with no way to manifest, and—more importantly—start to heal Lupo's human body.

Okay, now what?

He attempted to think rationally, but it was an irrational situation to begin with, and outside his experience.

Plus, Ghost Sam was not popping in with his homespun humorous suggestions, or directions. Lupo half-expected to hear his friend's ghostly voice, and he longed to. But there was nothing from the ghost, whom Lupo tended to believe was his own mental reflection of his friend's influence, brought about by the trauma of his death.

"Sam?" he asked calmly.

"Sam!" he shouted, when the calmness wore off. "Sam!"

He sniffled as he whispered the name once more. "*Sam?*"

He shrugged. He'd have to soldier on without Ghost Sam, it seemed.

The cabin fire seemed to have slowed, maybe even burned itself out. While that was good, it meant it was actually possible no one would have spotted the smoke, or would have thought it was a bonfire on some Indian's property. If neither the rez fire department nor the Eagle River FD were alerted, then no one would be coming, and if none of the distant neighbors had heard the blast or seen the smoke, ditto.

Lupo reached for his phone with the one hand that worked okay. Not in his pocket. He slapped himself silly, but the comforting and familiar flat rectangle was not in any pocket.

Shit.

He'd had it in his hand when he reached the back door. Now he remembered switching it to the other hand.

Maybe he could drive the Mustang out of the garage and get himself on the road even if he couldn't see. But...he couldn't feel his keys, either.

That was because he'd carried *both* his keys and phone with him when the door had exploded and sent him through the air like a puppet flopping off a stage. Which meant they might be laying around along with the hot debris. He propped himself on one shoulder and patted the ground around him, sharp gravel digging into his palm.

Nothing. Jagged pieces of wood siding and glass were scattered around him, but nothing that felt familiar.

Not much chance of that kind of luck, was there?

Ghost Sam might have led him to the phone, but it seemed that was not to be.

He remembered he'd rolled off the deck. Maybe he should work his way onto the deck, if he could get himself back up the three steps?

He was determined to try, but he realized it was very likely the keys and the phone had landed much farther away, which meant that he might never locate them no matter how much he tried. At least not until he could see again.

Dammit, I'm trying anyway.

It took him a half hour to crawl back onto the deck. All he felt along the way was still hot sharp bits of wood and a carpet of glass shards. His hand bleeding and riddled with splinters and scratches, he gave up and snorted blood out his nose again, too, just to keep things interesting. The stream gushed out over his clothing, but it was the last thing on his mind.

He was gasping by the time he got there, throat dry.

He paused to rest and reassess. Then, despite still laying on the deck, he tried his best to turn his face to three directions, hoping some light would seep through his sudden darkness, but it was no good. The light was probably going fast in any case, but he wasn't seeing even the glow or a halo or anything to indicate his sight was beginning to return.

Goddamn.

This was quite a predicament.

No eyes, no one really knew he was here, keys and phone missing in action. No police radio in the Mustang. No tools he could get to because they were in the trunk or in the blown-up cabin. Even if he found his way to the garage and the car, then what? Now he wished he'd learned to hot-wire cars, even just older ones that were easier. A new one would have been beyond his ability in any case. Plus he'd closed the garage and he could have used his phone to open it, but the phone was not letting itself be found.

No, he had to find an alternative. He had to stick with the proven.

He tried again to force a change, concentrating on visualizing himself going over as he always did, seeing himself as the wolf, the Creature inside, and then—*it's a fact, Jack!*—his DNA would mysteriously realign and in a split second he would be completely over and then he'd feel his body responding to the magical healing...

But he did all that again now, and there was no change in his body.

Fuck, it isn't working.

He growled, but it was a human growl of anger and frustration, not the growl of a wolf at all. The Creature was silenced for the moment.

He tried to quell his rising panic.

As if the pain wasn't enough, there was the fear that he would be undone by some asshole's bomb, just like that.

There was still fire inside the cabin. He could hear it crackle and consume some of the wood, but it seemed to be in the process of burning itself out. He sensed he wasn't going to burn up in a conflagration. No, this bomb had been designed to do its worst to him, right there at the door, and the rest was unimportant.

Maybe concentrating on who had wanted him dead would give his system a chance to reset and he'd be back in action in no time. He didn't believe it, but he had to keep his mind active rather than let it wallow in fear and self-pity. Even rage was better.

There were the obvious crooks and criminals he'd put in prison at one time or another, but he was fairly certain none of them knew his secret. The few who had, he'd...*neutralized*.

There were people who knew about him: Jessie, Heather, DiSanto.

Heather was a possibility. She was vengeful, jealous, conniving, backstabbing—and most certainly a murderer, although he'd never proved it. He suspected as a new werewolf she'd killed a raft of homeless people for sport and food. You just never knew with her—she was both dangerous and a magnet for danger. But she seemed to take her job as a journalist seriously, seeking out the criminal and the evil of Wolfpaw with singular dedication, even going undercover as an evil dominatrix—which hadn't been that much of a stretch for her.

And she'd been obsessed with him, hadn't she?

He glossed over this part, ignoring his own role in the obsession.

No, the bomb hadn't been set by Heather Wilson. She'd have done her killing in person, as either a human or a wolf. No bombs for her...

It didn't take him long to come down to Wolfpaw itself, or its backing nucleus, Wolfclaw. He'd become a target and he'd managed to thwart their plans too often, and they were surely not above a little bombing. But it seemed too *petty*, didn't it? He wasn't sure why he was tied into the Wolfpaw influence, but they'd sent alpha teams to kill him, and drones. A little contact bomb was just too unlikely an ambush for them.

So maybe that left only the Bastone family. At least this month.

Not Gus Bastone, the guy who wanted to be the Don of the Bastone family and take over the rez casino. He had been an unlikely survivor of the recent carnage at his Eagle River compound, but he might as well have been dead—he was hospitalized in a private facility and reported to be hovering near death. Even if he lived, he would not be walking or talking normally ever again. Or getting any boners, even though they'd been the basis of half his life.

But Joe Rabbioso, his one-time enforcer, looked pretty good for it. Rabbioso, who had also survived the inferno and had disappeared.

Who also happened to be a werewolf.

Rabbioso had improbably saved Jessie from being raped by a couple low-lives at the bottom of the family totem-pole, but he'd had no trouble slugging it out with Lupo, both of them in wolf form. He was a vengeful type, wasn't he? Came with the territory, for the average mobster. Even if he was kind to old ladies and little kids and puppies, none of that mattered when it came to money and honor—his own honor.

Working thesis, Lupo thought, *it's Rabbioso.*

The damned Expedition at the gas station in New London loomed large suddenly. Maybe that was the asshole himself, or more likely a bunch of henchmen on their way home after rigging his house. But how did they know he was heading there? Or didn't it matter, they just figured on hitting him whenever he showed up? *Whatever...*

Knowing who might have done the deed didn't help in any way.

So now what?

He had managed to ignore the pain in his veins and tendons and nerves for a few minutes, but now it all came roaring back in one wave and he cried out with the severity of the jabs, like lightning searing his insides. The silver shrapnel felt as if it was moving around, scorching his tissue wherever it went, making his blood sizzle. It had been a miracle he'd managed to set it aside so long.

Maybe not a miracle.

Maybe it was working its way out, losing its strength? Maybe his system was somehow neutralizing it?

He wondered if this were true, if it was what made him somehow *special*. Everyone but him seemed to think so.

The wave passed, then gathered strength again and redoubled the pain.

He writhed on the ground, almost helpless.

Chapter Fifteen

Heather

Running was part of the joy of *wolfing out*, as she sometimes called it, and she ran until her thick fur steamed in the chilly night air.

She'd left her partner happy and sweaty, snuggled in the mussed bed in her loft.

The sex had been great, better than great—it was still a pleasant scent in her sensitive nostrils—and the result was that right now Heather lusted for blood. She had learned this about herself since her life had changed when a lovely psychopath had bitten her: wolfing out increased her need for sexual gratification, and sex itself increased her need for a kill.

She wasn't currently into killing her sex partners (not that she hadn't before, mind you), so it meant she had to hunt.

The hunt was *all* right now. There was nothing else.

Her paws came down hard yet silently on the leaf-covered floor of the wooded Lake Park. Above the thinning trees were the lights of Milwaukee's small "gold coast," a pale imitation of southern rival Chicago's, but nevertheless impressive on its own. The park stretched along the same Lake Michigan shoreline, flowing down a long bluff to the beaches and marinas below. A half-moon beacon above welcomed her into its arms and she howled in delight, knowing she was warning the potential prey to keep to their lairs.

Tonight she sought different prey.

The moon's desires would not be denied, and tonight the moon wanted a less furry meal.

Heather rode along in the wolf's body and felt the desire course as electricity through her veins, her tendons, her muscles—*the wolf's,* but she was so very aware in there, unlike Nick Lupo, who had told her he'd struggled years to bridge his human and wolf sides—and soon she was following a scent.

It was a scent even a human would have been able to follow. *More like a stench,* she thought.

She came upon its source. A well-muffled homeless male had made a shallow indentation at the base of a large leafless maple, but the rancid smell of him spilled out much farther than his hollow.

The wolf didn't find the smell objectionable. It was what it was.

The wolf that was Heather approached stealthily, but she hadn't needed to. The man snored softly, and now Heather herself could pick out the smell of cheap wine as well as the body odor.

He would taste rather like a marinated roast, she thought and chuckled in the part of her mind that was separate from that of the wolf. And saliva drooled between the wolf's jaws as she crept closer, hoping to take him quickly. She was tired from running and wanted a sit-down meal, anyway.

When he awoke his eyes snapped open despite the crusts formed in the corners. He was staring right into her wolf's rolling eyes, colors changing like a kaleidoscope, and he opened his mouth to scream. His eyes were frozen open, inability to comprehend what was happening to him written there in broad strokes.

And she fell upon him, her jaws striking like a cobra's head and grabbing hold of the loose skin that ringed his neck, tearing through the muffler and scarves he wore for protection from the cold. As soon as she'd bared his neck, the jaws went back in like a flash and tore into his carotid.

Blood splashed into her open snout and she lapped it up even while tearing the homeless man's neck apart.

His screeches went unheard. If he had prayers at the end, she was sure those went unheard too.

Predator and prey were as far from the road as they could be. She saw lights rake across treetops above the decline, but their windows would be powered up and their iPods and satellite radios would blot out the sound of his screams.

One jerk of the powerful head and the screeching was cut off abruptly. Then she dug into his filthy clothing with her snout—not hard because the coat seemed to lack buttons—and started to rip and tear his lower torso apart, seeking out the tender delicacies that made up his internal organs.

She gorged herself on the tasty flesh and offal.

When she was done, she changed and stood still in her magnificent naked human form, letting some of his blood dry on her skin. She stared up at the moon, as if offering a sacrifice to the one who ruled her…

Then she quickly rolled up the remains in the multiple layers of coats and shirts, and dug down further into the loose soil he'd shaped as a shelter. A scattering of soil and leaves above him made him indistinguishable from a lump of roots at the base of the tree.

She found rather a positive message in the fact that if his body went unfound his fluids would help nourish the tree.

She knew she should worry about the homeless guy, but she hadn't taken one in a long while. By the time they did find him, his lumpy remains wouldn't give up much information. If they tested more thoroughly they'd find that he had been attacked by a dog-like creature with strange DNA. They would just connect the dots, figuring there had been an error in the testing. Besides, chances were nobody would find him until long after the winter, and by then even the DNA would be suspect.

Heather Wilson loved living on the edge. She'd proven her confidence worked often enough that she barely bothered to question her impulses, preferring to act on them — especially if pleasure was involved.

And Heather loved mixing pleasure with business.

Lupo

Ah, fuck, why does it have to hurt so much?

He was still on the debris-strewn deck and the fire within the structure, or what remained of it, seemed to have burned out. He had blacked out for a while, he didn't know how long, but the pain woke him and he groaned and swore aloud.

He was curled up on his side and still hurting, but the worst of the pain in his leg did seem to be fading.

Slowly fading.

Lupo rolled onto his stomach, feeling bits and pieces of sharp debris shifting under him, poking him.

He made sure his eyes were open, checking with a pair of fingers. Eyelids up. He blew out his breath in frustration.

The fact that his eyes were open but he couldn't see was disconcerting.

Blind!

He patted the area around himself, hoping to luck onto his keys or phone, but no, it couldn't be *that* easy. He widened his reach a little, but still nothing. He dragged himself a few inches in one direction and tried again. Then again, slowly traversing the deck toward the side. He had to be careful because at the far end, the deck was cantilevered above the sloping hillside that fell away, and he could drop off the open planking between railing posts and roll a long way down the hill toward the thin strip of beach. Some large pine would likely break his rolling fall first, but also break either an arm or a leg to go with his previous injuries.

Or skewer him with a sharp branch…

He was reminded that his left leg hadn't functioned before. Now it was sore, his bones aching deeply, but he could move it. He patted both hands around on the deck, still looking for the phone or his keys. Nothing, so he slowly shifted over…

And rolled down the hard-edged steps.

He grunted as his ribs and shoulders took the brunt of his rolling. He came to a stop a couple yards past the bottom step on the gravel.

Damn it.

He must have been rolling on an angle when he thought he was parallel with the edge of the deck, so now he was confused about where he was in actuality. He threw out his arms and checked around blindly, still hoping luck would bring him to his phone and keys.

No luck.

Why couldn't he see? And why couldn't he force himself to change?

He tried again, with no effect.

He visualized himself running on four legs, as he often did, and then he was over—*it's a fact, Jack!*—except that he wasn't. Instead of finding himself on four strong paws he was still lying on gravel, his aching, throbbing legs below him. Not broken, but not cooperating, either.

The pain *was* starting to fade, that was one good thing.

There were bad things, too. No phone or keys, being blind, nightfall coming and with it a lowering of the temperature, and no shelter.

No Creature to get him out of this. No inner wolf to help him heal whatever wounds he had suffered.

Maybe it was because he was blind that he couldn't turn, couldn't visualize himself turning, which was the way the mechanism worked.

Christ! Because I can't see, I can't see myself to the healing...

When he'd rolled off the deck, besides the pain of smashing his battered body onto every step edge, he'd also lost his perspective on where he was in relation to the rear of the cottage itself. If he went too far, he could still conceivably roll down the hill. It was steep enough that he'd find climbing back up difficult, unless he found the stepped path.

He shivered.

Reaction to the explosion? Maybe, but the temperature was also dropping.

He realized that the explosion and fire might have ruined the floor inside the cottage, so he was reluctant to work his way up there lest he fall through the floor into the grimy cellar and cause himself even worse trouble. Especially now that he couldn't just turn into a wolf and take care of it.

Slowly, he gathered himself and was able to rise, teetering, onto his knees. The sharp gravel bit into his scraped-raw knees, but he ignored it and carefully raised himself to stand on two feet.

Standing, yes, but wavering.

He wasn't very steady, and there was no wall, or railing, or even tree near enough to help him. Hell, he would have taken a scrawny bush.

He started to sweat. By the time he was mostly upright, unsteady as if he were drunk, portions of his body shook as if he had Parkinson's.

The *slap* of the shot came after the slug hit one of the deck posts, close enough for splinters to act like shrapnel and poke holes in his skin.

Another shot hit the post and another *slap* reached his ears.

He dropped to the ground, no longer worried about the sharp debris.

Fuck, where's the shooter?

This was a low-caliber, high-velocity rifle. A 5.56mm: maybe an AR-15, or a Ruger Mini-14. Something more exotic?

Crack!

Slap...

The third shot shattered the post into kindling and broke some glass in the remaining back window of his cottage.

He reached for his Sig, but he didn't have it. He'd left it locked in the car, inside the garage he couldn't get into. Along with the H&K submachine gun. And his Vatican blade.

Goddamn it.

Another shot slapped the air just over his head and he tried to burrow his way into the gravel.

Helpless.

It was not a feeling he relished.

Chapter Sixteen

Franco Lupo

On the Freighter Zeniča, crossing the Atlantic Ocean
December 1945

When Havlav arrived with the chains, it was obvious there had been a strong discussion. The priest, Tranelli, was less than pleased to learn Franco had coerced a crewman into helping them. Franco had told the priest to butt out—and stay in his cabin.

But when the chains were unlimbered, the priest was there, helping. Although he looked at the crewman with suspicion.

"We can trust this one?" he asked Franco in Italian.

Before Franco could respond, Havlav jumped in. "Yes, I am trusting!"

The three of them manhandled the two steamer trunks from Tranelli's cabin. The bodies were beginning to ripen, though they had yet to create a stench—but clearly they had little choice but to risk being seen and dispose of them.

Franco dropped a heavy length of chain into each trunk and spit on the bodies once more for the sake of his father and fellow partisans. Then he indicated to Havlav what they would do with them. For his part, the crewman seemed cowed by Franco, who had displayed his pistol in a nonthreatening but clearly suggestive way in case the big motorman wanted to back out.

Franco wished he'd traded Corrado his Beretta for the suppressed Mauser Broomhandle the partisan had used on the two German werewolves—if he had to shoot anyone it was most likely the reports would bring a crowd to investigate. Franco shrugged to himself, then set to shouldering the trunks and their grisly contents. It took the three nearly a half hour to maneuver the first trunk out of the ship's superstructure, past the rank of lifeboats on davits lashed to the starboard side, down an external companionway that brought them to the main deck but out of sight of the bridge (which was almost directly above them, though facing forward), and to the rail.

With three pairs of hands working somewhat in unison, the ungainly trunk was raised high enough and tilted over the side. It slid straight down the high exterior of the hull and into the backwash of the ship's churning progress, disappearing almost immediately into the oil-black water.

Sweating, Franco led them back to their cabin and they repeated the maneuver with the second steamer, this one made more ungainly by the occupant's greater girth and volume. However his steamer trunk made straight for the bottom as well, and Franco grinned at the thought of a job well-done.

"Now we will need to meet this woman across the corridor," he said to the garrulous crewman.

"This I cannot provide," said Havlav, stroking his flabby neck nervously. It was obvious he was frightened by Franco's intensity and single-mindedness.

"Not today," Franco said mysteriously, "but tomorrow is another one."

Havlav made sure he was no longer needed, then with a wave he stepped out of the cabin and stalked away down the corridor, leaving them there staring after him.

"He could be going back to betray us," warned the priest.

"I think not," said Franco.

Just as he shut the cabin door, the door across the way opened with a little crash.

A voice reached him just as he was about to turn away.

"Young man, will you help me a minute? I need a man's touch."

Chapter Seventeen

Lupo

He rolled, breaking suddenly so as to take the shooter by surprise, and for a few feet he went unchallenged, but then he heard and felt the familiar *slap* and he felt the wind of the slug as it passed only inches above his head.

He propelled himself harder and rolled some more, disregarding the sharp debris and gravel below him, until he reached some kind of brush or undergrowth whose leaves had fallen.

Another shot just overhead told him he was still in the shooter's sights.

Where the hell was he?

There was no higher ground nearby, no hills or drumlins here.

Then the thought hit him like a brick in the head.

Was the guy in a fucking deer stand?

That would explain why he couldn't get himself under cover. He feinted in one direction slightly, awkwardly, with his battered body, then rolled in the other. Sure enough, another shot and the wind from another slug seemed to part his hair.

The sniper was playing with him.

He was good enough, that was obvious.

So the guy could have shot him anytime, but he was choosing not to. The next shot kicked up gravel bits that cut Lupo's face painfully, but he barely felt the pain because he was too busy rolling again, hoping to surprise the bastard. Another shot just behind him urged him to roll faster, but he was blind and he had no idea anymore where the hell he was in relation to the cottage. All he knew was it wasn't the sloping side, which would have forced him to roll toward the small lake behind the property.

Lupo's sides were heaving with the strain of rolling, blindly, from place to place. He gasped with the combined stress and pain of all his cuts and bruises, and he blinked as rapidly as he could, but he could neither see yet, nor force a change.

The Creature could only watch from inside, as helpless as Lupo himself.

Jesus Christ!

He forced himself to his knees, cringing for the shot to come, but none came. So he forced himself to his feet and stumbled farther into what he thought was the thicker part of the wooded area.

No shot.

Maybe the bastard was done? No, more likely he was getting himself to another position. Another tree stand? Had somebody seeded the woods with tree stands? At this point, Lupo wouldn't have ruled out anything.

He tripped over a root or a branch or something and he ducked, in case a bullet headed his way, but none came.

He would have hated admitting it, but he'd been shoved around like a pinball and he wasn't at all sure where he was, or how far he'd come from the cottage. Earlier he might have been able to determine something by the sun's heat on his face, but not now that the sun was either gone or sinking.

Maybe he had left the shooter behind.

Lupo decided to head as straight as he could, rather than continuing the zig-zag routine. Otherwise he could be here forever, and frankly he doubted he could survive in the woods without the Creature to bail him out.

He picked up the pace, feeling less of the silver in his wounds. He'd never had so much silver damage, and now that the pain was fading—or at least becoming more manageable— he wondered again about whether he was learning something important about himself. But getting killed in the process wouldn't help, would it? Ignoring the vestiges of the burning pain of the shrapnel and whatever else had happened to him, he tried a trot, realizing that the odds of tripping were also increasing.

Lupo's breath came more rapidly now, and he started to sweat despite the cold. Trying to keep his feet heading in a straight direction, he gasped with the effort...

Crack!

Another shot. He ducked instinctively and his feet tripped over themselves and he went flailing into some bushes that scraped his face and hands and could have taken out his eyes if he hadn't been lucky.

Goddamn it to hell!

Another shot whizzed overhead. This one he felt, and he rolled again to make himself a smaller target, crashing through the brush that had caught him as he fell.

The ground was still frozen and he landed hard.

Rabbioso

He *was* in a tree stand, one of a series of them his man had spread through the woods around Lupo's cottage. Each was bugged with a tiny transmitter and he had a locator app that made it easier for him to find them, although a scrap of red cloth affixed to a nearby branch for each also made them visible to someone who was looking. Plus he had the night-vision sight on the rifle.

Rabbioso watched Lupo blunder about not far away, knowing now that almost certainly the cop had been blinded by the explosion.

It was accidental, a wonderful coincidence for which he couldn't possibly have planned, but which was making his day now.

The big cop was in bad shape—clearly the shrapnel had worked, to some extent. There *was* something different about Lupo. Even though Rabbioso had not intended the silver shrapnel to kill the cop, it should have injured him more. A *lot* more grievously. Somehow his body had taken the punishment of the blast and the silver, and he was still therefore a supremely dangerous opponent. But the wild card, the joker in the deck, was this new fact—that Lupo was blind.

And that, my friends, is what I call karma.

His powerful FLIR night-vision sight had shown him enough to determine that the blindness didn't seem to be related to a physical wound.

Ho ho ho, what have we here?

What gift have you brought me today?

He hefted the Sig rifle and sighted on Lupo with the FLIR sight. It would feel good to splatter his brains in the woods, yes, but it was too simple. Making him suffer some first was a good way to feel better—his own body still ached from the wounds the cop had inflicted that night not so long ago. If he could bring Lupo even a fraction of that pain, even a tenth of the suffering he had had to do, to suffer through, then it was all worth it and later on he could always splatter his brain all over Eagle River if he so wished.

How long before that moment came he wouldn't know until it was nigh. Would it be boredom with the game? Would it be anger? Mercy?

No, not mercy.

No fuckin' way.

Rabbioso had spent the last few years avoiding his boss's obsession with the past, with blood feuds and made-man ceremonies, with *vendetta* best served cold, and all that movie and TV show crap. But now that the shoe was on his own foot, he saw that there might be something to linking today with the past. He'd never wanted revenge this badly, lusted for revenge to this degree. But he'd given in to the feeling that he needed revenge, and it also dawned on him that if he wanted his takeover of the Bastone family to be complete, he would have to do something more spectacular than hire an accountant. No, he needed a *mechanic*, and he was good enough to be his own mechanic.

This would cement his standing within the family organization and, most likely, carry him easily to his real agenda—the takeover of the tribal casino.

Yes, it was still on the agenda.

After Lupo, it was the *entire* agenda.

He sighted again just past Lupo's head and squeezed off a shot, enjoying the cop's reaction as the bullet splattered into the trunk of a large pine just behind him.

This blindness really was a gift he'd had no right to expect.

Run, Lupo, run.

Today, you.

Tomorrow, your friends in the tribe.

Especially one friend.

Chapter Eighteen

Franco Lupo

On the Freighter Zeniča, crossing the Atlantic Ocean
December 1945

S*he was magnificent.*
There was no other way to describe her, certainly not in one word.

Franco had wandered across the corridor, ignoring the whispered protests of Father Tranelli from behind him. He had killed dozens, and had just thrown the remains of two men into the ocean. What had he to fear from a mere woman?

But even as he thought that, he realized that he might well need to fear her, for her call had instantly galvanized him and he recalled that he had thought of little else since he'd caught that one glimpse.

Now he crossed the Rubicon between them and then suddenly he was in her cabin and she was turned away, hunched over her luggage. He admired her from behind, barely understanding the primal sensation of lust that took control of his every function and reduced him to some sort of stuttering fool.

"Y-yes? Did y-you c-call for h-help, Madame?"

"Madame?" she exclaimed in a lilting, dramatic voice. "Madame? I think not, young man. Now step forward and help me unbind this bundle of clothing!"

She turned as she spoke and now faced him, and he could finally see her clearly.

The first impression was that she was tall, very tall, and lithe like a tiger or a jaguar. She wore not a dress, but riding jodhpurs tucked into shiny black leather boots that reached almost to her knees. She wore a suede shirt tucked into the woolen khaki breeches that accentuated two of her best physical features: her waist, which was small and shapely, and her breasts, which were full and pointed and widely-spaced. Franco imagined he could see her nipples, dark and bloated, thrusting behind the suede.

"Don't just stand there staring, help me with this bundle. Someone else tied it for me and I can't loosen it for the life of me." She spoke Italian with some kind of slight accent he wasn't sure about.

How had she known to speak Italian? But he and the priest had spoken in the corridor, and likely she had overheard.

Now his eyes had traveled up and down, taking in the rest of her.

She was magnificent.

Franco wasn't a virgin. In his travels since what had happened to his father, he had experienced moments of lust and release with various prostitutes as the city's normal economy had crawled back up from the underground. He had been with women often enough to accept that he was considered handsome, and he had certainly benefited from this knowledge. He'd lain with women of various types, but this woman in the cabin across from his was as sophisticated and beautiful as an international film star. She could have been cast in any of those giant, colorful American movies his parents had enjoyed before the war had robbed them of the joy.

Besides her lusty, full woman's body, her face was the very portrait of beauty. Lustrous raven-black hair fell in waves over her shapely neck and shoulders, framing wide-set eyes of the brightest green Franco had ever seen. Plump, red lips below a perfectly straight, long nose gave balance to her sculpted high cheekbones.

Franco was smitten.

He snapped out of his shocked silence when she snapped her fingers, lips curling in a mocking smile. Her teeth were movie-star perfection, to go along with everything else.

"Hello, young man, I need your help this century, not the next!"

Franco blinked and moved to help her, struck speechless by this incongruous presence on the shabby, decaying steamer. She should have been traversing the ocean on the *Queen Mary*, if that ship's troopship days were over.

"*Si, certamente, con piacere.*"

Together they untied the tightly-secured bundle of clothing and then she was hanging dresses and coats and a fur or two in the cabin's wardrobe, recruiting him with a smile that might have led him straight to hell without a single regret.

She continued to smile as his rough and calloused hands — hands which had strangled and stabbed — struggled to grasp the delicate materials without dropping. Or creasing.

When they were finished, she shook his hand. "*Grazie mille*, young man. I appreciate your help very much. If there is anything you need, feel free to ask me."

For a moment tongue-tied by the feel of her warm and shapely hand over his, he smiled shyly and blurted out, "Why don't you join the passengers and officers for dinner?"

"Well, young man, if the rest of that company is as charming as you, then I will certainly give it some thought."

He felt heat and realized to his horror that he was *blushing*. He shook his head as if the sluggishness would clear, nodded once again, and slowly backed away from her presence.

She followed him and swung her door closed as he stumbled into his, finally managing to open the latch and nearly trip his way inside.

With Franco's cabin open, there was a moment in which the woman, Franco, and Father Tranelli caught each other's gaze. Suddenly tense, Franco turned and nodded, closing the door before the priest could address their neighbor.

"What time?" she asked as the gap tightened.

"Eh?"

She smiled. "What time do they serve dinner?"

"Ah, eight."

"I shall see you there soon, then."

As soon as the door was closed, the priest was on him. "Sei matto?" *Are you crazy?*

Franco stammered, "We don't know if she is one of them?"

"And we should try to find out in some other way, not by inviting her to dine with us. Or going to her cabin alone. Are you being pulled along by your dick? I thought you were supposed to be efficient, not crazy. Corrado was wrong about you..."

Franco snapped. He grabbed the frail priest by the lapels and propelled him against the nearest bulkhead so suddenly that the priest gasped out all his breath, his eyes widening.

"You *are* crazy," he muttered when he could speak.

"Just stay out of my way!" Franco growled. "You are here because I am too kind, or you could join our old friends in the steamer trunks. Plenty of room in the ocean..."

They stared at each other until Tranelli lowered his gaze. His lower lip trembled, but he gave no satisfaction. Finally Franco blushed and released him, then turned away.

He wondered if the woman was still out in the corridor. If she had heard the commotion.

Mostly he wondered what lying with her would be like. His groin was painfully distracted, and Franco stripped and crawled into his bunk, turning away. The day's events erupted in his brain and he was lost to sleep almost immediately, those bright eyes in his mind and a ghost version of those soft lips on his.

Chapter Nineteen

Heather

She jogged toward the main door to the lobby of her building, still tingling from the sex and the kill.

Damn, what a cocktail!

There was someone in a parked car a few slots from the glass and steel doorway, and she slowed to determine who it might be.

Enemies abounded these days.

He was slouched down in the seat, trying to keep below window level, but her eyes were sharp, her senses honed and accustomed to predators and attackers. She'd had plenty of reason to beware shadowy people in parked cars.

She swerved toward the deep shadows near the building and crouched to avoid being large in his mirrors, then crept closer to the car's rear. It was a nondescript Ford and she didn't recognize it.

She sniffed the air, but as usual the human nose wasn't as sharp as the wolf's. She considered a change, but it really wasn't a good idea on the sidewalk in front of her building. In an emergency, really.

She stood tall and approached the driver's side like a cop on a highway stop.

And she did surprise the driver, who had been focused on the doorway. Her lights were blazing, so he'd likely assumed she was home.

In one angry, swift motion she grasped the handle and swung the door wide, leaning in to startle the driver.

It was Rich DiSanto.

He jumped and leaned back and away from her sudden attack, but she was already reaching for his jacket's lapels and dragging him bodily out of the car. She'd always been strong, and the wolf side of her contributed some extra power—Nick Lupo had told her his own reflexes and strength had improved enough to get him through the police academy at the top of his class, rather than where he belonged, at the bottom. She'd chuckled then, but now the extra brawn helped as she yanked the protesting cop out of the car in a neat turn of the tables, and tossed him onto its side panel hard enough to dent it.

"What the fuck are you—"

She slammed him again. "Well, if it isn't Robin to Nick's Batman!" She whispered mockingly, "Young DiSanto, are you here doing surveillance? Undercover? How did that work out for you?"

He would probably have responded, but the majority of her weight was jammed into his back and he was cramped up against the car and barely able to breathe.

She held him there until she sensed he was about to turn blue, then suddenly released him and backed off, and he fell toward her and slid to the cold pavement. He half-lay next to his car, now, coughing and gasping for breath.

"Well?" She restrained herself from kicking him. If she'd done so, it would have been only to make a point, because she really rather liked this young cop who knew her secret and had still cheated on his wife in order to fuck her. Often and in every possible position, for about a week.

And he was well-equipped, so at the very least Heather could appreciate him for something.

Oh yes, Heather knew him well. She held out a hand and helped him up now, while he grasped her fingers and glared at her as he slowly stood, almost shaking with the leftover pain and humiliation—mostly humiliation—of being taken down so easily by a woman.

Heather laughed at him. She liked him, but she couldn't help herself. He amused her.

"Ready to spill? What were you doing here? Why are you parked outside my building? Stalking me? What's to keep me from reporting you?"

Her snarl seemed to frighten DiSanto. After all, he knew what she was…

"I—I was just hoping to see you," he stammered. "So we could talk."

"Okay, you're seeing me, so now talk," she said, with more than a thin vein of cruelty obvious in her voice.

"Not here," he said, glancing around. "Upstairs?"

She smirked. "You just want to fuck me again."

He hung his head. "Maybe I do," he said softly.

Her eyes widened. She felt squishy and suddenly hot.

Minutes later she was pulling him inside her loft door, kicking it shut behind her and shrugging out of her running sweats while maneuvering him against yet another immovable object, a brick wall.

He didn't object. By then he was shucking clothing in no apparent order, and soon ended up with one sock on and his underwear, and a half-untucked shirt. The rest of his clothes lay in a scattered spread across the wood floor.

Heather growled deep in her throat as she slid out of the restricting panties and tore off her bra, simultaneously smothering him with her panther-lean muscular body, the engorged tips of her breasts digging into his chest while her long fingers dug into DiSanto's briefs and found him hard and ready. He groaned incoherently as she grasped his length with her red-tipped fingers and freed him from the cotton prison.

He sighed as she began to stroke him even as her body fit itself forcefully into his contours, their heat uniting while his erection grew impossibly larger between them as she caressed him. Meanwhile her lips, still damp with sweat from her run and recent excursions, sought his and clamped on, her tongue slithering inside. If he tasted the remainder of her take-out meal from the park, he didn't indicate it. Instead, he hungrily devoured her tongue, sucking on it as if it were a ripe fruit.

He stared into her eyes, and she knew he could see them starting to roll and change color, as they did when she was on the verge of changing.

He might have felt the long, narrow bands of fur that were springing up on her back, along her spine, and down her sides, too, but it didn't seem to deter his hunger or his needs.

One of her hot hands cupped his balls and the other his cock as they grunted, their mouths locked in a silent, violent dance of lust up against the wall, neither giving in, and neither willing to stop.

Grasping him solidly, she straddled him right there, still with his back against the brick wall. She gasped as the heat of his erection filled her and drove down onto him, impaling herself. She rocked against him and he grunted as her weight ground him into the rough bricks.

She was more assaulting him than fucking him. It was even worse than an assault—it could be deadly. And the line could be exhilarating. She felt the wolf inside her stirring, and tried to suppress her increasing excitement. In some cases, she'd thrilled as the wolf almost took over in such a situation, teetering on the brink of lost control, but she couldn't very well kill Lupo's partner. No, even *she* wasn't that suicidal. Lupo and his gang controlled the two Vatican blades, so she was only watching out for herself in the most basic of ways.

She suppressed harder and the wolf retreated, back inside to wherever *she* resided.

DiSanto was managing to thrust up into her, but their half-standing position was precarious, and she let him maneuver them away from the wall and down to the bare wood floor without letting his engorged penis slip away. She clutched him above and below as he rolled onto her and she opened her thighs to envelop him and he drove down into her. Her breathing became more rapid as he thrust machine-like but still somehow sensitively to her very core, and before she knew it she felt the waves beginning to take her.

This was unheard of! Hardly anyone had reached her so quickly, so thoroughly, and certainly not with anything so lacking in kink.

Heather panted into his shoulder, then bit into it (but gently, and as a human) as she came repeatedly when the friction of the action got to her and she screamed as the liquid fire flowed…and then almost immediately transmitted the success to him, and he cried out too. She grasped him hard and milked him and he stayed hard much longer than she expected, still thrusting and almost raising her back up to the same level she had just reached.

She continued to feel the wave rolling back and forth through her as his thrusting went on seemingly forever.

Finally he slowed and sank onto her, as if exhausted both physically and psychologically.

She let him rest a minute, then shrugged him off almost rudely. He got the message and rose up on his knees and they disentangled.

"All right, now that we got that out of the way, what the hell do you want? Or is that it?" She couldn't help the rude girl part of her personality. She could fuck them, but she didn't have to coddle them. She never had, and now that the wolf resided in her, she found she had even less patience.

He stood up looking hurt for a few moments, but then recovered and started to dress and adjust carefully, regaining his composure and his self-respect in steps she could follow. She kind of liked that: he was able to set aside what they'd just done, the rutting, and reclaim the parts of himself of which she would (of course) wish to deprive him.

"That was it," he said, with a toss of his ruffled hair.

She chuckled. He wanted to play it that way.

"I don't fuck just anybody," she said. "You should make good use of your time here."

"Maybe I already did," he shot back.

He was mostly dressed now. His face was ruddy with a flush of embarrassed anger. He really didn't know why he was there, did he?

She laughed at him. "Clearly you need me for something, something other than this. Are you going to tell me, or play twenty questions? Or are you just running out of here with your tail between your legs?"

Thoughts and emotions flashed across his features to join the anger that was already there. "All right," he said finally, fidgeting, looking into her eyes but then away. "All right, ever since I met you I wanted—I felt a connection…"

"Yeah, yeah, I get it. We just did *connect*, didn't we?"

He went on despite the redoubled flush. "What I mean is, we already have a connection. Nick. And what you are is what he is. I mean, you are both—"

"Yeah, werewolves. You can say it. It won't bite." She added, "But *I* might."

"That's just it," he mumbled. "I think I want that." He glanced nervously at his chunky silver watch, but it was a reflex and he didn't seem to have seen it.

"You want to be…like us?"

"I don't know. Yes. I'm not sure, but, yes."

She licked her lips. This was unexpected. He couldn't very well ask Lupo, so he'd come to her. Thoughts, pro and con, flitted through her mind. She could laugh him out of her place, or scream epithets at him. On the other hand…

It was kind of *hot*.

She could tell that having told her made him hard again. She sidled closer again until she was in front of him, close enough to feel his warm breath on her sensitive skin. She reached out and gave a little gasp-laugh—he really was growing hard again under her touch.

She sighed.

Lust had always been her downfall.

She sank to her knees and put both hands on the front of his pants. She looked up at him.

"Let me think about it," she said, as her slim fingers reached inside past his zipper and unlimbered him again. "I'll sleep on it, but first I could use a snack."

She opened her lips.

He groaned when she used them on him.

Marla Anders

The apparition's image kept fading in and out, as if he really did have a poor connection from wherever he was calling. Like the S.O.S. hologram in the original *Star Wars* or something.

She didn't know exactly why she was singled out for this reception, except for that her grandfather the shaman had dealt in apparitions and spirit guides and all sorts of great Indian folklore, not to mention some darker stuff that had gotten him thrown out of his tribe—and tossed out of his family, too, more or less.

So maybe she was *receptive*. She suspected she had always been, even though she had learned to suppress—or ignore—it to the point where she sometimes forgot her history.

She didn't *look* half-Indian, that was the problem. When she stared in a mirror, she saw her long, straight blond hair and Scandinavian features and really saw her father and his people, not her mother and hers. Someone had once told her she resembled Uma Thurman, and she supposed she did a little—a fact which had probably helped her get cops to open up, since they could slip a little flirting into their sessions, and she'd been a heck of a lot more popular than some of her old, white, male shrink colleagues. She wasn't one to take compliments well, but being compared to a glamorous beauty didn't hurt the old ego, even if she herself was getting a little too old for it.

But perhaps looking a certain way—or not—didn't matter. If the blood of Joseph Badger ran through her veins, and if he'd been plugged into the Other World, as she remembered him sometimes saying before he went to Europe on the trip that would change him and his life forever, then it was clear that the Other World existed and she was at least nominally plugged into it as well.

She was completely willing to buy in. But what was her role? What was the reason for her to get in the way of this strangeness?

The image of Sam Waters—the same Sam Waters in those photographs—had some message to pass on to Nick Lupo, her elusive cop.

When she tried to quiz the apparition, it became apparent to her that it was more of a one-way connection, because the Sam Waters image didn't seem to hear her, although it seemed to be able to follow her with its eyes. *It or him? Did it matter?*

So she couldn't ask any questions, really, but she could record what he said and she did.

The image of Sam Waters continued to fade in and out while sitting in her armchair—except how could he actually sit?—and his voice seemed to come and go, but she was able to put together most of what he was trying to tell her.

Nick Lupo was north, near Eagle River. And he was in trouble.

When she thought she understood everything the Sam Waters apparition had told her, she scooped up her phone.

Who to call?

Who wouldn't laugh her off the line?

Maybe Lupo's partner was the best one to call. Rob? No, Rich DiSanto. She called the station, got the dispatcher and identified herself, then requested DiSanto's cell number. As she dialed, she wondered how receptive *he* would be. From what she had seen, he and Lupo had a good relationship...and she'd heard plenty of rumors about the two of them being involved in bizarre cases and situations. So she really had nothing to lose...

"Detective DiSanto? Dr. Marla Anders here..."

DiSanto

God, he was almost feverish, as if her proximity had infected him with some disease.

Of course, that wasn't far from the truth, was it?

He couldn't believe what he had blurted out in her presence. He couldn't believe his half-formed thought had solidified right then, right while he was inside her, and then just minutes later had come bubbling out of his mouth like a goddamned beggar.

"Stupid, stupid, stupid," he muttered.

Oh God, she *was* extraordinary.

And dangerous.

And powerful.

And a monster?

Even so, did that mean *he* would be a monster? Lupo had managed to keep a handle on right and wrong, hadn't he? Or had he?

Locked away in a drawer of DiSanto's desk was a copy of the coroner's report on the gunshots that had killed that motorcycle gangbanger a while back. *Silver in the bullet fragments. Strange DNA, an error.* In the same drawer was a copy of an ME report on a gun dealer named Rag, from further back. *Silver in the bullet fragments.* No strangeness with the DNA, but Lupo'd caught that case with his old partner before the Martin gang had started blowing up Eagle River. Then there was Eagle River and the off-the-books ops he himself had helped Lupo with. And that drone control house in Minnesota. In that drawer was a veritable treasure trove of circumstantial evidence against Lupo that a talented DA might make stick, especially one working with a dogged Internal Affairs chief like Roman.

Roman was new, but then DiSanto had to tick off a couple more names in his head. Griff Killian had disappeared. Former head of IA just drops off the face of the earth, with the shrink Marcowicz. And what about *his* predecessor, Julia Barrett?

Jesus, did Lupo know the difference between right and wrong?

How much of a monster was his good-guy partner?

And if Lupo was a monster, why did DiSanto just confess to a dangerous woman who was possibly complicit in numerous crimes along with Lupo that he longed to be just like her? And Lupo?

He put his head down onto his cradled arms and cried with a mixture of shame and fear and disgust that he figured would have earned him a one-way ticket to the psycho ward in any facility in the country.

But at the end of the day, he still wanted to fuck Heather Wilson again.

And he still wanted to be a werewolf.

He jumped when his phone went off again.

Lupo

He'd been stumbling somewhere inside the tree line after making it out of the cleared area around the cottage.

It had to be late by now, but he was forced to admit he was disoriented in every way possible.

How long had it been?

He had no idea.

He had started to shiver. A reaction to his wounds, plus the cold. Winter was starting to give up the North Woods, but it still owned the nights.

Small miracle he had managed not to drown himself in the tiny lake that spread out from the front of Sam's old place—*his* place, now—and instead he had entered the thickest part of the woods surrounding the reservation's land. There was a lot of ground to cover here, but if the hunter was merely playing with him, then he was doomed because he still couldn't see, he still couldn't change, and he was bound to walk into a bullet sooner or later.

Or freeze to death.

Lupo had been thinking, though, as he bumped into trees and the occasional boulder that was probably a glacial artifact...

He was certain by now that the explosion couldn't have been intended to kill him. Just to hurt, maim, stun, and render him as helpless as possible, so he'd be more fun to hunt. They could have loaded the damn thing with five times the C4 and a mound of silver, money being no object. Yes, there *had* been silver—it was still burning inside him—but it was a smaller, measured amount. Just enough to make it harder and more painful to bounce back from, making it a part of the intended result.

Hell, the shooter didn't have the Wolfpaw or Wolfclaw stamp, as far as he could tell. That bunch would have dropped a bomb the size of a Cadillac on him. A rack of Reaper missiles. Overkill was their middle name. No, this had the stamp of a sadistic mob asshole playing with his dinner before eating it.

Face it, it had to be Joe Rabbioso, because who else knew this much about him? And who else had a grudge that would lead him to play a cat and mouse game?

Hell, Lupo was Italian—he knew how to hold a grudge. Just add C4 and silver shrapnel.

Joe Rabbioso, where are you?

Funny, he'd just been thinking the asshole was now on the run, but if this was him then he'd decided to double down and get a slice of revenge while it could still be served hot. He wondered how large a crew he had managed to scrape up, or was he going it solo? Clearly somebody here had helped set it up—and now that made him think of Jessie.

Was Jessie also in danger? What if Rabbioso had decided to take them both out?

Christ, how was he going to check on her if he couldn't even help himself?

He *had* to outflank the asshole. There was no trying, he had to just suck it up and do it.

Still shivering uncontrollably, he tried to put the cold out of his mind. As a wolf, he would have laughed at the cold. As it was, he was lucky to have had a coat on.

Lupo had gone back to walking in a rough zig-zag pattern continuously interrupted by inconvenient trees, now trying for a general easterly direction as he tried to see a map with his mind's eye, and simultaneously continuing to urge the Creature back from wherever he had crawled. It was as if his wolf side had taken a time-out.

You're always trying to suppress the damn Creature, and one time you need him...

Another slug splattered against a nearby tree trunk, taking out a chunk of raw wood and spraying it and shrapnel across Lupo's chest like tiny javelins.

Goddamn it, the pain was intense where the slivers jabbed through his damaged clothing and into his chest.

If the slugs were silver, and they seemed to be, then one or two of them hitting any major organ would do it and you could kiss Nick Lupo good-bye. The fact that the shooter kept missing was indicative of how much of an asshole he was, giving Lupo the so-called sporting chance. It was more like torture. And giving himself a boner while doing the torturing...yeah, that was something you never heard of. Especially with the mob. Some of these guys went around with hacksaws and propane torches and a gleam in their eye at every limb they could threaten to slice off.

Plus he must have had a night-scope on his telescopic sight.

Just for the hell of it, Lupo tried to force a change again.

But his *it's-a-fact-Jack* fell on deaf ears. Nothing happened.

He had no doubt that if he were able to change into wolf form Rabbioso's shooting would get a whole lot better. Lupo had a hunch the bastard was trying to drive him in a general direction like a tiger in those old-fashioned Indian hunts he'd read about as a kid. But how long would his blindness last?

Was it all in his head?

Some kind of short-circuit, the same circuit that usually let him see Ghost Sam.

If it was in his head, how could he fight against it?

Was he blind for life...and therefore no longer a werewolf?

Chapter Twenty

DiSanto

S *hit.*

This wasn't going to help him here or at home. He was already paranoid, fearing he had Heather Wilson's musky smell all over him, and now Jessie—Doc Hawkins, as he liked to refer to her—had a little problem.

Okay, a major problem.

She'd killed a guy. One of *them.*

"Christ," he blurted out when she told him. Now he understood why he'd had so many voicemails and missed calls from her, but he hadn't been paying attention to his phone.

No, last thing he'd been paying attention to.

"Christ," he repeated. "What the hell was he doing?"

"Well, I didn't ask him, did I? He was clearly about to turn. He was naked. I...I had no choice. Did I? I'm so confused. I thought maybe we'd gotten rid of them."

"Werewolves?" he whispered. "Hell, not hardly. I've got a feeling Nick's just poked the hornet's nest with a very short stick. He keeps winning these little skirmishes, but don't you feel there's more going on than we can see?"

Shit, what was he rambling about?

"Maybe…" she said, tentatively.

He got back on track. "Listen, what did you do with the body?"

"Nothing." She paused. "Well, I covered him up with leaves and drove his truck to a remote spot on one of the old logging roads up here. Otherwise, I just left him. Usually I'd be on the phone to the sheriff's office and report what happened, but I can't very well do that and expect anyone to believe me, can I? And even if I could spin it that he was threatening me, there's too much weirdness. The fact that he's naked, the silver in the wounds." Her voice softened. "I really don't think I can do anything but get rid of the body, and I don't know how."

"Did he have a phone?"

"Yeah, I got it. He made some calls just today, to a 702 area code."

"Crap," he said. "That's Las Vegas."

There was a pause as that sank in. "Oh…"

"Has it gone off?"

"No, not that I'm aware, but it could be in silent mode. I'll check, but if it goes off I'm not going to answer it, so…"

"Okay, we better assume somebody's noticed your guy's not answering, or will notice soon. Somebody else might show up."

"I have the Vatican blade—one of them, Nick has the other—so I can deal with it, I guess. But Rich…" Her voice cracked. "I don't want to have to do this again."

"I know, Doc, I know." He felt stupid, but what else could he say?

Did this mean the Bastone family, what was left of them, was making a move for the casino again? Or was this personal, just a little payback for the Doc's role in thwarting their last bid? He had to talk to Colgrave—organized crime was her beat. He told Jessie.

"Okay, that makes sense," she said, sounding calmer. "Then what? What do I do?"

"Then I guess I'll have to come up. You tried Nick how many times?"

She told him.

Shit.

Either he'd gone off the grid—and off the books again!—about something, or something had happened to him. Lupo was not one to ignore phone calls, especially not from Doc Hawkins. He'd made her life miserable and complicated, sure, but he was crazy about her. Hell, DiSanto could have been crazy about her himself, so he understood. Although his problem was the size and shape of one Heather Wilson. Still, it applied. Sometimes the course of true love just doesn't run so smooth, right? Paraphrasing the Bard.

None of this could help Jessie, though.

"So maybe we got two problems," he said, reiterating what he'd just thought through.

There was a long hiss of exhaled breath. She said, "Okay, I've got enough to worry about, and now you're saying something's happened to Nick."

"Not saying that, but you had to be thinking it."

Her silence confirmed it.

"Okay," he continued. "I'll check with Colgrave, tonight or tomorrow if I can't find her, then get on the road as soon as I can. And Doc?"

"Yeah?"

"Don't panic. We'll figure it out."

They clicked off.

He drove way too fast from the Third Ward and that damned loft where he had left his pride and self-esteem and hit the precinct, hoping the goddamned task force guys were out in the field, or getting laid, or eating brats and cheese somewhere.

First thing he did was check his locked drawer, where all that circumstantial evidence against Lupo was stashed. It was secure.

Better find a new hiding place for this shit.

He didn't know what he was going to do with it, if anything. Ever. But he had it anyway, and he planned to keep it.

Time to check for Colgrave. She sometimes pulled some night duty or stuck around late to finish up something.

He stood from his desk, exited his cubicle, and within a half-dozen steps he found Agent Barton blocking his way.

Fuck.

Just the person he wanted to see...*not*.

He tried to go around the Fed, but the guy danced with him and he was stuck.

Barton was smiling, the predatory non-smile he always seemed to display when dealing with either DiSanto or Lupo.

DiSanto had no choice but to stop. He could see from the corner of his eye that the new IA guy, Roman, was standing in his doorway, obviously interested in this tableau.

Christ, everybody was hanging around.

"Heading somewhere important, Detective DiSanto?"

"Yeah, the can."

Crooked smile. "Isn't it that way?" He pointed in the direction from which DiSanto had come.

"I need the special stall," said DiSanto, pointing the other way and smiling back with the same bullshit grin.

"Ah, don't let me stop you." Barton waved the detective past. But as they drew even, the Homeland Security agent added, "You know where Lupo might be hiding? He's ducking us."

"No, I don't know. He doesn't check in with me."

"You sure? I thought you guys held hands while pissing."

DiSanto blanched but walked away without slugging the bastard. He noticed that, farther away, Roman was still interested, staring at him.

He decided to avoid Colgrave for now and instead hit the washroom as he'd said he was doing. When he exited, Roman was right there, apparently about to head in. But blocking his way.

This is ridiculous. Now what?

"Detective DiSanto, isn't it?"

He knew damn well it was, but DiSanto just nodded.

"You're looking a bit harried. Something going on? Anything I can help you with?" He grinned in a way that made DiSanto's buttocks clench in a most unmanly way.

So far Roman was filling old Griff Killian's shoes perfectly, as no one DiSanto had talked to liked him one tiny bit. But then, that was Internal Affairs—cops weren't supposed to like the cops who watched them. Still, the guy did have a way of skulking around like Dracula or something...

Shit, is he one of them?

DiSanto realized suddenly that he would forever have to think in such terms, because his whole world had changed when Lupo had come out, as it were, and then suddenly the fuckin' creatures were everywhere.

For now, though, he had Jessie Hawkins to help. Lupo wasn't anywhere to be found. Really, other than talking to Danni Colgrave, what else could he do?

"Uh, no thanks," he said to Lieutenant Roman, who was giving him some kind of vulture-eye. "All good and quiet on the Western front." Stupid clichés, sometimes they bugged even him.

"Just wanted to mention that you can feel free to come talk to me anytime, Detective." There was that grin again. DiSanto shuddered imperceptibly. He hoped.

"I'll keep that in mind."

"See that you do."

Whatever *that* meant. DiSanto sidled away and finally decided it would be best to call Colgrave from a safe location. Maybe best not to be spotted together right now. He went out to the lobby and dialed her phone, then spent fifteen minutes on the call. They managed to get on the same page after a bit of wrangling, and he hung up thoughtfully.

The music made him jump.

His phone again.

Jesus!

He glanced at the screen before answering. *Marla Anders?* The new shrink? Now?

"Uh, hello?"

Colgrave

That call was disconcerting in more than one way.

What had Lupo stumbled into?

She'd told DiSanto his partner had decided to head north, stealth-mode. But she didn't figure he would refuse calls from the love of his life, either.

So the conclusion had to be that something had happened to him. Maybe he'd been in the crosshairs and they just hadn't figured it. But they should have known. And what DiSanto said the doc had been forced to do...for one thing, it meant they had been moving on her. Maybe moving on them both.

She ran her hands through her hair, worrying at the scalp until it hurt.

Sometimes she was her own worst enemy, especially when she was about to embark on something bad. Something *not quite kosher*, as DiSanto would probably say.

She'd agreed to help, though, so now she had to make a plan. For all she knew, it was too late. But she couldn't let DiSanto swing in the breeze. Off the books was the only way to go—there was just too much they couldn't tell anyone.

They'd lock me up if I tried to explain.

She had to find a way to shove this whole dark op under the umbrella of the new concern regarding organized crime's push into the state's Indian gaming. The chatter was there, all she had to do was hook into it. She had some connections, and most of the nation's law enforcement community was keeping an eye on resurgent mob activity, so the changes to the Bastone Family had been noted.

Hell, she knew this monitoring by both feds and locals was on-going, so she was only getting ahead of it, and if it could serve as an excuse for her to get involved with whatever was going on with Lupo, then all the better. What he'd told her before leaving was startling, not least because of how far back his story stretched, and how wide the implications were. Or might be. Even he wasn't sure how much was folklore of one sort or another, and how much was reality.

But she had seen a fair share of reality that didn't seem possible, so who was she to wag her finger at it?

She unlocked the large file drawer of her desk. Inside was a gym bag with some of her off-book gear. She'd been involved in more than a few questionable ops in her career, always willing to skirt the law, the end justifies the means. *Dirty Harry Syndrome*, a former lover had called it...

Maybe.

Inside the bag there was an Uzi submachine gun with a dozen loaded 32-round magazines, plus a couple off-duty weapons, .40-caliber Glocks and extra mags for them. And there were a few more goodies not currently endorsed by the Milwaukee homicide division, but she'd always had connections.

She zipped the bag closed and pulled it out, then selected a heavy military-style parka from her old-fashioned wooden coat tree. Gloves, a heavy sweater, a knit cap...she was almost ready.

DiSanto said he was driving overnight, but they should meet at one of the Mexican diners just south of downtown.

Lupo had indicated he was heading north, flying solo, clearing his head. So now she was going to join DiSanto on a trek to find out if he'd fallen prey to some mobbed-up guys looking for revenge. She noted that Joe Rabbioso had fallen off the radar pretty quickly, and if Lupo was right and the guy had healed up, now she knew where he might be. Even so, she checked on the BOLO she had put out on him, but there was nothing yet. As for the rest of his prior Bastone crew, they were either dead or scattered to the winds, which meant either he had no one or had recruited anew. When she'd told DiSanto this, earlier, he had gasped.

"If he's recruited from Wolfpaw, then we could be dealing with a bunch of *them*..." he said.

"And they don't die easily," she muttered.

"No, they do not." He looked around, making sure no one could hear, and raised an eyebrow. "But I do have a stash of the right kind of ammo."

"Hope it's 9mm," she said.

"Most of it. We're good."

Then he had called Jessie Hawkins, Lupo's lady friend. Colgrave liked her—liked her a lot—but she felt funny, since she'd started to feel that uncomfortable pinprick at the pit of her stomach when thinking about big, gruff Nick Lupo.

Felt a little like betrayal. Did she want to go there?

"Well, let's go see if we can get him back."

"Hopefully he's just sitting on his couch, chillin' with one of those fancy drinks of his, watchin' a movie, and his phone fell in the toilet."

"Yeah, I don't buy that either."

DiSanto was grim-faced. "Hey, we can hope."

They discussed a plan. They couldn't very well simply take off together without some sort of reasonable excuse.

"I'll drive up first," DiSanto said. "Jessie's problem won't solve itself, unfortunately."

"What are you going to do?"

"I'll figure it out when I get there. Lupo taught me to stop playing by the rules, 'cause the rules are made by people who don't know the score. I mean, I wouldn't have agreed a year ago, but now I think I do."

"Hell, I wouldn't have agreed a *month* ago," said Colgrave. She smiled but it held little humor. "Even so, I've seen and done enough to know where I stand when it comes to rules."

"Yeah, I thought you and Nick were more on the same page than you even knew."

He was sitting on the edge of her desk when he said it, and somehow the mundaneness of what was happening started to register. As if they were discussing last night's episode of whatever the hell people who had time watched on television. She didn't have time, really, but she could at least grasp the feeling.

By the time DiSanto had left, she had spelled out just how she would get them cover with the new OC chatter. She'd been given a fair amount of latitude, and she meant to use it. He had promised to call, and now that he had, their plan was coming together.

"Where the hell are you, Lupo?" she muttered now. They'd both continued trying his phone, but it went straight to voicemail. Between the two of them—and probably Jessie Hawkins—they'd left a hundred messages by now.

It was time to figure out what had happened to Lupo.

Before it was too late.

Maybe it already is, she thought. She wanted to beat back the thought, but it was out there in her brain, rattling around. She tasted a bitter taste on her tongue. She'd bitten it.

Chapter Twenty-One

Franco Lupo

On the Freighter Zeniča, crossing the Atlantic Ocean
December 31, 1945

Christmas came and went and the ship slowly steamed across the Atlantic, bearing southwest to begin aiming for the South American coast.

Things had cooled between Franco and the priest, who now acted as if he were a prisoner while the young man stalked the ship's corridors and attempted to make friends with the crew. Havlav had kept quiet about their shared midnight mission, and if anyone missed the two original passengers, no one said.

A scratchy radio in the officers' mess played some Christmas music, and that was the extent of the festivities, along with a more or less festive meal of some kind of fowl and various side dishes based on potatoes and root vegetables, of which the larder had plenty.

The woman did not show for dinner, but continued to take her meals alone, although occasionally she donned a full-length fur with a hood and made her way to the ship's railing to smoke long American cigarettes. When she bumped into Franco she smiled and nodded, but conversation was kept to a minimum.

Franco was bursting. Every time he saw her his groin reminded him painfully that she was the most beautiful, sultry, and stimulating vision of a woman that he had ever seen, on the screen or off, and he wanted her. For her part, she sometimes winked at him and half-smiled as she sidestepped him and walked away to be on her own. He ached to follow her, to grab her and run his hands over her, his lips finding her neck, her cheeks, her lips opening...

Is she one of them?

The question burned in the pit of Franco's stomach—and lower—and he began to sweat through his sleepless nights, wearing hooded eyes the rest of the day, walking the cold corridors as if her image was summoning him to her but he could never reach her.

At mealtimes, the officers had subsided their conversation when it came to politics, and soon it seemed the voyage itself and the often inclement weather that surrounded them were the only safe topics. For his part, Tranelli ate his meals in silence after a quick silent prayer and stumbled away from the table to return to the cabin. Franco made small talk with his elders, but his attention was elsewhere and soon they began to talk amongst themselves without addressing him at all.

On New Year's Eve, everything changed.

The dinner was mostly a repeat of the Christmas meal, with the addition of various sweets afterwards such as dried figs and nuts, crumb cakes, and a surprise: two well-preserved *panettoni*, the traditional tall Italian holiday cake. There was some cheap French *champagne* and Italian *moscato*, beer for the nonbelievers.

Franco's heart skipped more than a beat—a whole measure of beats—when the woman entered the mess hall wearing one of her furs, long woolen trousers and fuzzy fur-trimmed boots. All conversation faded away as she looked around (never yet having visited the mess), located Franco, and immediately approached him...to the accompaniment of an immediate pained jealous gasp uttered by most of the other men in attendance.

"Ciao, Franco," she said brightly. "Buon anno, caro!"

He wondered how she knew his name, as they'd never been introduced. He also wondered why she would address him as *dear* in public, as if their connection were closer than it was. He felt the stares and smiled crookedly, enjoying their distress.

He stumbled through a new year's greeting as well, and she rescued him. "My name is Caterina Cavalli. There's a boring land title that goes along with it, but since it has been meaningless for a decade I don't bother to use it. And you, Franco? What is your name?"

"Mi chiamo Francesco Lupo, Signora."

"Signorina," she corrected haughtily, but she playfully extended her hand. He felt a spark fly between her dry, soft hand and his suddenly damp palm.

At least she didn't wipe her hand afterwards, he thought.

All through the meal, while Caterina chatted politely with most of the officers and the surly captain, she ignored the priest and lavished most of her time on Franco, who was both embarrassed and secretly pleased.

She switched easily from Italian to Czech, to Spanish, English, and to a passable German, and while Franco could only follow in the German and the English, besides the Italian, there was more than enough conversation to go around, centering mostly on the coming new year and its lack of war—the first such year in too many.

The cheap champagne and wine flowed, and even Tranelli seemed to catch the spirit of things by the time the ship's clock showed 11:30 p.m. on the eve of 1946. The remains of the sweet after-dinner courses and cracked nuts, eviscerated figs, and scattered crumbs, covered the table but the captain clinked a steak knife against his empty glass for attention and conversation stopped. Caterina finished a low giggle at something someone had said, and then all heads turned toward the ship's commander.

"Even though the new year shines upon us, I must remind everyone here what an absolute shit of a year we have just ended," he said, perhaps more than slightly drunk. "In fact, gentlemen...*and lady*, there are more shit years behind us than I care to count." He ignored the grimaces and headshakes of his officers and soldiered on. "So let's drink to this new year and hope there will be less shit in it for all of us."

Nervous laughter followed as glasses clinked. The first officer nervously announced that there would be fireworks at midnight, "if the Chief doesn't blow us all up," and the group slowly adjourned to retrieve coats and parkas, then headed in groups up the companionway toward the bridge.

"Come," Caterina whispered to Franco, "escort me." She took his arm.

His skin tingled where she touched him. She laughed when she noticed his discomfort, her wide mouth mocking and alluring and enticing all at once.

Tranelli took a bottle and followed. In fact, most of the officers took bottles and glasses.

When they reached the bridge, they fanned out around the wheelhouse along the extended exterior deck. "Watch off the starboard side," called out the first mate. Toasts clinked in the night, which was chilly but no longer so cold as to be uncomfortable as they approached the equator on their journey south. They could see the rest of the crewmen lined up along the rail of the main deck, sounds of their own celebration reaching the bridge in snatches.

Just before midnight, an officer begin to call out the countdown.

"Ten...nine...eight...seven...six..."

Everyone made sure they had a full glass, but long glances were only for Caterina, whose sparkling laugh lit up the night. She held on to Franco, both of them with full glasses in one hand.

"Four...three...two...one!"

"Happy New Year!"

"Happy..."

"...Year!"

Above them, a series of weak fireworks bloomed in the night sky and illuminated the dark ocean in brief, colorful flashes that reminded all too many of them of guns and artillery in the night. But they pretended it was a joyous display and cheered.

As glasses clinked and the men chattered, Franco felt himself pulled closer and the scent of her was beyond intoxicating, as she laughed in his ear and then turned his face and her lips were on his, opening, and he was responding in more ways than one, clinging to her as their tongues met and the kiss seemed to go on forever.

When they parted the sensation of their mouths together lingered and Franco felt the stiffening in his groin that told him she had reached into his depths.

Is she one of them?

In that moment, Franco didn't care. He pulled Caterina closer again and she didn't resist, and then their lips met again and she laughed happily—or was it mockingly—as her red lip color smeared all over him again, and then they just continued to kiss, not stopping until they realized the fireworks had all been shot and the officers and crew of the freighter had abandoned them and headed off to continue serious drinking. Of Tranelli there was no sign.

Caterina took his hand and pulled him along as they slowly headed back to the ship's superstructure and the nearest hatchway.

Chapter Twenty-Two

Barton

He had to get out of the central precinct. Ryeland had been hounding him all day, and apparently even the threat of Homeland Security sanctions wouldn't put him off.

Nick Lupo was missing. Maybe he wasn't just ducking after all.

That was the hushed word going around the station, after some uniform had overheard Lupo's partner on the phone with someone, all hush-hush and secretive. Barton had tried connecting with some of his people, but no one had seen the big homicide cop. Somehow he had slipped surveillance and disappeared. It was likely he'd headed north to that backwater he liked so much, Eagle River, but so far he hadn't been spotted. Now Barton wanted to talk to other sources, but Ryeland was huffing over his shoulder, certain the DHS agent had done something to his star detective.

On a whim Barton had tried to brace the partner, DiSanto, but the kid was all wire-wrapped electricity and of course had gotten in his face—Barton had *some* idea what was going on there, but he didn't want to visit it—and then he'd disappeared too, stalking out of the police building.

So now Barton stood outside the block of unattractive gray marble, huddling in his too-light suit and getting slammed by the chill winds everybody told him swept off the lake. His phone, a government-issue satellite with built-in scrambling, tweeted or chirped (depending who you asked) and his speed-dialed number went through.

The voice that answered was curt, as always.

Barton said, "Lupo's disappeared."

The other party said nothing.

"I don't know whether this is connected to our thing, or one of the hundred or so he might be involved in, or some asshole from his past..."

"Surveillance?"

Barton sighed. "Failed. I've got people out there trying to get eyes on him, but so far no luck."

"Keep trying. Find him alive, if you value your career."

Barton didn't want to admit it, but he was sweating. "He may get himself killed without our help."

"Just make sure he doesn't."

Barton said, "All right." But he had no confidence that he or his connections could do anything at all about Lupo's sudden disappearance. So much for him keeping an eye out on the guy.

The voice said, "And make sure the other thing is finished. Once and for all."

He sighed. "Yes." The phone went dead in his hand.

Fuck.

Barton knew he couldn't go around those orders. They came from above and outside his DHS sphere. He called his teams and redoubled their efforts. Lupo had to show up eventually, but was he gone of his own will, or had he been snatched? If he was off the grid, what was he up to? If he wasn't, what was up?

It had been a long while since Barton had felt so helpless.

He dialed and Corrado answered before the second ring. *Does that guy ever sleep?*

He jumped right in. "You have any idea where Lupo might have disappeared to?"

Corrado was silent for a moment. "I gave him a lot to think about, I think. When he wants to think, he heads north."

"Just like that?"

Corrado chuckled. "I gather he is not really in the loop—is that the right phrase?—with this task force of yours, so what is to keep him? Besides, north is where his lady friend lives."

"Possible. I can get eyes on him there. I just thought—I figured he'd had enough of the place after, uh, recent events."

"He wants to be free."

"Whatever that means," said Barton.

"It means that he does not like being the center of all this attention."

"*Humph*, it's too late for that. Well, I'll check out the up north angle."

"I am sure you will."

"I'm not convinced it's just him being elusive."

"Neither am I, Agent Barton, neither am I. This is why you should probably hurry. Our mutual enemies might be making a move. Or it might be a monkey-wrench. A rogue, acting on his own."

Barton barked a humorless half-laugh and clicked off.

Corrado gave him the creeps. Too bad they were tied together. It felt like chains and an anchor and they were standing on the edge of the Marianas Trench. Whatever went wrong would bring them both down, a long way down.

He sighed. He was but an instrument of others' will, and his understanding or agreement wasn't needed very often.

He called his teams and directed them to head north and converge on Eagle River. He made sure they all had Lupo's picture on their phones, in case it came down to a missing persons case.

It would take them some time to get there, and it was his fault for not moving faster.

Despite what he'd told the old man, he had not considered it a possibility that Lupo would have run away, which in essence is what this would have been. No, he didn't figure it. *I must be slipping.*

DiSanto

He drove his not-so-new Ford well above the posted speed, but he'd learned from Lupo that a well-placed call to the State Patrol could keep the bulls off his back, so even though he kept sneaking looks at his chunky Invicta watch in the shifting bars of light from the overhead poles, he really was making good time as he raced toward Vilas County. He didn't have a lightbar like Lupo, though. *Have to get one of those.*

Poor Doc Hawkins was probably going through the roof. Killing a guy, having a body to dump, and Lupo was nowhere to be found…

DiSanto was both miffed at Lupo for choosing *now* to disappear but also grateful because he could feel Heather Wilson turning his head—both heads, really—and if he was honest with himself his marriage was over. Wilson was like a fine wine that forever made you swear off the twist-top stuff. She was an animal in bed, which was certainly understandable under the circumstances, while his wife had become a breathing mannequin. In bed and everywhere else, it seemed.

DiSanto drove, silver ammo in the trunk. The doc had insisted he load up in case things went to hell. It had been so short a break from the shit, why had he thought there would be down-time? With Lupo there was *never* down-time.

Where the hell are you, Nick?

And what about the psychologist, Marla Anders? She had babbled on about dreams and messages, some kind of ranting about Lupo being in trouble.

Thing was, she was right. Now, was she right because of something *woo-woo*, as Lupo might say, or just because she knew something no one else did? Had Lupo talked to her more than he'd let on? DiSanto didn't think so…as far as he knew Lupo had been avoiding her.

Hell, she was an attractive one, especially after the last two who had sat in her chair. DiSanto thought he'd have been willing to tap that…if he thought that way.

But he did think *that* way, didn't he?

A tendril of guilt found its way into his mind, but he chased it out.

He had confirmed to Anders that Lupo was missing, but then he'd bitten his tongue and wished he hadn't. He'd tried walking it back, but she was perceptive, damn her (*better remember that*, he told himself), and she'd picked up on his concern.

He hoped she wouldn't do anything stupid. He wanted to tell her about Julia Barrett, and what had happened to *her* after she'd driven north. She'd had the bad luck to run into both a serial killer and the first pack of werewolves Lupo'd ever faced. No, she hadn't been lucky at all after going up north.

Fuckin' weird shit always happens up north.

Yeah, that was why he was heading up now. The darkening landscape flew by in a blur as he made good time, left alone by the state patrol cruisers that presumably haunted the roads especially at night. That Lupo, he was always finding ways around things.

At this rate, he'd get there no later than dawn. God, he wished they still made Benzedrine. He could have used it as an upper to keep him going. He'd stop for a quick coffee when he reached Antigo, wake him up just before he got there.

He stepped on the accelerator a little harder, roaring around a series of rumbling semi-trailers. Hell, what was the point of the blank check if you didn't take advantage of it?

Chapter Twenty-Three

Lupo

He was still blind.

No other way to describe it. His eyes were open but, as the song said, they might as well have been closed.

The freezing cold was seeping into his bones, and his wounds—though not serious as far as he could tell—were beginning to take their toll on his stamina and endurance. He was grateful there wasn't any major snow cover here. It had all melted in a recent thaw, but then the ground had frozen again. But it had to be late, given how cold it had gotten. He had no way to know for sure, but he thought he'd heard an owl hooting just a little while ago. *Looking for his dinner*.

The bastard who was hunting him wasn't far behind, either. Occasionally Lupo heard the sound of someone crashing through brush or dried, felled branches, not far behind. He almost thought it was intentional, that Rabbioso was making noise just to remind him he was there, and driving him in the opposite direction.

Like the helpless tiger of the hunts he had pictured.

Except that a tiger in the wild wasn't completely helpless, and neither was Lupo. Wolf or no wolf, Nick Lupo had learned enough in his decades on the force to figure out how to survive a situation like this. And now, worried that Jessie might be compromised too, he realized he had to go on the offensive.

But how?

He stopped moving for a moment. It was a miracle he hadn't tripped badly enough to break an ankle. Without the chance to heal while in wolf mode, his running would be done. Rabbioso would just walk up and put a silver bullet in his head.

Lupo wondered if the silver loads were hurting the bastard. He hoped so, but it was likely that in the same way he himself had been able to withstand the pain, so could Rabbioso. Then again, perhaps he himself was more impervious to the silver than he realized.

Another thought hit him hard: *Maybe we're* both *more impervious to silver than others*.

Now that he wasn't moving, he could hear the crashing around better.

He had considered just backing up to a wide enough pine or juniper trunk and resting there for a while, hoping Rabbioso would sneak past him unawares. If Lupo could outflank him and come up from behind...

The problems with his plan were obvious: he couldn't tell whether or not his cover was adequate, and he might well never see or hear Rabbioso pass nearby unless his luck was phenomenal...and he had never had phenomenal luck. *Ask various Vegas casinos*.

No, he decided all he could do was use his senses to continue moving, staying out of sight of his hunter. The guy's night vision was giving him a huge advantage over Lupo, whose normal vision was not functional.

It was "The Most Dangerous Game," a classic short story he had read while in grade school.

He almost laughed at the paradoxical aspects of the main thrust of the plot. Human finds that the most dangerous, and therefore the most exhilarating, game to hunt is a human. But here was Rabbioso, a werewolf in human form, hunting another werewolf who was forced to remain in human form, but normally wasn't.

He didn't laugh, however, because a shot rang out and a chunk of wood was blasted out of a tree, near his head. He felt the sizzle of the bullet as it parted air close to his ear and almost deafened him.

He stumbled away again and jogged blindly, hoping he wouldn't find the next tree by smashing his face on it.

Goddamn it, Sam, sure would be nice to see you now.

Instead he heard another owl hooting.

He felt sympathy for the owl's prey.

Rabbioso

He was glad he'd dressed for the cold, but even so he was starting to feel shivers climbing up his arms and down his legs. He could abandon all this *game* idea, drop the equipment, and take the wolf form that would make him almost impervious to the weather, to the dropping of the freezing shroud of the northern forests. But he'd lived in the desert *over there*, and in the desert surrounding Vegas, and this wasn't so bad.

Lupo, on the other hand, since he couldn't seem to let his wolf out, had to be suffering more and more the frigid fingers of the lingering winter. No snow didn't by any means mean *warmer*, not here.

Rabbioso chuckled.

This was an ego thing, he could admit that, but the bastard had pissed him off and all he wanted was to make him suffer. He wondered if his man Jacko had gotten the woman doctor yet. After telling him he'd spotted Lupo on his way north, sooner than expected, Rabbioso had given him the go-ahead.

"Take her," he'd said. "She's all yours."

Jacko had salivated audibly on the phone.

Jacko had been one of his best guys *over there,* one of the guys who'd been with him the day they had come face to face with a bunch of Flags and had no choice but to erase them. Rabbioso didn't think about it much, but occasionally he remembered that Jacko was the one who'd initiated the action that had saved them all from a fate worse than court-martial.

Rabbioso heard the owls and it occurred to him that a blind Lupo wouldn't know what time it was, at least until he heard the owls.

Damn owls, he thought. *Couldn't you just shut up?*

Chapter Twenty-Four

Franco Lupo

On the Freighter Zeniča, crossing the Atlantic Ocean
January 1946

The companionway corridor was empty, as if everyone had already disappeared.

When they arrived at their respective cabin doors, Franco hesitated then reached for his. But her long hand also reached out and enveloped his. He looked from her red fingertips, along her arm, and up to her face. When his eyes met hers, she— perhaps subconsciously—licked her lips and exerted the slightest pressure on his hand.

"It's cold in my cabin," she said softly. "It's a new year and no one should be cold. Or alone. Come keep me warm."

"What about…?" he stammered. He inclined his head in the direction of his door.

"I trust your priest friend will understand, and if he does not…he can always pray for guidance."

Her smile softened the blow of the words. She pulled and he let her lead him to her side of the empty corridor, where she opened the door.

And then, without knowing exactly how it came to be, they were inside her cabin and kissing passionately. Picking up where they had left off up on the bridge.

Franco had no idea how much time passed, but suddenly it seemed they were naked on her bunk, and she was pulling him gently onto her, her thighs held spread wide. Gently at first, then more intensely, almost violently, she drew him in, and when he pierced and entered her she gasped and arched her back. She licked his shoulder as he bore down on her, then she moved her face beneath his and their lips met again, old friends from before, on the deck, and they tasted each other as he began to thrust into her slowly, fully, pacing himself.

Her breathing increased in speed as he increased his rhythm, filling her and then withdrawing before once again thrusting to the hilt as her hands on his shoulder blades urged him deeper. And he tried, driving into her as if his life depended on it, or hers.

Then, sweat dripping from their bodies, they uncoupled and as if their thoughts were linked they reconfigured with Caterina on all fours and Franco behind her, the dark mane of her hair in his hands as if he rode a wild horse. And the new rhythm began to build as they rocked on the bunk, their bodies in sync and their groans increasing in speed as their pleasure rose with each thrust, each withdrawal, until finally they reached the crest together and screamed out as they climaxed. Franco collapsed on Caterina's back and thus they lay, still united, until their sweat began to dry.

Franco closed his eyes when he thought he saw a ripple on her skin, like a wave, but he chose not to see it or acknowledge it, and perhaps he had seen nothing at all.

Later, they coupled again, this time finishing face to face as Caterina bit her lip and nipped at Franco's until she drew blood, which she wiped off with one long finger.

It was dawn of New Year's Day when her hand found him, coaxing him to fullness yet again, and then she rode him as if *he* were the horse, her hair falling wildly onto his face, their eyes fixed on each other…and he thought he saw a flicker there, in her eyes, but it was a trick of the new light streaming in from the nearest porthole, and he ignored it.

By the time Franco found his way to his own cabin, the sun was high on the horizon and the ocean air had picked up a slight warmth that even the day before had seemed unlikely. It didn't last, but it pointed the way to South America. The connecting door to the priest's cabin was pointedly closed, and Franco shrugged, climbed under his covers, and lay shivering until he fell into a fitful sleep.

The next several nights found Franco again in Caterina's bunk, covered in a heady mixture of sweat, musk, and spent sex, while during the days Father Tranelli avoided him.

The fourth night after New Year's Eve, an accident occurred that left a crewman dead. At least, the boiler crew chief called it an *accident*, but Franco had his doubts. When he peered past the crowd that had gathered, it looked to him as though the crewman had been slaughtered. His neck was torn open, his belly an eruption of blubbery flesh and entrails, and parts of his limbs were missing.

"Teeth marks," Franco whispered to the priest in one of the rare moments they occupied the same orbit.

Tranelli made the sign of the cross. He muttered something, but Franco couldn't catch it.

The funeral service and the burial at sea for the man with no family were mercifully brief, and Father Tranelli officiated on a gray day in which the much warmer air was pregnant with the coming rain. When the fat droplets started to pelt the ship, the few assembled mourners escaped to their cabins or crew's quarters and the sinking human vessel that had been a werewolf's meal quickly disappeared below the ship's hull.

Franco set out to determine who among passengers and crew was a werewolf, but his determination was hampered by the voracious Caterina, who demanded the youth occupy her bunk longer and more often. Like her namesake, her wild horse's body was too luscious for Franco to ignore, and became his forced playground as she coaxed more and more of his once endless stamina for her own pleasure. Though Franco had to admit that his satisfaction was not ignored, as she used her lips to revive him time and again, drinking from him while staring at him from below with those mesmerizing, otherworldly eyes. He learned that besides being ridden hard, she loved when he thrust deeply down her throat, and she held him at bay with such games for seemingly hours on end, after which she required him to service her while her thighs squeezed his head and her feet rested on his back.

As the crossing neared its end, Franco found himself more and more exhausted, sleeping during the days because Caterina's insatiable needs had taken the nights hostage.

Tranelli mumbled curses when he saw the sallow-looking youth skulking about the deck on the increasingly sunny, warmer days.

And then came the day, less than a week from sight of port, that Tranelli—who had been investigating either with the help of the nervous Havlav or on his own (when not imbibing some of the surprisingly tasty rum he had discovered by spending time with the crew)—decided he was right and informed Franco that he had determined who their shapeshifting killer was. And what they were bound to do about it.

Franco shook his head, but inside he knew they could let no werewolf survive this voyage. As far as he could figure out, there was only one, and Tranelli had identified him after shadowing him and having Havlav also keep an eye on him.

Tomas was the last passenger to board, taken on at Genova just an hour after Franco and Father Tranelli had made their own switch with the two original Nazi officers. Perhaps Tomas wasn't acquainted with the two Franco and Corrado had killed, as the ratlines out of Europe often brought together both escaping Nazi war criminals and shapeshifters and in many cases they were unknown even to each other. Corrado had learned in the weeks before finally attempting to infiltrate the escape route that the ratline operating through the port of Genova tended to involve shapeshifters from the Werwolf Division, therefore Franco was already inclined to suspect this bland-looking Tomas, last name unknown, who kept to himself and rarely appeared on deck even when the weather was pleasant. He was one of the reclusive passengers who rarely turned out for communal meals.

He appeared to have come from one of those German-occupied areas of lower Europe in which collaborators had been hunted down savagely as the war ended, and Tomas seemed to have been through the wringer. Although he might just as easily have been a victim himself.

Uncharacteristically, Franco was indecisive and dismissive when Tranelli could hold back no longer. They were nearing port, the priest begged, and they needed a plan. Franco waved off the concern. He was trapped in a web of his own desires and Caterina's sexual escapades, a novelty for a boy who had had no childhood and indeed had been a killer for years by now.

When the knock on Caterina Cavalli's cabin door came, Franco was on his knees, his tongue exploring her scandalously shaved sex while she reclined on her bunk, her head thrown back in abandon. He faltered, and she looked at him, fixing him with her penetrating stare.

"Why are you stopped?" Her sensual lips were set in a red frown. "We agreed you were free to spend this afternoon with me."

Franco thought, *Am I a lover or an errand boy?*

I am not 'with' her—I am here 'for' her, a servant wearing a tight leash.

But then he set the thoughts aside and deferred, knowing he could feel no anger with this woman who had opened his eyes to the sensual world—one he hadn't known existed. He'd known men took their pleasure with women, often violently, but her version of the sex act transcended the hurried, awkward experiences of his youth, approached the level of art, and deprived neither of the ultimate satisfaction.

Whoever she was, however she had ended up here, Franco saw her as a goddess, and he was all too willing to worship.

When he opened the cabin door, the enraged priest turned red and—speechless—slapped the boy soundly across the handsome face.

"You smell like a brothel, boy! You've become a tramp, a plaything for that *creature* behind you!"

Caterina Cavalli's sonorous laugh reached them from the bunk, where she made sure to keep her thighs spread wide.

"Really, *Father*, you flatter me!" she said in perfect Italian.

The shade of red on Tranelli's face deepened and, for a moment, he appeared ready to brawl his way into the cabin and backhand her like a wayward serving girl.

"What do you want, priest?"

Franco's voice, full of sarcasm, apparently brought Tranelli back to earth, although his rage simmered visibly beneath.

"Remember your mission, boy?" the priest whispered. "It's time to finish it. This Tomas is likely to take another victim soon. He can't survive without fresh meat, and the meals we take are not satisfaction enough. He thinks of the crew as his larder."

Indeed, by now Franco had all but stopped taking his own meals with the officers, eking occasional sustenance from Caterina's delivered trays or occasionally the crew's galley, where food was available for the asking. Franco remembered the hunger he had suffered through the length of the war, and while the lust had dulled the sharper pangs of his appetite, he still suffered from the vestigial hunger borne of near-famine. On those occasions when not dining with the woman as they lolled in her bed, Franco accepted the cook's platters of excessive food and stuffed himself as if the meal was his last.

Across his face, a flicker of shame that felt like a fever to him, and then his demeanor softened and he whispered, "I will be there in a minute."

While he closed the door, he ignored Caterina's languorous query. The priest's rage had broken through the spell. He made fists and felt his muscles tighten, adrenaline start to flow. When he left her cabin, the blade of the Vatican dagger seemed to burn in his grip.

Chapter Twenty-Five

Marla Anders

After talking to Lupo's partner, DiSanto (who seemed nice enough, if a little spacey) she had decided she could offer help. She had assumed Lupo was just ducking her, and he had been…but now he was missing. DiSanto said they were stopping just short of declaring him officially missing because his position was delicate, and a manhunt could easily backfire and cause him harm.

DiSanto hadn't actually said that, but she was good at her job and reading between the lines of dialogue her patients sent her way was something she was *very* good at. She'd sensed the panic behind his calming words—it sounded as though several people, some of whom should know what Lupo was up to, had lost track of him.

She'd spotted Lupo talking at length to Sergeant Danielle Colgrave, so she figured that was one of his inner circle. Marla called Danni and found her somewhat standoffish, sounding hurried and short of patience.

"Yeah, Lupo and I have worked together on some OC matters, and we're cooperating on some new information." The sergeant was widely respected, but she sounded short when she said, "Dr. Anders, is this about anything specific, or are you looking for background? I don't have a lot of time right now."

"Can you tell me what he might be investigating?"

"Sorry, I just don't know."

The pause told Marla she did know, but wasn't going to say.

After they hung up, Marla sat and thought at length. In her office, the image of Sam Waters seemed incongruous. He was speaking to her.

"I don't believe any of these people will include you in their efforts, but it will take them time to get there and find Nick Lupo. You would have an advantage—I know where he is, and I suspect I know how to save the day, but the problem is…there's always a problem, isn't there? The problem is that while I can see him, he cannot at the moment see me."

"What can I do?" she asked in a whisper. "How can I help?" She wasn't sure he could hear, but his eyes held hers and he waited for her to finish.

"I believe your blood connection to Joseph Badger will cause a change in his situation, in his condition."

"But why?" she asked. Her door was closed. She didn't want anyone to see her talking to herself. The police shrink was already regarded with enough suspicion.

Sam Waters—or his ghost, or his spirit, or whatever he was—inclined his head sadly, as if he didn't want to say the next words. "Because Badger was responsible for making Nick Lupo what he is…"

Marla's breath caught. "And…what is that? What is he?"

"He is—"

"Yes?"

"Not like us, not like most people. You must trust, and you must be patient."

"But why?" Marla couldn't believe she was conversing with the apparition now, and reception was better. But he wasn't talking enough, was holding back.

"You'll learn the truth, but now there's no more time to waste. You must head north. Just map it, head for Vilas County, and I'll lead you. The others will go, too, but only you will give Lupo the jolt he needs. Think of it as Joseph Badger making amends, through you, for what he did to Nick when he was young."

Marla wanted to shout, but instead she whispered, "What? Tell me! What happened, what is he, what did my grandfather…"

But the image flickered and was gone.

She put her head in her hands. Was she going crazy? Was she nuts if she followed directions from a vision?

She checked her calendar. There were no appointments. It was destiny.

She fired up her browser and searched for a route, printed the map and jotted down basic direction notes, then grabbed her parka.

Somehow she knew she was doing the right thing. If she was wrong, she'd pay the price. It was that simple. It seemed possible that there *was* some kind of destiny involved here, and she wasn't one to stand in front of destiny.

Lupo

He was still disoriented and freezing, but his head was clearer. He'd shaken off the effects of the last close slug, but his ear still rang. Yet, he was thinking more clearly now than since the explosion, as if the fog was lifting.

He was starting to suffer hypothermia, having shivered for the past couple hours, but now it was pure numbness. His hands were slabs of cold marble-like meat. It had to be past midnight. How long had he been wandering around? Shit, it had to be *well* past midnight. He recognized the sounds of the night predators chasing their prey. The wind had picked up, rustling through the bare branches of the deciduous trees and the needle-laden branches of the evergreens.

He could barely believe he hadn't stabbed himself on a low-leaning branch yet.

Plenty of time for that.

He hadn't planned on being trapped in the outdoors. He should have been curled up in front of a fire—maybe lonely without Jessie, but at least comfortable as he tried to think through his problems and his choices.

His mind wandered. Anything not to fall down and go to sleep. Therein lay death.

Jessie wanted to become like him.

Yeah, like that's going to happen.

Well, he had other things to think about now. He tried to think warm thoughts. Jessie's loving face was in the back of his mind, giving him some comfort now that Ghost Sam was nowhere to be found. Comfort, but no warmth.

Ghost Sam. Where was he?

Something to do with his blindness, Lupo guessed.

Whatever the fuck it was, it was screwing him up. Making what should have been an easy situation into a goddamn crisis.

He shambled slowly, stiffly downhill, movements jerky like those of a movie zombie, but luckily finding that he had a bit of a sixth sense about trees in his way. Occasionally he stumbled on a root, or grazed a trunk with his shoulder, but mostly he seemed to be avoiding them almost as if he could see them. Maybe part of the wolf's influence was similar to radar, like that of a bat. But if that was the case, why not have the wolf emerge as Lupo had been trying to force?

He heard a rustling not far away, but it couldn't be his hunter—there was no way he had caught up so quickly. Lupo knew he wasn't moving fast, but he wasn't moving at a snail's pace, either.

The rustling grew louder, and Lupo stopped, listening. He heard it—a low growling.

Jesus!

One of them? Rabbioso?

Did Rabbioso bring a partner?

Lupo had assumed not, that the asshole wanted all the fun, but what if he was wrong?

No, it wasn't a werewolf.

It's a wolf. An actual wolf. Not a lycanthrope.

He could hear it sniffing, almost as if confused, maybe catching his human and wolf scent cocktail. Just because Lupo couldn't smell the wolf's scent, it didn't mean that a wolf would be so hampered.

Wolves in Wisconsin had made such a comeback in the last few years that their protected status had fallen out of favor, and politicians pandering to landowners and farmers who claimed the wolf population was dangerous and would cull their herds and domestic animals had given in and allowed sanctioned hunts. Wolves had been massacred by the dozen throughout the northern parts of the state. Lupo's run-ins with actual wolves had never gone well—two predators meeting in the same territory couldn't—but he had always respected the wolf. A cousin, after all!

But now, blind, cold, defenseless, unable to change and fight tooth and claw, unable to outrun a hungry lupine...now was not a time Lupo wanted to come face to face with a single wolf. Or a pack...what if this was an alpha male, with a pack for back-up?

He or they would sense his helplessness. His own lupine nature was no help, it wasn't on display at all.

The growling intensified as the creature approached. Lupo imagined the displayed fangs, the drooling snout. The cold, predatory eyes. He did respect his wild cousin, but was that respect mutual? He didn't think so.

He debated. Should he stand still, wait for the wolf to lose interest? Or should he redouble his efforts to put as much distance as possible between him and—

The wolf's growl rose in pitch suddenly and Lupo was startled. It was much closer than he expected.

It was only feet away.

The beast's paws scrabbled for purchase on the cold, hard ground, and Lupo tried to twist away, knowing the wolf's body was hurtling toward him, pouncing on the intruder.

He was the intruder. And for once he wasn't the strongest of the match-up.

He braced for the impact of heavily muscled body and tearing fangs that would come at any second...

DiSanto

When he pulled up behind Jessie's old Pathfinder, he was startled to see her sitting on her tailgate looking very dejected.

"Doc, you okay?" he called out, jumping from the car while the engine still ticked.

She slid off her perch, her lovely face lighting up at the sight of him. "Dee! Thanks for coming! I don't know what I would have done otherwise..."

DiSanto flinched. She looked terrible. Her eyes were swollen. She'd been crying, and her classic beauty was marred by lines of preoccupation he didn't remember seeing there before.

She hugged him briefly but warmly, tightly, and he felt a stirring as her body touched his.

Christ, man, what's wrong with you?

It was still a good hour before dawn, but a filigree of light was beginning to spread from the horizon, though still mostly hidden behind the tall tree line.

He also felt her shivering. She was freezing.

"Jesus, Jess, you been out here all night?"

They broke their embrace and she nodded. "I didn't know what else to do." Her teeth were chattering.

"Wait," he said and went back to his car. He brought back a tall to-go coffee container. "It's hot 'cause I drove through the joint in Three Lakes. I figured we might need it."

She nodded her thanks but was already slurping up the hot, sweet liquid. "I can feel it warming me up," she said when she stopped after downing half of it. DiSanto knew how hot it had been. The woman was *cold*.

Afterwards he asked her to recount what had happened. By the time she finished the dawn was announcing its arrival with occasional glimpses of light touching the treetops, slowly moving downward.

"Good thing there's just no traffic up here right now," she said, then drank more coffee. "Sorry, I think I left you just a few drops."

He shrugged. "Jessie, why don't we just call the sheriff? I mean, it was self-defense. Everybody up here knows you and Nick, and everything that's happened before. This would be a done deal, the guy attacked you and you did what you had to do, right?"

Jessie half-smiled. Color had returned to her cheeks. "I thought about it, Dee. But listen, the guy? He was naked. Any M.E. worth his salt's gonna figure that out even if we tried to dress him. I shot him when he was about to change into his wolf form. I used silver, and it...burned him. Badly. There's just no way I can figure out to explain it all, so we have no choice but to just...make him disappear."

"Yeah, I get it. Makes sense."

She was crying now, suddenly. "I can't take this any more, Dee. I'm a doctor. I'm sworn to save people, not kill them. I went a little crazy there for a minute."

DiSanto touched her arm awkwardly. "But he was a monster. He was going to kill you."

"Sure, but if he's a monster...what is Nick?"

He said nothing for a beat or two. He'd been having the same thought, and it hurt to think it. He didn't really want to think these things, but what the hell had Lupo dragged them into now? On top of everything else? Sure, it wasn't all his fault, but...

He shook his head to clear it of these destructive thoughts. He was having a lot of destructive thoughts lately.

Nick was his partner. Lupo was always trying to do the right thing; no matter how things ended up, his intentions were always good. He knew that Jessie agreed, but it was easy to fall prey to the darkness.

"Nick's not like these assholes, Jessie. We both know that. He only kills when he has to, and these guys are stone cold. Hell, some of 'em love to kill. I've seen the bloodlust in their eyes. I know this guy would have killed you, and he would have enjoyed it. Maybe it wouldn't have been quick, you know. Maybe..." His voice faded. "Let's just do what we need to do and find Nick. This guy coming after you and Nick's disappearance are too coincidental."

"I've been thinking," she said, some pain still etched on her features, "and Nick doesn't usually come up here without telling me, but if he did, then there's one place he would go."

DiSanto snapped his fingers. "Sam's cabin!"

"That's right, it's not a stretch at all."

"Okay, let's move. Did this guy have a vehicle?"

"Yeah, huge SUV. I drove it into the woods about a quarter mile from here, far enough that you can't see it from the road at all."

"Well, if anyone searches for him they'll be able to find it pretty fast from the air, especially with the thin cover. We may have to move it again. Any deep lakes around here? Ponds?"

"Man, I don't know about doing that..."

"Jessie, we're stuck. Either we follow through or now we get pulled into it to our necks. I'll take care of it. Wipe it down, whatever. Maybe we can make it look like a mob hit. You think he was mob?"

"I assumed. I think the Wolfpaw guys always attack in packs, or teams, whatever they call them."

"Okay," said DiSanto. "We'll deal with that later. First, the body. Then we find Nick."

She told him. She had rolled the remains down a ditch that led to an incline down from road level. He'd gotten caught in the undergrowth that remained between the bottom of the ditch and the gentler incline. She led DiSanto down to where the swollen, scorched body had come to rest. DiSanto nodded — she was right, they never could have explained this. He had brought a shovel and a pickaxe, standard equipment when working with Lupo lately, and the two of them made a shallow incision into the incline below the gruesome body, and then rolled him in.

"Need to make sure it's deep enough to keep scavengers from digging him out," she had said.

He brought down a red can and sloshed it on the body, sent a match into the hole, and they stepped back as the flames finished what the silver had started. They stood well back, gagging, eyes watering. Then went about covering it up as best they could.

"Leo McCoyne still sheriff?" DiSanto asked as they cleaned up and stowed away the tools of their crime. It had taken almost two hours. Now the day had definitely come, a weak sun pouring a few beams down to the floor of the forest but heating it not at all.

"Yes. Leo's a good man."

"Well, let's hope he's both not too good, and barely good enough in this case."

"He's already had the wool pulled over his eyes so much..."

"And that's best for him, Jessie. Believe me, they wouldn't hesitate..."

"I know."

He slammed the trunk of his car. They checked their phones, but there was no message from Lupo.

"Again, thank God there's no traffic around here. Okay, let's go see if Nick's at the cabin. Maybe his phone's fucked up and we're all panicked over nothing. Have bacon and eggs with him in his kitchen."

"Yeah," she said, but it was obvious neither of them believed it.

Colgrave

She was making good time, driving north following DiSanto's directions. She'd already been to Eagle River, but frankly it wasn't a place she felt attached to, so she'd forgotten the best way to get there. Old roads vied with newer wide highways cut through the nice forests—that she remembered, that the new was squeezing out the old again. She shook her head. Maybe she'd caught that sadness from Lupo himself.

She'd gotten on the road long before dawn, spurred by another call by DiSanto filling her in and it was bad enough there was no reason to wait. Now she was edging up to 85 miles an hour, using Lupo's trick of calling ahead and getting the State Police prowlers to back off.

Cop on the job.

Seemed to work too. She spotted cruisers here and there, slotted within the meridian, but ignoring her after a glance.

She realized she would have to call for better directions once she got closer. The northern part of the state was a warren of old drives, circular and circuitous routes, and county roads that were so dark at night you might as well give up trying to see anything at all outside the range of your headlights.

Nick Lupo…

Had he gotten himself in some kind of trouble, or was he just incommunicado? She couldn't guess, but his friends seemed to be intent on finding him. She'd caught DiSanto's responses to Jessie Hawkins and wondered whether the fact she'd almost been attacked was why they had assumed Lupo was, indeed, in trouble.

Though she couldn't imagine him not finding a way out of it on his own.

He was a resourceful guy, she was sure of that.

Again, there was that tingle.

She'd felt it with Brant, whom she'd helped out on occasion. Richard Brant was a Vietnam vet and post-Vietnam spook who'd gone rogue a couple times, and she'd gotten crossed with him when an old lover—a crooked cop—had tried to put the screws to Brant.

Yeah, there was a tingle for Brant, but he was probably too old for her. He'd told her that he was, regretfully.

But Nick Lupo wasn't too old.

It was as simple as that.

Colgrave smiled as she thought of him, coming into her office and spilling his guts like that. Maybe he felt a tingle too. She knew he was in deep for the good doc, but...*well, even the good ones stray.*

And she'd caught a hint of some kind of history between him and that impossibly hot reporter chick, Heather Wilson. Like maybe he'd strayed with *her.*

She could see why people—*women*—found him intriguing. There was sense of tragedy about him, maybe hanging around his neck like a noose, she thought. And yet he was lusty, a drinker, a cook, a rule-bender when he needed to be, but a good guy who always had your back.

So now I have his back, she thought. *We'll see what else, down the line.*

She was about an hour behind DiSanto, from what she gathered when he called her while he was getting gas and coffee. They'd still not heard from Lupo, and neither had she. He hadn't gone into detail, but she knew they had done some bad stuff up there—stuff that law enforcement would frown upon. But law enforcement had no context for werewolves, did they?

Colgrave grinned mirthlessly. No they didn't. But she did, now.

Lupo

Crack!

The wolf uttered a cut-off whimper and the body was flung away as if it had never been there in the first place. Seemed like a high-velocity bullet had taken it squarely in the snout. Lupo only surmised that was what had happened—he heard the wolf crash into the undergrowth somewhere off to Lupo's left as if it had been swatted down by a giant hand, but there was still some movement there, rustling.

Crack!

The second shot made a wet *smack* sound and the wolf's body lay still.

Lupo ducked as if it would save him from the next bullet, throwing himself to the ground in a sloppy evasive move that ended in a roll until his ribs violently connected with a very solid tree trunk.

"Oof!" The air was kicked out of his body as if a mule had taken aim. The pain was just one more on a long list, but he still had a hard time regaining his breath.

He kept low, expecting another slug.

Rabbioso, playing guardian angel, hadn't wanted to share with the doomed wolf.

Lupo lay there, winded, letting his body start to respond again, and then slowly tried to roll to his knees, holding on to the trunk so he could stand.

Then a slug took out a chunk of tree above him.

Crack!

The slivers hit him like shrapnel once again, but even before the echo had died he was already in motion and he didn't stop, rolling up on his feet and ducking to where he hoped he was covered by the tree.

Crack-Crack!

Two quick shots found the tree, but by then he was running, bent over in a crouch, keeping the trunk between him and where he figured Rabbioso had taken up a perch.

Lupo's strength was fading fast, and he had to admit to himself that this time he might not find a way out of this predicament. Middle of the night, miles from anywhere. No Sam to help him, strength running out, bullets getting closer.

Fuckin' drone missiles missed, alpha teams, rogue werewolves…and now one fucking psychopath with a rifle's gonna do me.

Wasn't fair.

Jessie.

Damn, he wanted to see her one more time.

Chapter Twenty-Six

Franco Lupo

On the Freighter Zeniča, crossing the Atlantic Ocean
January 1946

He was running, running, steps clanging loudly on the deck, then stumbling into the door of their cabin, breathless.

"Havlav's dead!"

Tranelli leaped up from the bunk as quickly as his aging body allowed. "Where?"

"One of the storage rooms he showed me, where we met a few times. I told him earlier I wanted to meet tonight, right after you talked to me, and I went to meet him and—God in heaven, I hate those monsters! He's chopped into pieces, not much of him left, but they made sure to leave his head for me to find. *Bastards!*"

"That's it, we must trap this Tomas." Tranelli plucked his Vatican dagger from under the thin mattress, drawing the blade partially.

Franco thought he saw the blade glow, but it was a trick of the light. He drew his own dagger, checked his Beretta, and turned to stalk back out into the corridor.

"Wait!" said Tranelli, grabbing his arm.

Franco shrugged it off.

"Listen! You can't just barge into his cabin and kill him!"

"Why not, we are agreed it is him. Havlav was going to confirm it. It's why he was butchered. It's mocking us..." Franco hadn't realized how much the tension of the voyage had built up. He thought his head would explode.

"And what about...*her*?" The priest pointed across the corridor.

Franco blanched. "Leave her alone!" he hissed. "What has she to do with this, you drunken old man?"

"Where was she? When Havlav was killed?"

"How should I know?"

"You know the taste of her ass—"

Franco slapped him and knocked him back into the cabin.

For a moment, Franco looked as though he would use the dagger on the priest, who stared at him silently, stunned.

Then he snorted and left, heading for the cabin they knew belonged to the reclusive Tomas.

Tranelli dragged himself to his feet and followed. Someone had to keep the kid from getting killed. He gave chase as quickly as he could, but when he reached the open door and rushed in, he found Franco stalking from one side of the square chamber to the other. Tomas wasn't there.

"He's out hunting," Franco said. "He's hunting *us*."

Tranelli nodded. It was possible.

"We split up, walk the decks in opposite directions. See if we can flush him out."

Franco snorted again. "And then what? Alone, we're vulnerable. We must watch each other's back. We must find a way to drive him to where we can corner him, like one of those tigers in India. Once we have him trapped, we shoot him until he's incapacitated..."

"But—"

"And then we step in and slit his throat with our blades."

It was no plan at all, Franco knew. It was his temper, his anger, his need for revenge. Not for Havlav, not really, but because the monster had killed under their very eyes. It was the insult he couldn't swallow.

He turned to make his final point, but his voice faltered. The priest had gone deathly silent, pale, his drinker's complexion so white he might as well have worn a sheet like a child playing at ghosts.

"What's wrong?"

But then out of the corner of his eye he saw a ripple, a strange rippling of the air, and he knew—*knew*—though it was too late, that Tomas had trapped *them*.

In his cabin.

The grotesque wolf-like creature stood on four gigantic paws, head down and snout displaying rows of sharp fangs. Drool was pooling under his head as he fixed them with a ravenous red-eyed stare. A low growl came from the depths of its throat and it opened its maw and licked its chops like a rabid dog contemplating a raw steak.

"Come get me, fucker!" Franco shouted, pushing the priest away and simultaneously leaping in the opposite direction, trying to divide the wolf's attention and draw its attack.

It didn't work. The wolf pounced without any sort of preamble, aiming for where the priest had stumbled.

"Noooooo!" Franco screamed, and he was able to only redirect his momentum to a point, but still he threw his bulk back toward where the wolf's body was crashing into the priest.

Tranelli was saved by his last-second stumble, which changed his profile just enough so that the snarling airborne wolf was no longer centered on his chest and couldn't recover in time.

Two of its great paws struck the priest a glancing blow; through sheer luck the razor claws didn't connect with anything but his clothes.

Franco's response was lightning-quick. He followed through the wolf's trajectory with a pursuing trajectory of his own, and the unsheathed Vatican dagger flashed as he drove it home into the monster's muscular flank.

The wolf shrieked as the blade carved into its side and made its blood sizzle. Franco's grip never faltered as he slit the beast open, cutting through ribs and organs both. A bath of its blood exploded from the wound and Franco followed the body to the deck, never letting go of the dagger's grip.

They ended up against the bulkhead, sliding around in the blood and gore from the wolf's torso, as it attempted to bring its snout around to snap at Franco, eyes blazing with pain and rage, but mostly pain. Franco lay across the wolf's body, his dagger still buried inside its chest cavity, evading the snout's frantic snapping jaws.

"Now, priest, now!" Franco shouted.

Tranelli recovered from his near-miss and lunged into the corner, landing atop the writhing monster and managing to avoid the fearsome and deadly jaws long enough to drag his own blade across the wolf's thick neck. The fur and flesh parted like lard under his attack and the stench of scorched hair and flesh enveloped them as did a gout of the unholy creature's horrible blood.

The red haze slowly faded from its eyes as both men twisted their blades into the awful wounds they had inflicted. It squealed as it died, shuddering, then flickered between its wolf and human forms almost faster than the eye could see.

They withdrew the blades from the human form of Tomas, and stumbled away in near fatigue to sink down in the cabin's opposite corner, chests rising and falling.

Franco sheathed his dagger and wiped sweat from his eyes.

But now he smiled, a grimace of hate. He *enjoyed* killing the monsters. He caught the priest staring at him and felt his face color under the scrutiny.

He turned away. "Let's get to it."

Chapter Twenty-Seven

Jessie

As soon as they turned into the curvy drive that led to Sam's—now Lupo's—cabin, they knew.

"Jesus!" said DiSanto. "Look at the place."

"What…what happened?" Jessie's face was plastered to the side window.

DiSanto stopped the car a ways from the damaged, still smoldering cabin. The whole rear wall of the place was blown out, the kitchen ruined, parts of the roof collapsed. Water had spurted from a broken connection and half-flooded the kitchen floor, which had probably helped keep the rest of the place from burning down. Debris was strewn in a semi-circle the radius of a hundred feet or more, but most within twenty feet.

They left the car doors open in their haste and raced up to look for signs of Lupo, avoiding the larger chunks of debris.

Jessie had never known so much dread.

She heard her own voice, far away, screaming a mantra:

"Jesus!-Nick-Nick-Nick-Nick-Nick!"

It was as if she were calling him and reminding herself about him at the same time, her brain empty except for his name and an image of him, his rough and tumble dark brown hair uncombed, a smile wide on his expressive face.

She reached the cabin's damaged rear deck before DiSanto, looking around desperately. Tears tugged each other out of her eyes, spilling down her cheeks unheeded.

"Nick!" she screamed, voice cracking.

But he wasn't there.

She searched desperately, flipping chunks of paneling and drywall that still smoked a little into the early morning chilly air.

There was no body.

DiSanto had reached her by now, and stopped her from entering the blasted hole of the back of the house.

"Wait, Jessie, it's dangerous!" He grabbed her and she tried to shrug him off, but he held her captive. "Listen to me, that roof's gonna collapse all the way. And it's still hot."

She could barely hear him, but his grip was steel. She tried once more to break it, but then gave up. She felt tears gushing down her face and didn't wipe them away.

DiSanto was talking and she had to focus to hear his voice past the roaring in her ears.

"Looks like a device set to blow when he opened the back door," he said. Then: "Look!"

He was pointing to a splash of blood like a Rorshach inkblot, but it wasn't large. And it was *outside* the worst blasted portion of the house.

Her heart slowed its thumping and she felt as if she could be almost rational again. DiSanto must have felt it, too, because he released her.

Jessie bent over and her doctor's experience took over, also helping to quell her panic. "If that's it, it's not much," she observed. "You're right, he never went in. If we don't find any more blood, then he didn't get hurt all that badly."

"And he should be able to heal, right," DiSanto said. "All he'd have to do is, what, turn into a wolf and let the thing happen that happens whenever he gets wounded." He stopped. "Right?"

"Yeah, but then why isn't he here?" She looked around, hoping to suddenly spot him walking toward them, grinning.

But he didn't.

"I dunno." DiSanto surveyed the scene. Suddenly: "Hey, there's his phone. And keys." They were at the far corner of the deck, but below the top surface level so they could barely be seen. He went over, picked them up. The screen was cracked, but the iPhone was operational. He touched the home button and "67 missed calls, 32 voice mails" showed on the screen, which he held up for her.

She shook her herd. The panic was threatening to return. "How long ago was this?"

"Still a little warm here. Not long. Maybe last night?"

"And the blood is fresh, I think," she said, her voice breaking up.

She felt his hand on her arm. "I know Nick," he said. "He's fine. I just know it."

Jessie stepped away, staring around them, looking for clues. Or something worse, but she didn't want to admit it.

But then...

"Dee, look at this."

He went back to where she was looking at the ground just off the back edge of the deck, where the steps were jagged and broken.

She said, "It looks as if he rolled down, fell onto the ground." There was more blood they hadn't noticed. Not much, a trace. The ground was furrowed.

DiSanto said, "He was trying to get on his feet. Maybe his knees. Hell, I'm no tracker. I don't know."

"No, you're right," said Jessie, following the furrows. "He was dragging himself. He's hurt, Dee! I don't know why, but whatever happened he definitely walked away, but he's not in good shape."

They followed the crooked, meandering path Lupo—or someone—seemed to have made through the debris field, crossing the place where they had messed it up with their running approach.

DiSanto spotted it first. "Somebody was shooting at him." He pointed to a long white crack of raw wood on a tree trunk. The ground showed more scuff marks. "Looks like he walked away from this, too."

"My God, what happened out here?"

DiSanto whispered a name. "Has got to be Joe Rabbioso. Guy's old school. We thought he was on the run, but maybe he's not. Maybe he's out for some good old-fashioned *vendetta*."

"He's the one who—?" She stopped. "After Bastone almost got me, then he stopped his guys? He's the one?"

"Yeah. Nick hurt him pretty bad, he says. Guy disappeared, but maybe not so much."

They jumped as his phone went off, the poppy ring tone loud in the quiet woods.

"Colgrave," he said as he looked at it before he answered it. "Yeah, Danni."

Jessie could hear Colgrave's voice, a questioning tone. DiSanto outlined the current situation in a few broad strokes.

DiSanto turned and said to her as he listened, "She's almost here. Can you guide her in?" He handed her the phone, and Jessie gave Colgrave clear directions that would get her to the rez faster, then to the relatively remote cabin at the reservation's far edge. DiSanto went back to the car, opened his trunk, and rummaged around until he plucked out a black composite case and hunched over it. He came back cradling an H&K MP5 submachine gun with a 30-round magazine, and another Remington tactical shotgun for her. She'd forgotten hers hidden in her Pathfinder.

"We can't wait for you, Danni," Jessie added, speaking into the phone. "We *have* to follow the trail. Somebody's shooting at him. I don't know why he's not—well, why he isn't in better shape, on four legs I mean, but it seems he isn't."

Crack!

It was far enough away that at first it barely registered as what it was.

But then they looked at each other. It *was* a rifle shot, with a long echo.

Then again, it wasn't *that* far away.

Crack-Crack!

"Shit! Christ, let's go!" said DiSanto urgently, setting off at a lope.

Jessie shouted almost incoherently into the phone. She told Colgrave she'd have to follow *their* path now. She hoped Colgrave got it, and the directions. Then she hung up and caught DiSanto as he stopped to stare at another gouged tree trunk.

He said, "Looks like Nick was headed closer to town and the shooter's right behind him. McCoyne can get to him before we do."

She nodded furiously. "Call the Sheriff," she said. "Hurry!"

"Okay." DiSanto took the phone and made the call after finding the sheriff in his contacts list. He identified himself without any preamble, then outlined the situation. "We're following now, but maybe you can head them off. We think they're coming your way."

He made a face and hung up.

"What did he say?"

"He's sending some squads, but he sounded pretty…neutral."

"What?"

"I dunno, like he was just waking up."

"We can't wait for him, Dee. We'd better go."

They set off in the direction they thought Lupo and his hunter had taken, and from where the shots had come.

"Fuck, look at that!" DiSanto was pointing up.

She was almost annoyed, but followed his pointing finger. There was a new-looking tree stand fastened to one of the more bare pine trunks.

"What you wanna bet he's using deer stands to fuckin' play with Nick?"

"They would have had to set up a bunch of them, though, right?" she pointed out.

"Maybe they never intended to leave the area. Their big compound went up, but who's to say they didn't leave behind a contingent? Check real estate firms later. Maybe—"

"Yeah, Dee, later! If this is true, we *have* to get on their trail!"

"Got that right," he said. Grimly, he pulled back the bolt on his MP5.

She bit her lip as she made sure the shotgun was ready, safety off, and followed the cop closely through the alternately thick and thin late winter woods. Looking up occasionally, shaking her head at the folly of male humans. And male werewolves.

Her ears were attuned to the sound of shooting, almost more obvious in its absence. The silence made her nervous. Made her heart beat faster, the expectation driving her crazy. The fear making her shudder more than the cold morning air.

And then, there it was again.

Crack!

Lupo

Cold, hands still frozen from the long night of running, he thought maybe by now it was morning. The wind had shifted and maybe he felt sunlight on his face, but he couldn't be sure. He hadn't died of hypothermia yet, but the jury was out on how long that would last—the day wouldn't likely get warm enough to save him.

He stumbled down the slope, bounced off a trunk he hadn't sensed, bruising his shoulder and adding another to his long list of aches and pains.

Some were worse than others.

The silver was still smoldering inside him, but seemingly it had faded into a dull throbbing ache no worse than some of his human muscular throbs. It wasn't sizzling anymore, at least.

He felt the hard forest floor suddenly become a pebbly surface beneath his feet.

A path of some sort.

He weaved drunkenly, feeling out its width. This meant he wouldn't crash into any trees or bushes, not if he followed the path. On the other hand, he was more visible to his phantom hunter.

The grim reaper.

Lupo had started to visualize him that way, dealing death at the end of his high-tech scythe.

Didn't matter whether it was Rabbioso or someone else.

Death.

For some reason Lupo hadn't thought much about death after surviving the firefight at the Bastone compound. Maybe he'd come to believe—impossibly, he now knew—that he was leading a charmed life. He spent all his time worrying about protecting and rescuing others he loved, like Jessie and Dee, and even the reckless, sometimes murderous Heather, and had started to believe his own press when it came to his longevity.

Screw that, I could die right here, any second from now. One of those silver slugs could enter my brain and splatter it all over the ground, and instead of healing as a wolf it would scorch me from the inside out and that would be that...

But Jessie and DiSanto could find him, too, track him down and take out the Grim Reaper. They *were* nearby, he told himself, ready to intercept his hunter.

Shit, I'm hallucinating.

He wondered why he hadn't yet done so. He should have been hallucinating all night.

I'm alone and I'd better face it. Get myself out of this one. No cavalry, no rescue. No Ghost Sam to hand me cryptic hints and advice.

He gave it another try.

He tried to visualize himself changing, feeling his DNA realigning and—*it's a fact Jack!*—he was over.

But he wasn't.

No shedding his useless clothes.

No coming down on four paws.

No howl from the newly-freed Creature.

Instead, he tripped over his own feet and went rolling and tumbling down the incline and suddenly he crashed headlong into a wooden barrier that stretched straight across the path, blocking his way.

What the fuck, it's a wall...

And then he wasn't sure whether it was a hallucination or a memory or he was just dreaming, but he thought if he looked at a map, after bouncing around the woods like a pinball all night, this could have been that boys' camp—what the fuck was it?

Camp O-Jew-Boy.

He remembered first what the assholes called it. They'd held Jessie there, trying to lure him to their silver-loaded guns. Martin Stewart had led the chase there, hoping to trap him.

It was actually Camp Ojibway, named after the Indian tribe.

It had been closed then, and as far as he knew it was still closed.

Christ, how did I end up here again?

Maybe his Grim Reaper had led him here, placed his tree stands in advance and hoped to be able to hunt Lupo like a tiger, driving him toward the camp where he could finish him off.

Was Rabbioso that Machiavellian?

Shit, he's Italian, isn't he?

Lupo grinned, wondering just how terrifying his face must have looked now.

He also thought—or maybe hallucinated—that this might be the perfect place to turn the tables on his hunter.

Just like that time, so many years ago now.

Corrado

They met early in a café in the Third Ward, and he was mindful that he wouldn't have picked it if Lupo and his partner were in town, because they often grabbed lunch or coffee in one of the many Italian-style establishments that dotted the revitalized area.

Corrado still enjoyed ordering espresso, Limoncello, an occasional Negroni cocktail, and other Italian delicacies, so he gravitated to these places in the repurposed warehouses of the district. This particular building was only a couple blocks from the Italian Community Center, so to say it helped him feel at home was an exaggeration, but still also true.

He stirred way too much sugar into his espresso as he watched the door. He'd always preferred it sweet, due to time he had spent in South America, Cuba, and Turkey—all places in which coffee was a specialty, but who tended to favor sweetening it. He added a squeeze of lemon, a completely invented American thing to which he had become accustomed in any case. In the end, he knew he wasn't sipping an "authentic" espresso, but he just liked it that way.

He was blowing on the demitasse when Ari Ben-Shalom entered the long, narrow establishment and spotted him down the side, along the light brick wall. Corrado raised a hand and Ben-Shalom nodded, approaching.

Ben-Shalom was almost supernaturally handsome, Corrado thought, truly his father's son.

Corrado had come to know the elder Ben-Shalom—Yaacov—after the war, when he and Franco Lupo had turned their weary eyes on Communist werewolves after having spent years hunting the Nazi variety. Ben-Shalom and Corrado later aided in the Adolf Eichmann abduction from Argentina, though Corrado had never documented his role in the affair. The two had formed a strong friendship, and Corrado had worked with Mossad on more than one occasion since then, although he had been forced to change his identities for obvious reasons. Though the Cold War had included a fair number of lycanthrope agents and assassins, Corrado and Ben-Shalom had spent most of their time on former Nazis and their disciples, many of whom continued to entertain Fourth Reich dreams, which included resurrecting the wartime experiments that had led to the hybrid super-wolves. Corrado knew well what all this had led to, and Wolfpaw Security Services had only been the tip of it...

Now Corrado had been working for a few years with Ben-Shalom's son, who had followed in his father's footsteps and taken up the mantle from within the Mossad.

"Hello, Ari," Corrado said, lowering his still-steaming cup.

"Corrado, nice to see you."

A waitress approached as Ari sat and asked him if he needed anything.

"I'll have that, but leave off the lemon," he said, pointing at Corrado's demitasse and smiling. She walked away, charmed as usual by the younger Mossad agent's boyish looks.

"I know, they don't do it in Italy," Corrado said. "But it tastes good, what can I say?"

"I'm a traditionalist."

"Like your father."

Sadness crossed Ari's fine features, but then was gone. "Yes. What have you for me this time, Corrado?"

"Well, Barton and I are trying to keep an eye on our valuable Nick Lupo, but he's a marked man—first Wolfpaw, then Wolfclaw, and now…"

"Yes, yes, I know. We'll just have to make sure there's always a guardian angel around him."

"That is so Catholic of you," Corrado said.

"When I have to be, I'm a man of many faiths."

"Indeed. Barton has a bead on the bus shooter—a sad story, that, very sad. He has no choice but to bring it to an end, or more innocent people will die. It's another how do you say, side effect, of the mess Wolfpaw made in the Middle East and here. But once Barton resolves it, he will have lost his excuse to stay here and keep an eye on Lupo."

"You and I will have to do. Barton will be a call away. Your DHS has much sway."

Corrado said nothing, but nodded slightly.

"You've made direct contact?" Ari asked.

He barked a low laugh. "Oh, yes. It was not pretty. And those camera things you supplied, they worked perfectly, but Lupo was enraged—he almost killed me, I think. My connection to his father saved me. But he knows about me and what I am—he figured it out because of my age, and how I do not look so old as I am."

"Sometimes paranoia is just a warning they really are out to get you," Ari said, not entirely appropriately.

Corrado sighed, then sipped his strong, sweet coffee. "Your father would be proud," he said.

Ari nodded once, clipped it. Looked away.

"I hope he's close to ending all Middle East conflicts, where he is."

Ari inclined his head as if praying. "Thanks."

Notoriously atheist in his views, Ari was a reflection of his father. "Once you die, you're gone," Yaacov had often said. "Everything else moves on, you don't. It's annoying to think about it."

Now Corrado said, "It's good you inherited your father's conviction. Me, I'm not so sure. I go with all ways. How do you say, I hedge my bets."

"A wise approach, perhaps."

Corrado sipped again as the waitress brought Ari's aromatic coffee. "You might as well bring me another," he said to her. When she was gone, he said, "We are any closer to the final goal?"

Ari's face clouded. "No. It took many years before we were able to convince anyone to look, and now that we do look we are unable to find. They have had many years too, to hide in plain sight. Their infiltration is more insidious than we knew."

"Yes, insidious," Corrado said, pensive. "At least we know they have had much dissent within their ranks."

"Which is being taken care of. Soon there will not be any."

"I worry about that."

"You know for years my father suspected. He was a laughingstock within the intelligence community."

"No more?"

Ari half-smiled. "No more a laughingstock in some quarters, but it does him no good, does it?"

Corrado shrugged. His coffee came and they sipped amicably, the older man and the younger man, who together knew a secret that would explode through the world news if it were revealed. It was a secret that, together with the existence of shapeshifting humans, would change the course of humanity.

They had pledged to wipe it out without allowing it to be shared with the world. But the odds continued to stack against them.

Now was the time, and Corrado told Ari what he'd been worried about. "Nick Lupo's missing."

"What?" Ari put down his cup. "When were you going to tell me?"

"Right about now, when the caffeine is surging through your veins."

Ari smiled with his mouth, but not his eyes. They were killer's eyes. "Details?"

Corrado explained Barton's intel. Despite his joking manner, he was very concerned indeed.

"So you think it's the mob? Nothing at all to do with our, eh, operations?"

"If I were a betting man, I would say the odds are even, but I have a feeling it's a home-grown problem, as they would say. That bastard Rabbioso, he escaped the firestorm Lupo caused, and now he runs the Bastone family. I think the current problem is caused by him and his desire for *vendetta*. A fine old Italian word, wouldn't you say?"

Ari nodded. "Indeed. Anything I can do? I have resources..."

"No," Corrado said. "Better to let it play out. Lupo has a good team around him. I think he can get himself out of trouble, and his team can help. And our little problem is on hold, is it not?"

Ari nodded. "We believe that dissent you speak of may be over soon, perhaps even as we speak."

"They're moving this quickly?"

"It only seems quickly to us, I think. The snake has many heads, but one is in charge of all the others, and occasionally it cuts off one or two. But soon they grow back." Ari finished his espresso, sucking out the last drops daintily. "Much too soon they grow back.

Corrado nodded. It was true.

He wondered whether they were taking care of what was left of their problem right now, as Ari had suggested.

He shivered. Even at his age, knowing what he himself was and what he had done, he would not want to be there when they *took care of* their problem. Chopped off one of their heads.

Soon they shook hands and went separate ways as the weak winter sun rose above the buildings of the Third Ward.

Chapter Twenty-Eight

Marla Anders

She had driven most of the way following her own jotted directions, feeling a deep sense of déjà vu, because she remembered her youth and spending some time with her grandfather up in the woods, the reservation, the poverty and the hopelessness all around them.

Her grandfather had always seemed like a man from another time, but not altogether old-fashioned. He had seemed plugged into the earth, plugged into nature (more like *Nature* with the capital N), plugged into his people's heritage. Not at all the way he was portrayed at the end, a criminal, an evil man, mastermind of evil, dark plots against Indian values. He was derided for his beliefs, but then he was banished for whatever he had actually managed to do. She barely remembered him, but what she did remember was not the way the stories made him sound.

Things were said about him, things she had blocked out of her tender mind. Things that, if they were true, would have made her love him less. But because she had blocked them out, she had continued to love him. Even after he was gone, something he had done—given to the tribe, maybe—had been controversial. Elders had fought over him and his legacy, whatever that was.

But he had been connected to Sam Waters, a man who straddled the white world and the Indian world in a way so few managed—somehow ending up respected by both. She knew little about him except what she had heard, but she knew he was dead.

And yet here he was, sitting in her car's passenger seat. He didn't seem to cast a shadow on the Altima's upholstery, but still he was visibly seated.

"I still don't know what this is about," she said. When she glanced over, he had flickered out, so she looked like she was talking to herself. Then he came back, as if the connection was spotty.

He said, "There's a place, Nick Lupo is going there right now. I can see him...when you don't see me, I am there."

"But he can't see you? Has he seen you?" She remembered her notes, even those she wasn't supposed to have.

The apparition ignored her. "This place, it is a boys' camp long since closed for its last season. Nick has been here before, a time of strife. It is important that you reach him before he leaves this place, and before the one who hunts him succeeds."

"I'm driving as fast as I can," she said. Indeed, she had made great time. She was passing through Antigo, a short way south of Eagle River. She had slowed due to the speed laws of the tiny town, but she edged the responsive car faster and faster, and when she reached the edge of town she opened it up and there was a roar of agreement from under the hood.

It was a straight shot north now, U.S. 45 through Pelican Lake, then Three Lakes, then Eagle River.

"You will turn off when you reach Three Lakes," said Sam Waters.

His ghost, or whatever he is.

He flickered out, then came back into focus.

"You must hurry," he said.

It freaked her out a little, the way he came in and out like that.

He had convinced her she was the only one who could save Nick Lupo. If she hadn't been a sensitive, maybe even a psychic receptor, she would have taken ibuprofen and gone to bed. Or maybe a good Cuervo margarita, one of her weaknesses. *With salt, damn the bloating.*

Hell, if she'd had the margaritas before the strangeness occurred, she would have thought it was the booze. But she was stone cold sober. Maybe she didn't want to be.

The road sped by under her, and the ramrod pines and other evergreens hugged the shoulder. The car was almost roaring now, and she fought the wheel a little, feeling it start to elude her control. It wasn't slippery, fortunately, or she would have planed right off and into the deep ditch that lay at the feet of all those trees. If a deer loped out of the woods now, she was dead.

Then the sign told her she was almost there, and the apparition came and went, came and went, and then he pointed. "Cautiously, turn here."

She didn't ask, she just did. He pointed straight, then left, then along a winding road with the occasional cottage hidden in the woods on one side, then right and close to some kind of water—a river, a channel, a pond or lake, she didn't know, and she followed his lead. She was parallel with the water, not iced over as winter's last gasp was milder than average, and she caught glimpses of its surface, and then she saw a clearing or a parking lot carved out of the forest and graveled but shot through with holes and dried weeds, and she was turning under an old-fashioned faded wood and iron sign that still stretched over the road, though lopsided, its paint cracked and peeling.

Camp Ojibway, For Boys, it read. She could barely make it out.

When she couldn't take the car any farther, she stopped and left it, door open and its engine ticking like some kind of IED getting ready to blow, and followed the path the ghost of her grandfather's friend showed her.

Crack!

She jumped at the shot, but didn't slow down.

Crack-Crack!

Jessie

"He went into that campground!" DiSanto pointed at the overgrown parade ground surrounded by ramshackle cabins and a much larger long-house with a collapsed roof. Several flagpoles leaned unsteadily in front of that building.

Jessie stopped to look. It was Camp Ojibway, long ago dubbed Camp O-Jew-Boy by the anti-Semites of the area because it had operated mostly for Jewish families. She remembered it well, not only its operational days, but also when the Martin Stewart gang had taken her and Nick had rescued her just before one of the redneck psychopaths could rape her.

She hefted the Remington. "Have to get there, Dee, he's in trouble."

From what she could tell from that glimpse, Lupo was stumbling around and had crashed into a wall, bounced off, and continued drunkenly out of sight. She had no idea what was wrong, but he didn't look in control of his movements.

Wounded? Blind?

Maybe.

Then she saw someone else.

"Look!" she said in a loud whisper.

He was climbing down from one of those deer stands—they'd spotted a few more while following Lupo's trail.

She wasn't sure, but she thought it was indeed that Rabbioso guy, the mob guy who had been here on the ground for the Bastone family invasion. He was handsome in a roguish way, and she'd liked him a little when they'd met briefly. He might even have saved her life, but now the story was different and she saw that he was carrying an assault rifle. He was stalking Lupo, following barely a minute behind. As they watched, mesmerized, Rabbioso stopped and put the rifle to his shoulder.

"Noooooo!"

She couldn't help it, she shouted and Rabbioso stopped and turned, looking for them. Too far away for the Remington, she could only stare as he turned and raised the rifle again.

Crack!

He paused, glanced at them, then leveled the rifle again.

Crack-Crack!

The gunfire took barely two or three seconds, but the echo lived longer as it bounced through the woods.

Beside her, DiSanto said, "Shit!" and let go with a burst from his MP5. But it was like splattering lead—and silver—at random, because it didn't affect the shooter. He was just too much out of range.

They had to get closer.

She gripped the Remington with a vice-like grip and stalked off toward where that murderous bastard Rabbioso had just been, intent on defending her man.

Nothing would get in her way.

Rabbioso

Goddamn them!

The crackle of full-auto fire made him half-duck, but as he did he realized he was well out of range of whatever the cop was carrying. *Maybe a fucking submachine gun.* He might be too far right now, but they could close the gap fast enough. He couldn't very well go back to his last tree stand.

He had no idea how those two had managed to find him and Lupo, how the hell they managed to show up right *now*, right when he was about to finish it. He had been so patient, he could *taste* his triumph like a fine vintage or fresh and bloody cut of human meat.

Fuck! Anger surged as he realized he was no longer in the hunter position. He could still fight them off, but the odds had just shifted. He could kill Lupo—now he *wanted* to kill Lupo immediately—but then he would have to fight off those two raging assholes.

What were the chances they were as loaded up as he was?

His hands were seared from carrying the silver-loaded rifle so long, but he had learned to control his pain back when he'd earned his stripes in Wolfpaw. He knew he was different, special, and now he was certain Lupo was, too.

Yeah, he wanted to kill Lupo once and for all, but ever since he'd bounced off that cabin wall, he had managed to disappear among the camp's other dilapidated structures. He could be anywhere, and Rabbioso had those two on his tail now.

He had no choice. This was no longer a solo first-person shooter.

The radio was clipped to his harness. He was nearly breathless. "Come in, Matty. I need covering fire here at the campground. Tell Brujo to leave my guy to me, but he's got a cop and a woman, both armed. It's open season, man. Over."

The radio crackled for a split-second. "Got it, boss," Matty said. "Heading in now."

"Ten-four."

Rabbioso picked his way carefully over the cluttered gravel incline, which was slight and probably led to the water of the swift, black-looking channel, avoiding half-buried roots and other winter debris. He tried to keep as many tree trunks as he could between himself and the two meddling assholes, but they seemed to have figured it out and were starting a flanking maneuver of their own. They were keeping even with him and so he had to keep moving.

Annoyed, he thought about dropping his rifle and clothes and tearing after them as a wolf, ripping out their throats and then taking his sweet time catching up with the strangely powerless Nick Lupo...

But then he decided against it. He had lost visual contact as the bastard cop must be weaving in and out of the two dozen cabins as if he'd figured out where he was. Rabbioso still wasn't sure why the cop hadn't done the obvious.

Why is he not defending himself? Why isn't he a wolf, fucking stalking me?

He had assumed it was a reaction to the explosion. Lupo had seemed blinded, as well as wounded by the shrapnel he had included in the little surprise IED package his man Jacko had left. Whatever it was, Lupo had not been able to effect a change, and apparently he still couldn't.

All the more reason to catch him and kill him with my bare hands, up close and personal.

He tapped the Gerber Mark II combat knife hanging upside down from his sling.

He wanted badly to feel the blade entering Lupo's goddamn neck, to open his mouth and tap the spurting spray of hot blood even while keeping his human form. He didn't have to beat Lupo as a werewolf...he would beat him man to man.

But first, he gave directions for his team to swat the niggling mosquitoes who had started to buzz around his ears.

Marla Anders

She was running into the old campground, aware of the ruined cabins and their collapsed roofs.

The ghostly apparition who had led her here seemed to hover before her, showing her the way like some bizarre version of Dorothy's Scarecrow. The thought reminded her how silly this would all sound if she told anyone, but she knew too much from her own life had edged into the strange—not to say definitely supernatural—and she was a willing receptor.

Besides, she'd heard the shots. Something was happening, even if she wasn't sure what it was.

She felt the same sense of urgency shown by the ghostly shape that shimmered in her path. She had no idea what she would find—would it be too late for Nick Lupo?—and she had only a scant idea of what to do if she came under fire.

But she gripped her own Glock.

Though not technically an officer, she had the training and the permit, and she wasn't stupid. She knew the sound of a high-powered rifle when she heard it.

She transitioned from a badly frost-wedged, crumbling concrete path to a widening parade ground, a pebbly, pocked expanse that spanned from one irregular row of cabins to the other. A longer lodge-style log cabin, probably the office, kitchen, mess hall, and equipment storage lay across the way, forming a large U surrounding three sides of the parade ground. However, she saw that footpaths on either side of the large cabin converged at its face, also spilling into the inside of the U.

And someone was stumbling crookedly down one of those side paths, heading almost straight for her.

She came to a sudden halt, kicking up a spray of gravel, and raised her pistol.

It was like a scene from one of those silly zombie movies, except it didn't seem quite so silly right this second.

Her finger slid from outside the trigger guard to inside and brushed the trigger itself. Only a small amount of pressure would fire the weapon.

The staggering, tottering large form took the shape of a bloodied, battered male unsub and Marla tightened her grip on the curved metal, feeling the pad of her index finger spreading on its cold surface.

"Freeze! Hold it right there!" she said in a hiss. She realized immediately that this person was not carrying a rifle.

The form lurched to an unsteady stop, his head down and his features still shrouded in shadow.

"Now hands up, get on your knees," she called out, surprised at how calm she was.

But she glimpsed her shimmery ghost next to the man who stood panting in front of her, and it seemed he was shaking his head.

"Oh God," she blurted out before the shape could follow her command. "*Lupo?*"

It *was* Nick Lupo. Now the shadow seemed to lift off its surfaces and she could see his face, but it was him lifting his head. He seemed stunned, exhausted, hurt.

She lowered the Glock.

How close had she come to shooting him?

"Lupo, are you all right? We were all worried, figuring you were dead."

"Anders? Marla Anders?" Confused, puzzled.

She was silent for a beat, and then...

Crack!

Near Lupo's feet gravel flew like shards of glass.

He leaped aside and suddenly seemed to find a reserve of energy, for he immediately zig-zagged raggedly toward the corner of the large log cabin. He found it with his body, grunting as he struck the corner hard with his shoulder. He ignored the pain he must have felt at the glancing blow.

His eyes were open, but glassy.

"Anders, get down! Or come here!"

She had no time to question, no time to assess his revived state, or his quickness. He did not seem like the drunken stumbler from a few seconds ago, but he did seem to be blind. Another shot rang out, and this time *she* was the target.

Crack!

She felt the bullet's passage nearby and it almost deafened her.

"Goddamn it, Anders, I don't know if you're like a hallucination or what, but if you aren't you'd better get down or come here before he takes your fucking head off."

She turned in his direction, knowing he wasn't seeing her.

It was at least twenty feet.

Can I do it without getting killed?

She sensed the sniper was just waiting for her to make a move.

Lupo

Against the odds, he'd recognized the voice.

He couldn't process the reason Dr. Marla Anders was *here,* barely more than a fucking stone's throw from Eagle River. *Right now.* It made no sense. He had stumbled into the camp unseeing, barely aware of where he was. He had crashed headfirst into a dilapidated cabin, taking that solid blow on his right shoulder, but then he had bounced off and careened down the inclined path and...

He was startled by the voice in front of him, not only because of who she was, but also because he hadn't expected someone in front of him. He had heard the rustle of water flowing nearby and had taken a chance on finding it, using it to somehow evade the Grim Reaper.

But then the sniper had started shooting and Lupo's memory had correctly placed where the wall was that he had found moments before, so he sought cover. And called Anders to get the hell to cover.

Anders?

Anders, the doc, had ambushed him?

The Creature would never have let it happen, let him get taken down so easily, but the Creature was dozing somewhere inside and he himself was still blind and handicapped — not to mention hurting as if he'd been fed through a grinder.

"Goddamn it," he said again, "get over here now! Before he takes another shot!"

His hands hurt like hell as slivers seemed to leap off the unpainted, decomposing wood and jabbed him like miniature javelins.

And then he sensed her body hurtling toward him and stepped back slightly just in time so she crashed into the wooden wall, bounced off, and apparently sat on the ground, stunned.

"Anders? Anders, you okay?"

Funny how the roles reversed. He tried again. "Anders, we've got to find better cover. He's not far behind me." He reached out his hand to where he thought she might be.

Everything was still dark.

"Lupo?" she said. "What the hell's—"

And he was laughing quietly, without a stitch of humor. "I got blown up. Can't see at all, nothing. He's been hunting me all night. How in hell did you get here, and why?"

"I think— Maybe later, Lupo."

"Are you armed, Doc? I hope so, otherwise we're fucked. Pardon my lan..."

She grunted in pain.

"*Doc*, you hurt?"

"I smacked pretty hard into this wall. I dropped my gun, but I can see it. It's right here."

He reached out a hand, to where she seemed to be. "Here, can you see this, my hand?" he said.

"Yes!" she said.

And she touched him.

The spark jumped from one to the other like the bolt off a Tesla coil and she shrieked more in shock than actual pain. They seemed stuck together for a split-second, then the current dissipated and...

And he could see.

He could fucking see again.

"Jesus," he said. He blinked hard. No, she was still there, and it wasn't some sort of weird hallucination. Crouched near his feet, awkwardly positioned after taking the hard line into the building. Her Glock was on the gravel just a foot or two out of her reach. "I...I can see now, Anders."

"What?" She sounded confused. She'd barely processed the news of his blindness, and now he wasn't blind.

"Yeah, it happened when you touched me."

"My God, that's why he was urging me to find you!"

"Who?" he said, still amazed that his eyes worked, still trying them out, fearing they'd go black again. "DiSanto?"

"No, you're gonna think I'm nuts, but..."

Then the Reaper's rifle started to speak again, evenly-spaced shots like probes.

Crack! Crack! Crack! Crack!

All they could do was duck as the slugs started taking apart the scant cover provided by the cabin wall.

"Christ!" Lupo called out desperately. He snatched up her Glock and started returning fire, both keenly aware that he'd run out of rounds and yet that consistent fire was the only thing to keep the Reaper away.

He hoped Anders had another magazine.

He fired the Glock until the slide locked.

Empty.

DiSanto

"Jesus Christ!"

They were in the open on the incline leading down to the camp, and he could see flashes of dark water between the cabins, on the other side of the row of sentinel pines that must have been lining the channel or river. The campground had been on the water, of course!

But now they looked up in awe—and fear.

Maybe the trees had dulled the sound, but suddenly a bright royal blue helicopter lunged over the tree line and came in close, hovering barely a few hundred feet above them. They were so exposed they might as well have been naked.

It must have come in over that channel down there, DiSanto figured, an old wartime chopper pilot maneuver like you saw in the Vietnam movies. Whoever was at the controls was good. They hadn't seen or heard him coming.

They were both staring up, distracted from whatever Rabbioso might be doing as he reached the parade ground. For a few seconds, DiSanto thought it was Sheriff McCoyne's people arriving in grand style to effect a daring cavalry rescue. He started waving up at the sleek chopper that tilted and came around when they'd been spotted.

"Dee..." Jessie said uncertainly, standing beside him.

He kept waving, but slower.

"Dee," she repeated, and he saw that she was starting to raise her Remington.

"What the...*fuck*?" But his voice faded before he got the words out.

Now the helicopter was facing them broadside, and one of the rear doors popped open and stayed that way. That was when he realized what was about to happen—what he was actually seeing.

Down at the camp, Rabbioso's rifle started to bark repeatedly—and then a pistol responded in kind. *Was Lupo armed?* But they were too busy to make any comment.

For what DiSanto was seeing was death from above.

A dark figure seated inside the belly of the chopper was hunched just at the open door, and DiSanto saw the glint of a reflection.

"Get down! Down!" he shouted, and he leaped sideways and dragged Jessie down to the ground under him in a heap.

Too late.

Chunks of ground exploded up all around them like miniature volcanoes spewing hot, deadly lava.

"Agh!" was all Jessie managed to get out before the *Crack-Crack-Crack!* of this new assault rifle reached them, climbing over the lower-pitch of the hovering chopper's engines on idle.

DiSanto grabbed her and pulled both of them over and over so they rolled down the very slight incline, the same one that would lead them directly below to the camp—except that now all he thought about was keeping them moving so the airborne gunman, suspended in mid-air as he was, would have a better chance of missing than hitting his targets.

He could barely hear the shots, but the guy was just above them and he must have been having trouble with his shaky platform, but he couldn't miss forever.

Slugs hit the ground all around them as they rolled painfully down the rocky slope.

DiSanto tried to get himself over Jessie's body to protect it as best he could, but the jagged little hillocks set into the slope drove them apart and they continued to roll their separate ways.

Later, DiSanto would have to ask what happened next, because he was too busy rolling and praying to not feel the high-powered slugs tearing his body apart.

He rolled on and on, grunting.

Somewhere nearby, Jessie was doing the same.

Colgrave

She'd been hoofing it as fast as she could from where DiSanto and Jessie had guided her in, then she followed their trail. She spotted the tree stands, the torn-up trees. She heard the shots, far off but getting closer—or maybe *she* was getting closer—and she had no trouble figuring out what was happening.

Now there were lots of shots.

She heard the reports of a high-powered rifle, a burst from DiSanto's MP5, and then a pistol.

It was a complete honkin' firefight.

"Christ, Lupo, what did you get yourself into?" she muttered.

She wasn't completely aware of it, but she was smiling. Her friend Brant would have nodded in understanding.

She was carrying the Uzi over her shoulder on a sling, but now she stopped her full-on trot so she could pull back the bolt on top of the breech and cock the weapon. Whatever was happening, it sounded as though she needed the firepower, though it was short-range. The rifles worried her. But she felt like a reincarnated warrior as she continued to gallop toward the action.

She ran between tree trunks, jumped over dangerous roots, and all along knew she was almost there.

Suddenly she broke out of the thin cover of the woods and found herself on a slight hillside, but off to its side. She scanned its width and spotted Jessie and DiSanto. They were pointing.

Pointing up.

Right over her, a bright blue helicopter burst above the opposite tree line like a Martian war machine from one of those *War of the Worlds* movies. It was like a dragonfly as it swooped in low enough she could count the rivets in its belly. She thought it was the local cops, until it flipped sideways and someone aboard started shooting his own assault rifle.

She watched as Jessie and DiSanto hit the ground and realized they were the targets.

Then they started to roll crazily down the hill, toward a group of rotting cabins tucked into a wooded area right above the same river or channel the chopper had flown over. There was gunfire down there, too.

It's like a war.

That Lupo, always having fun.

She was more or less below the helicopter, one of those expensive Italian machines the U.S. Marines had almost purchased in bulk. They hadn't seen her—they were too occupied with DiSanto and Jessie, who were still avoiding the bastard's shooting...but not for long. She saw the pilot getting his shit together and holding the chopper more steadily so the gunman could draw a bead on her friends.

No way, Goddamn it.

Before the chopper could slowly work its way past her, she made sure she was squeezing the Uzi's grip safety, and then she aimed almost straight up at the rivets and let fly with a long burst.

Lupo

The Glock empty, he swore loudly. Anders was too far away to hand him a magazine, if she had one. Gunfire seemed to have erupted somewhere away from the camp. He thought he heard the sound of an MP5 and his hopes soared—DiSanto? Then there was another rifle, farther away.

And was that a helicopter?

The fucking cavalry?

Then he heard stumbling footsteps as somebody—his own Grim Reaper?—approached with unsure footing on the gravel. It had to be him. He had emptied his rifle as he approached and now he was here, maybe trying to reload while walking and keeping an eye out for whoever had been shooting at him.

Barely able to see, but Lupo spotted an open doorway leading into the log cabin. It was black as night, but he'd just been blind for almost a full day, and it was cover.

He staggered over to Anders and pulled her halfway to her feet, shoving her ahead of him into the doorway. She went without complaining, but she looked hunched over in pain. He followed her inside, glimpsed some sort of open game room or mess hall, and turned to face the doorway.

Lupo figured he had a half-minute at best.

He felt as if he'd been dragged behind a three-ton German truck like good old Indy, then the truck had backed up and rolled over him a few times. But he could see...and if he could see, then maybe...

Anders was still stunned by the smacking she'd taken against the cabin.

He called out in a whisper, "Anders, I want you to close your eyes and just ignore what you hear. Or anything you see, understand?"

She hesitated, then nodded. Closed her eyes.

She's a peach, he thought.

He stripped out of his outer clothes, his body screaming in pain. The footsteps were just outside, moving slowly, cautiously. He set the sheathed dagger nearby. It was a case of needing two things almost simultaneously, but one had to come first.

Lupo visualized himself going over, and started to feel the familiar sensation of his DNA realigning.

It's-a-fact-Jack!

It was what his brain always said at that moment, wherever it had come from.

The Creature was there, ready to pounce. Lupo made it stifle its automatic snarl.

First, this...

He focused on his hurt, battered body, and almost the same second he felt relief as the magical healing began. Who cared why this worked, but it did and that was all that mattered. He told the wolf to be cautious, a predator was approaching, but the wolf—his familiar Creature, back from a long nap—already knew, and lay in wait.

Lupo felt the healing work on his more serious wounds, his aches and pains, and even his near hypothermia.

Then a shadow reached the doorway, the rifle held at the ready. Maybe he'd reloaded? Lupo thought he could sense the silver loads from here. If it *was* Rabbioso, how did that guy hold it?

Lupo had to weigh his timing carefully. Use the wolf as a surprise, but keep from getting drilled with silver slugs. But if he could do that and keep Rabbioso from shooting him and then also from changing…

No guts no glory. A sardonic tribute to DiSanto's love of clichés.

He held the Creature back to the last second then sprang, catching the entering Rabbioso off-guard.

The wolf snatched the silver-loaded rifle out of the gunman's hands and shrieked with the pain as the silver burned him like a live wire, but it followed Lupo's internal commands despite the quick jolt of agony and shook its head violently, sending the gun clattering across the claustrophobic space where it lay out of reach.

And then the two of them faced each other.

Rabbioso, clearly startled, saw that Lupo had changed — after all those hours, something had allowed him to do it. But what? He turned and his eyes widened as he saw Anders, huddled in the corner.

He smiled.

He smiled and started his own change.

But Lupo timed it perfectly and lunged, taking the mobster enough by surprise that he stumbled backward as the wolf snarled and bit, ripped and tore at him. Blood flew as Lupo's fangs shredded Rabbioso's human flesh.

Screaming now, Rabbioso tried to complete his process.

But Lupo willed himself back to human form, and when he was over he reached down to the cracked plank flooring with his human hand and picked up the Vatican dagger. In one motion he unsheathed it, unmasking the silver blade so any werewolf would now sense it. It didn't matter anymore.

Even though he wanted to go for the kill, Lupo did not—in his weakened state, a full-strength Joe Rabbioso would be like a psychopathic killing machine. Lupo wouldn't stand a chance. Instead, he leaped forward and caught Rabbioso just a split-second before the air around him would have started to ripple...

Lupo's grip on the dagger strengthened as he slashed across the top front of Rabbioso's face, from cheek to cheek.

Rabbioso shrieked again, but this time it was the very sound itself that was frightening, as blood and gel-like vitreous humor spurted out of his ruined eyes and caused him to resemble a twisted, bloody parody of Oedipus.

And, as Lupo had hoped, Rabbioso became unable to complete the change. Blind, he could not summon his wolf.

The wounded mobster threw himself backward and out the doorway, staggering across the parade ground. Lupo made sure Anders was all right, then gave chase as best he could, although he wasn't faring much better than his enemy. When he looked up, Ghost Sam was standing there pointing the way to where Rabbioso had stumbled.

"Nice way to miss all the action," Lupo muttered at the apparition. "Now that it's safe you show up."

"He's making for the channel," said Ghost Sam, ignoring the sarcastic remarks.

"Yeah, thanks."

Right then the ground was shaken by an explosion.

Christ, Jessie and DiSanto!

But he shook himself and tottered off in the direction of Rabbioso's desperate escape, splashes of blood and whatever was leaking from his ruined eyes marking the way through the trees.

Lupo caught up to him just as he reached one of the several rickety piers that jutted into the channel. Rabbioso didn't seem aware of the piers, only of the channel and the current's rushing gurgle. He half-tripped and landed hard halfway along the pier, becoming aware of it when the planks creaked.

"Goddamn it, you sonofabitch, where are you?" He was scrabbling for his combat knife.

"I'm right here," said Lupo, and he visualized himself crossing over again, and this time the wolf was right there—*it's-a-fact-Jack!*—and he lunged for the wildly swinging killer. Snarling, his huge wolf's body had almost reached Rabbioso when the mobster twisted away and was struck a glancing blow, sending him careening off the pier and into the swift black current, where he disappeared. An arm broke the surface momentarily but was dragged down again and then the water took a gentle curve and it was out of sight.

Lupo allowed his Creature-self to stand at the pier's edge, peering downstream to catch another glimpse, but the enemy was gone. Blind and unable to change, he would have been too weakened to crawl out of the current's grip, or so Lupo hoped.

He let the healing touch of his magical form work some of its wonders on his bruised and battered body, then he loped back to the log cabin. By the time he reached her he was human again, subdued due to his wounds. When he ducked into the doorway, she held out his clothes.

"Better not ask, Doc," he said gruffly. "You wouldn't believe it."

"After the last few hours," she said, raising an eyebrow, "I'd pretty much believe anything." She looked away and he looked there, too, and maybe that was Ghost Sam flickering out of sight.

Then he set off on a painful run up past the cabins to see what had happened to Jessie, and his partner, all the while trying to hope the explosion was a good thing.

Colgrave

The last thing she remembered, she was emptying the Uzi's magazine upward, into the belly of the blue helicopter.

It was so low that she clearly heard some of the slugs twanging off the rounded body, but she also heard glass exploding and some solid-sounding hits. The Uzi went silent when all 32 rounds had been fired. The chopper hovering above her was wobbling crazily, like a dragonfly trying to hold its course, and its Pratt & Whitney engines were stuttering as they misfired badly, a thick tendril of black smoke pouring from under the rear rotor. The nacelles below the pilot had been blown out, and somebody half-hung from the still open side door. Suddenly the helicopter's body itself started to spin rapidly as its hovering power faltered and the unchecked main rotor took control.

The pilot seemed to try and right the craft, but it was spinning and tilting too quickly, and the ground was just too close.

Colgrave realized too late that she was standing exactly where the blue machine would crash in seconds.

Gathering her wits, she leaped as far as she could downslope, hoping the extra space would get her away from the smoking helicopter before it hit the ground.

With a mighty crash, the helicopter dug itself into the hillside, its rotor disintegrating on impact and sending out a hail of shrapnel. The air was sucked out of the scenery as Colgrave rolled downward, never realizing that a six-foot sliver of jagged rotor carved a rut right next to her, close enough to cut the sling off her shoulder and turn the empty Uzi into unrecognizable junk. The explosion slammed her back into the hillside and nearly ruptured her eardrums, and then she was rolling away again, as the metal body behind her blew apart in a ball of flame.

Gee, I did that, she mused as if looking down on herself from somewhere else.

By then Jessie and DiSanto were running up and screaming at her, but all she could do was sit up, groggy, and watch their lips move because she couldn't hear anything at all. The blue paint blackened and peeled off the Agusta as she watched, bemused, too stunned to bother worrying about the heat of the fire. Only when she was dragged away did her ears pop and then the entirety of her hearing came back with a painful *whoosh* that made her cry out and hold her ears, and she heard the helicopter immolating itself like some phoenix out of a fantasy tale. Except this one would never rise again.

DiSanto left Jessie to tend to Colgrave, and he rushed up and pulled the pilot out of the burning wreck, only managing to do so because he'd been tossed out when it hit the ground.

The gunman, she noted, had been turned to bloody mash — something had first sliced him to ribbons, and then the copter's body had crushed what was left.

Jessie was checking her pulse and her limbs and she smiled at the doctor, wanting to thank her.

Instead Colgrave lay down and when her head hit the ground she blacked out.

Jessie

After making sure Colgrave was okay, that she'd only fainted, Jessie finally stood and pulled DiSanto into a kind of embrace as they watched the helicopter burning itself out.

In the distance, she heard sirens.

The sheriff and his group, arriving just in the nick of time, she mused, thinking a little like DiSanto.

And Nick?

She realized then that her face was sodden with shed tears she hadn't been aware of until now.

Whatever had happened here, it had taken over her tiny universe for the last three or four minutes, probably no more than that. In that amount of time she had gone from seeing Nick still alive, to not seeing anything else and not having time to think about anything other than the trauma happening to her universe—DiSanto and Colgrave both putting their lives on the line for Nick. And for her.

She was profoundly grateful.

But she was profoundly sad, because she sensed this time she had lost everything.

She knelt, weeping, and DiSanto awkwardly put his arm around her. For once he was at a loss and not even one cliché came out of his grim face.

"Look at him, this guy always comes out looking good."

It was Colgrave, unaccountably awake again, and staring behind them.

Jessie turned, not daring to hope.

It was Nick, making his way gingerly toward them on the hillside, his clothes half-trashed and his features obscured by blood and open cuts. He was aided by—

Dr. Marla Anders, from police headquarters!

She held him steady as he walked like John Wayne after a bad gunfight toward them. He was smiling, though, and instantly her head cleared and she ran to him, almost knocking him over in her haste to wrap her arms around him. He was shivering and unsteady, but she sensed that he'd been worse not long before.

He winked at her.

"When you throw a surprise party—" he began, and then she slugged him.

Part Three

Chapter Twenty-Nine

Heather

She had picked up her recent conquest and they'd gone out on the town. Not exactly clubbing, these were more small restaurants than night clubs, although half of them featured live music on weekends. As they were in the Third Ward, they were easy to get to. The two of them dressed and made up to impress from afar.

Heather was nothing if not practical. There was nothing better for her than finding a way to benefit from something on two levels.

And she was in the middle of working an angle, which made her genitals hum with constant tension.

Displaying out in public was such a rush. She was reminded of her cozying up to that cop, Sheila Falken, and how they'd put on a show in the bars.

Nothing turns on boys more than seeing two amazing woman brazenly flirting, eating each other up with their eyes, and playing footsy.

Except this new one was a whole new animal. Falken had been dangerous, but Marina was a question mark, and this implied she might be even more dangerous.

Sitting on padded stools in one of the narrow drinking establishments, trading sips of their different martinis, laughing at the surreptitious looks headed their way by the many single guys trolling for company, they made a point of being hands-on—hands on each other's thighs, hands on each other's elbows, hands caressing each other's hair...there were a million ways to intrigue.

"All this flirting is making me horny, I'm warning you," Heather whispered in her ear. She pushed her point by licking the earlobe before nibbling at it. She winked at a middle-aged man in a rumpled suit who was staring at them from down the bar and drinking fast.

"I hear you, honey," Marina said, her voice a little boozy, almost husky. "I want your tongue and your teeth somewhere else."

"I'm all for that."

"I'm ready, you know. My panties are soaked."

"I know," Heather said. "I can smell them."

"You cannot!" Marina giggled. Her wide mouth was perfect for kissing, and Heather leaned forward and they touched lips. The guy at the end of the bar squirmed. They shared a little tongue, just enough to catch every guy's attention. The place was rocking, but they were in a bubble all their own.

Heather ran a hand up Marina's thigh, stroking the tight leather pants she wore so well. She wondered if there would be another visitor later. She made a mental bet. Yes there would be.

Once you hook a fish, you can pretty well plan on dinner. *If you handle him carefully*, she thought. *Very carefully*.

Heather stroked the inside of Marina's thigh, laughing. Her plans were coming together in all the right ways.

DiSanto

He had tried to stay away, God knew he had, but there was some sort of magnetism drawing him there.

He sat in his car one hour, then two, then three—hoping to see her jogging by again. But when she didn't show, he gathered his courage and went into the lobby. Buzzed her. He knew she was home, her lights were on and her silver Lexus SUV was parked in its slot in the garage. Yes, he had checked. Unless she was on foot, she was home.

"What?"

He leaned into the tiny speaker grille. "It's me."

"I'm supposed to know who 'me' is?" There was amusement—no, mockery—in her tone.

"DiSanto." Maybe he shouldn't have growled.

"Ooooh, sounds like you've been practicing. Come up."

He pushed open the buzzing door and rode the elevator in a haze of lust and expectation.

She opened her door and stood framed in the doorway, nude. She smiled lewdly when his eyes nearly popped out of his head. It was just amazing, how incredibly sexy she was. He was straining the front of his trousers, almost trembling with the lust. She reached out and took him none too gently in her hand, pulling him inside by his groin, grinning at his discomfort.

"I guess you really are happy to see me," she whispered into his ear, her breath hot and her scent overpowering. The door closed behind him and she continued to pull him inside. Her fingers were like a live wire wrapped around his manhood, and he let her maneuver him toward one of her deep sofas, this one facing the wall of windows.

DiSanto had lost his connection to reality, the physical world. All he could think of was raw sex, the slap of flesh on flesh, the slurping sounds and the moaning, all things he had experienced here, with her.

"It's nice that you came back," she said, and her words were deep down in her throat, giving her voice a husky, whiskey quality. If he tried, he could hear the wolf side of her, he mused.

"I...I couldn't stay away," he said, and immediately wanted to slap himself silly. "That is, I was in the neighborhood..."

Stupid, stupid, stupid...

"If believing that makes you feel better, it's no fucking skin off my teeth."

"Well, I..." His voice ground to a halt. After all, her amazing breasts were thrusting toward him, those perfect nipples waiting for his lips, his tongue, his teeth. That cleft below her navel, with the jewel now hidden, the landing strip above it signaling the way in. Those hands, tipped in crimson and waiting to grab and tease, manipulate and milk him. Her raven hair was tied in a loose ponytail today. Her lips shone in the intimate lighting of her place.

She pulled him a little farther, around the sofa.

He was startled.

On its length was another woman, also nude, reclining as if she'd been asleep. But her dark-rimmed eyes were open, and she was licking her lips.

Heather said, "This is my friend Marina."

"Hey," Marina said, her eyes like slits but a sly smile curling her lips upward.

He nodded dumbly.

Heather said, "We've been discussing this urge we had for some three-way action. And then the bell rings and it's you. Imagine our surprise, and the pleasant shock of you arriving just in time to help us with our...discussion."

DiSanto's eyeballs were going to burst. He thought the guilt would give him a heart attack or a stroke. It seemed all his major organs were racing toward failure. But honestly, his lust was winning the war, and he was simply wallowing in the view of these two naked women who were so out of his league that if he had stopped to think about it he might have had second thoughts about the whole scenario.

He stood there awkwardly as Heather released him, then bent over and gently lowered her lips over her friend's and they kissed long and hard.

Wet, sloppy kissing, guaranteed to arouse.

They teased him with both lips and tongues, putting on a show for him and eyeing him the whole time. His own lips dry, he felt nothing but the pain of exclusion. When Heather finally reached out for him, he barely registered approaching and became a melting puddle in her hands. Somehow his clothing dropped off, forgotten, and when legs opened and musk enveloped his senses he was there, his manhood dipping into the forbidden while other body parts and slick lips found his, and after that his view shifted with the lean, muscular bodies which wrapped themselves around each other and around him.

Four arms maneuvered him, four hands manipulated him, two questing mouths explored him, and sweat-slick limbs entwined him and each other in turn, and there were moans muffled by wanton flesh, and DiSanto was in another world, one of sensation and pleasure and a tiny sense of guilt that he quickly suppressed.

They massaged and licked and drew from him his strength and essence again and again until he screamed out and felt sharp teeth on the skin of his shoulder and also on the sensitive underside of his genitals, and he wondered very briefly who was in control, who was devouring whom, and whether he would see the day again as a normal man, or whether he would see it differently.

Or whether he would die at their hands. The thought niggled, but did not bear fruit.

It was for him a world where nothing but pleasure mattered, and the only rational thought was a questioning of when the next pleasure would come and what form it would take.

When he lay between them, spent again, his skin drying, Heather fed him water from a bottle she'd had nearby. It was almost the image of mothering that surprised and disgusted him.

"Why are you here?" she whispered as he drank. "What do you want?"

"You know what I want," he said in a strangled voice, annoyed yet grateful for the water. He glanced at the other woman, who seemed to be dozing now. "You said you would think about it…"

"And I have," Heather said, coyly. "But I haven't decided yet." She stretched languorously. "What's the hurry?"

As he watched, a shocking change began.

There was a rippling of the air around Heather Wilson, as if she were vibrating so quickly that it couldn't be quite perceived by the naked eye. A long run of thick, coarse fur sprouted quickly in patches along her forearms and thighs, and across her bare chest, first surrounding then enveloping her breasts. Her face, features still sated by the lustful activity, elongated and turned into a snout, her jaws filled with rows of fangs and sharp canines. Her eyes swirled like kaleidoscopes, pupils changing colors in waves. Suddenly her look was predatorial, but not only sexually. She seemed ready to pounce.

Just in front of her, Marina dozed on, unaware.

DiSanto was startled, but also enthralled. Having seen Lupo's transformation, he wasn't totally unprepared for this close-up look, but he hadn't expected it in this context, in such close proximity, and his muscles tightened as the fear swept through him like a river of molten fire. He felt sick in the pit of his stomach and his testicles seemed to shrivel, his flesh betraying him.

The monster that had been Heather and was now somewhere between lupine and human stared at him with ravenous hunger he could read in the gold-flecked eyes. A low, low growl rose up from the bottom of the beast's throat and DiSanto thought he would piss himself. His buttocks clenched involuntarily. His hands shook. His throat, just moments ago watered, dried up like a desert.

The Heather-wolf seemed to smile as she opened her jaws at an impossible angle and slowly, gently pinched Marina's head in a vise of frightening fangs. Her tongue lolled obscenely off to the side of her snout, tickling her friend's face until she stirred from her deep sleep.

DiSanto knew right then, knew that Heather would snap those jaws shut and tear Marina's head from her body, rip into her neck and shower them all in hot arterial blood. DiSanto tried to close his eyes but couldn't, caught like a snake in front of a charmer's basket.

He gasped as the Heather-wolf smiled despite the lupine snout.

Marina grumbled, her eyes fluttering, perhaps feeling the further tightening of those jaws.

DiSanto wanted to shout, to warn her, but he couldn't generate a sound.

He stared, helpless, as the Heather-wolf positioned itself to close its jaws like scissors.

Marina's eyes snapped open.

DiSanto blinked, mouth open, tongue bloated and useless...

And then it was Heather Wilson again, lying behind Marina as she awoke, unaware and blissfully ignorant of what had almost taken place. Marina reached up and scratched her hair—blonde but showing dark roots—where the wolf's snout had been, her look bemused.

"What?" she said, startled. "Were you staring at me sleeping?"

DiSanto felt faint. Not even the gunfight at the abandoned campground had done this kind of number on him. He nodded, weakly.

Heather winked at him, her grin evil. "Still thinking about it," she muttered.

"About what?" Marina asked, half-turning.

"Nothing my dear." She stroked Marina's hair. "Come, lick my pussy."

DiSanto's head threatened to explode.

Chapter Thirty

Heather

St. Michael's was a private hospital, clinic, and rehab facility about a half-hour out of Minocqua, an hour away from Eagle River. Tucked into a lush, still-forested swath of acreage west of town, it was an exclusive, private, big-bucks kind of facility that looked nothing like private hospitals out of old movies, but more like a resort hotel. Indeed, an eighteen-hole golf course curled around one side of the property with only a stand of sentinel pines between them.

It didn't seem like the kind of place that could be sustained by local business, until you factored in the upper-crust level of the resort town, and the fact that its biggest business drove in from Minnesota and Illinois.

Heather parked her Lexus near several Mercedes and Audis and looked at Marina, making her expression as soft and caring as possible.

For her part, Marina rested her head back on the padded rest and sighed, long and hard. "I hate coming here," she said, her voice tinged with sadness.

Heather reached over and took her lover's hand. Just touching the slender fingers awakened Heather's lust and she wished they were at the hotel, a nice little inn in the center of town, but Marina had insisted they come here first and she get her visit out of the way.

Heather figured she was making progress anyway.

They walked into the lobby, which was reminiscent of a modern hotel and spa combination, except that a few discreet wheelchairs and gurneys were wheeled here and there in the background as Marina checked in. They headed up to the fourth floor, the more serious ward in which the nearly hopeless cases were kept at arm's length from those who were famous and recovering from cosmetic surgery or undergoing substance abuse rehab.

They passed the low-key nurses' station without seeing anyone. Marina frowned and marched faster down the hall. Heather had a longer gait but almost had trouble keeping up.

Marina steamed forth like a dreadnought of old, reaching her father's room and barging in without preamble. Heather followed in her wake, slower, standing just inside the door.

The room was larger than most hotel suites, with skylights along one portion of the ceiling, and woodwork worthy of high-cost yachts or luxury lofts. Beautifully appointed, none of it mattered to the shrunken body on the high-tech hospital bed. Machines and tubes surrounded the head of the bed, but the patient didn't seem aware of them. His eyes were closed, his skin sallow, his limbs rail-thin.

Marina stood at the foot of the bed a minute, her hands—fists, really—on her hips.

"Oh, Daddy," she said, and she sounded like a little girl.

Heather wasn't sure why, but the voice turned her on. She half-smiled, but hid it when Marina turned suddenly to look at her.

"This is just…this is incredible!"

Heather raised an eyebrow and came closer.

"Here," Marina said, taking hold of the blanket that covered her father's legs. "Help me."

"Okay," said Heather.

Together they lifted the blanket gently.

"Goddamn it!" Marina's breath hissed in and out. "Look at this shit!"

Heather saw, but didn't say anything. She reached out and took Marina's free hand in hers. Marina shook it off.

"Do you know how much we pay for this room, for the medical staff, for the *care*?" Her eyes were blazing. "Do you even have any idea?"

Heather knew it was a rhetorical question. She wasn't intended to answer it. She might have shown some anger otherwise—she didn't appreciate being talked to this way. The wolf inside stirred, annoyed. Angering, if not quite yet angry. Heather suppressed, giving Marina her space.

Walking around the bed, lifting blanket and sheets, checking under her father's limp arms and legs, half-rolling him, the smell hitting them at the same time, the look of the exposed skin, the soiled bedclothes. Marina continued to fuss with the bedding, her motions clipped and jerky, body language telegraphing her state of mind.

"Motherfuckers." Heather could tell by the way the language rolled off her tongue that it was not unfamiliar.

Marina swept out of her father's room and headed down the hall, past the untended station, ignoring the beeps from the machines in open rooms. Heather snuck a look and saw more patients, none of them looking too good.

They elevatored to the first floor, stormed past the lobby and into the administrative wing according to the brass plaque on the wall.

"Wait here," said Marina when they reached a waiting area that led to a series of plush offices. She barreled past a distracted receptionist, who said, "Hey..." and then gave up, because Marina was already past the doorway, the door itself closing behind her.

Heather smiled wolfishly at the receptionist, who seemed to be trying to reach someone on her headset phone.

Security, most likely.

Heather sat in one of the visitor chairs, ready to be entertained. Whatever happened, it would be interesting.

She heard voices from the office, muffled by pretty good sound baffling in the walls and a rather thick metal and wood door with huge shiny aluminum fittings. It didn't sound good. She'd expected something like this, just not all at once. The chance to accompany on a visit had come up innocently enough, and she had taken the opportunity to suggest it could be a mini-holiday. She offered to get them a nice room, and to drive.

God, that drive was a killer for boredom. Good thing they'd gotten up to some mischief while on the road. Having your nipples licked while truckers and extra-wide pick-up compensation vehicles pass you, weaving a little, certainly makes for interesting observations about men and their huge, solid...toys.

She couldn't have planned it better, finding Daddy Bastone in poor condition, getting Marina all steamed up. Being the supportive one wasn't Heather's style, but she knew how to act the part, and the sex was a happy by-product.

Marina must have been on a tear in there. She wondered whether the story would be told or withheld, but ultimately she didn't care. She wanted to be on the inside, and she'd edged a whole lot closer today.

Voices raised behind the walls made her itch to march in there herself. Instead she smiled crookedly and shrugged at the irritated receptionist.

Heather waited patiently, wondering when the guys from security would show up.

Marina

As soon as she'd stormed into the office, the dark-haired woman with the axe-shaped nose who sat behind the desk had half-risen in surprise.

"Sit down!" Marina ordered, and something in her voice made the smaller woman obey. The hospital administrator froze, then sat back down and visibly placed a straight-edge smile on her thin red lips. Her dark eyes showed a flash of anger, however.

Marina reached the desk and stood off-center in front of it.

"I think you know why I'm here."

"Miss Bastone..."

"I'm married now."

"I'm sorry—"

"Don't patronize me," Marina said with a snarl. "If I didn't show up unannounced, how long would my father have been kept in that condition? His sheets are soiled, he stinks, there's no one in the ward. He has bedsores, you goddamn bitch!"

"Now listen here," said the administrator, whose name plate said she was Dr. Amanda Chambers. She started rising again. "You have no right to come in here—"

As she spoke, Marina had edged closer to the side of her desk. Now she reached into her handbag and plucked out a large chrome revolver. Chambers gasped, but by then Marina was too close, her voice all hard tones and sharp blades.

"Do you know who my father is? Do you know who my husband is?" Now she was standing only inches away and she poked the revolver's muzzle into the woman's forehead. "Better yet, do you know who *I* am? *Do you?*"

Chambers froze, terror in her eyes, her lips stretching back in a grimace that parodied a smile, her skin going pale as if a veil had been lowered over her face. Her eyes crossed as they turned upward and tried to focus on the cold gun muzzle that was pressing a forceful circle into her forehead. She obviously determined that silence was her best bet.

"I will be back tomorrow," said Marina, putting an extra beat's pause between each word. "I expect to see a huge improvement in my father's care, and I expect to see you personally supervising the staff on his floor. And I expect to see staff on his floor, not empty chairs. I expect to see something as a result of the check I write out to your pathetic little scam of a hospital every fucking month. I expect to see you wipe that patronizing look off your battle-axe face, and I expect to see some evidence that you're not gonna just wait for me to disappear and then go back to this...this fucking fake concern you have always shown. Are we clear?" She put a little more pressure on the gun, pushing the Chambers woman's head back just enough to redden the circle on her forehead.

Chambers nodded, as furiously as she could with the muzzle pressing against her.

Marina nodded once, then replaced the gun in her bag, turned around and marched out without a glance back.

Outside, she approached Heather with a sweet, innocent smile.

"Are you ready to go, sweetie? I'm a little horny."

"Did you have a word in there?"

"Oh yes, I did have a word or two."

The elevator made a loud *ding* not far away, but by then they were stepping into the staircase.

Chapter Thirty-One

Barton

Chicago's south side

Corrado had come through.

He wasn't sure how, but the Mossad contacts were always solid in the end. They had quietly but enthusiastically encouraged his life's work, and when Barton had been approached he'd climbed aboard. Corrado Garzanti was the Simon Wiesenthal of werewolf-hunters, someone had once said jokingly, but the joke fell flat because by now Barton was convinced it was true.

He climbed the grimy outdoor concrete staircase to the second floor of a Red Roof Inn that had apparently never seen the recent renovations. Or maybe this one was an independent, trimmed off by the company. Whatever the case, it was probably one of the most dilapidated buildings Barton had ever seen still in operation, barely a rung above living in an alley.

Reaching the second floor, he was faced with a long series of doors and large windows set next to them, each pair representing another motel room with some loser's name on it, if not empty and raided of its meager valuables. He crouched lower than the window sills and crab-walked his way to the third door on the landing, his .40-caliber Glock in hand. The pistol was outfitted with a long cylindrical suppressor, not at all standard issue for DHS agents. It couldn't completely silence the gun, as in the movies, but the reports would be reduced to the sound of a backfire in the street, if that much.

When he reached the right door, Barton tried to peek over the sill into the room, but the heavy plastic curtain was pulled tightly.

Well, no other way to do it.

He didn't identify himself. There was nothing official about this visit, and he was gloved and prepared to leave no evidence behind. A thin Lycra sleeve covered his own sleeves past his latex gloves. He had slipped a Lycra cap over his head, which also helped distort his features. His brass was polished before being loaded into the pistol magazine, so when it was ejected it would still be a dead end. He took a couple steps back, touching the wood-slat railing with his rear, then wound up and delivered a strong, practiced kick to the door. It collapsed inward as if it had been made of balsa wood, taking most of the jamb with it.

Barton was already inside before the dust settled.

The shooter was lying on the bed. He was out of it, trembling and moaning as he slept fully clothed. The smell that permeated his clothing implied he hadn't seen a Laundromat in ages, as well. REM under his lids indicated some sort of waking dream state. Barton didn't care. The professionals had been given a chance, but they'd failed. The system had failed. By the time the intersection of their worlds brought them both here, now, the former sniper had become Barton's problem.

The agent came in close, standing next to the bed on which the shooter writhed. The guy'd been a good Marine, an outstanding sniper, probably a good human being. But a switch had been thrown and he had become a problem, a liability. A killer.

Barton wouldn't have admitted it, but due to his upbringing he uttered a short prayer.

"I'm sorry," Barton whispered. "I really am."

A tear coursed its way down one cheek, followed shortly by a second.

He extended his hand, but not in mercy. The Glock coughed once, twice. Both rounds hit the former sniper in the head. The spent brass skittered over the carpeting.

Barton stifled a sob.

Then he was gone, the door pulled back into place as best he could. He doubted anyone would find him anytime soon. When they did, they would eventually link him to the bus shootings—he'd seen enough weaponry there to tell the story.

But Barton's name would never appear in the report.

This problem had been handled off the books, as more and more of Barton's job was being handled these days.

By the time he reached the street where he'd parked his non-official vehicle, his cheeks were dry.

Heather

She could tell from Marina's flushed face that something had gone down in there, and she smiled.

Marina calling her *sweetie* was funny. It was not typical of her demeanor, but more in line with Heather's own sense of humor.

She wondered, not for the first time, if she would have to kill Marina sooner or later. She knew the woman carried a piece in her bag—and she wondered if it had made an appearance in that office. How much did the woman know about her new husband? How much did she know about the family business?

Joe Rabbioso had moved fast, swooping in to marry her after only a few months of sporadic dating. He had clearly been in the middle of setting up the internal coup when the whole Eagle River casino takeover thing had gone down, nearly killing the Don. Lupo had really tossed a grenade into the Mafioso's family, but that had opened up a whole new avenue for Heather—as well as for Rabbioso, who had taken his opportunity when it came.

She mused that he was a lot like her, as a matter of fact.

If she had to kill Marina, there was definitely a chance for her with him.

Heather followed Marina to the parking lot, feeling the vibe.

There would be great hotel sex tonight, if they even made it there. The Lexus was pretty comfortable, after all.

Heather smiled secretly as she drove them away toward town and Marina's hands, and lips, were all over her.

The threat of violence was an aphrodisiac, and no one understood that better than Heather Wilson.

Colgrave

She had a concussion, cuts and bruises, but no major wounds after almost being squashed flat by that fucking helicopter.

She was back at work, fending off questions and admiration and offers for dinner and drinks, as everyone wanted to know how she had gotten on to this new attempt by Organized Crime to take over an Indian casino.

It was a good thing she had made the obvious inquiries beforehand, put out the Rabbioso BOLO, and generally papered over the possibility that her whole story was nothing but gossamer.

Ironically, Lupo said that he'd seen Rabbioso go under when he was taken by the current, but his body had not washed up anywhere. Lupo was convinced he'd managed to slither away again, and Colgrave was inclined to agree. Blind or not, Rabbioso was a powerful werewolf, Lupo said, and he was tough to kill. Lupo was hobbling for real these days, and he joked that if the asshole hadn't been blinded by his own ego, instead of playing a game he would just have drilled a couple of those silver slugs of his into Lupo's brain and that would have been it.

Ryeland was buzzing behind her like a friendly bee. He was talking commendation, certificates of bravery, laurel leafs—you name it, Ryeland wanted to reward her. Her actions had looked good to the sheriff up there, he said, even if she thought McCoyne had managed to show up just late enough to avoid getting his hands too dirty.

She'd heard a nasty rumor about him, and she would have to run it past Lupo.

It appeared Lupo had plenty on his mind these days. But she had added to it when she'd approached him in the hall.

"Proposition for you," she had said on approach.

"Oh oh," he joked. "Always worry when a beautiful cop propositions you."

She fake-slugged him, but his smile faded at that.

"Really, I just want to be part of your team."

"Team?" he said, puzzled.

"You know, the people you go to when *things* get heated."

"Are you an adrenaline junky?" he said, gently joking again.

"Maybe."

Actually I think I have some sort of death wish.

I want to look Death in the face.

She had no idea where that came from, but it explained why she was willing to go off-book so often.

Ryeland wasn't so pleased at how his homicide detectives had been involved in the whole affair, but he had to allow that Joe Rabbioso had been out for sadistic revenge, and Lupo was an innocent victim. DiSanto and Colgrave had figured it out, and the rest was easy to fit together.

Barton looked at her funny, but he also smiled at her in the hall now.

She wasn't sure what to make of that.

Have to ask Lupo about him.

But Lieutenant Roman was another story altogether. He stared at her the way a snake stares at its prey before his jaw unhinges. She was going to talk to Lupo about Roman.

She realized she was listing all sorts of reasons to talk to Lupo.

Goddamn it, no.

Not this again.

She wanted to ask him to show her a change again.

And she wanted to ask him more. A lot more.

She smiled. There was time.

Chapter Thirty-Two

Franco Lupo

On the Freighter Zenica, crossing the Atlantic Ocean; Arrival in Buenos Aires
January 1946

From the ship's rail they watched the mainland approach, the wide Rio de la Plata estuary narrowing as they reached the large seaport's *Nuevo Puerto*, the New Harbor. The heat of the southern winter season was upon them and they sweated in the heavy humid air.

Franco was pensive, having retreated into himself since the death of Havlav and his killer, the passenger Tomas, who was a werewolf (although Franco had not been able to determine whether he was also a Nazi).

Their struggle to dispose of the bodies and clean up the evidence wore on them physically, and cost them several heavy bribes that guaranteed no questions, but also cleaned out their wallets (which, fortunately, were those of the Germans they had replaced). Still, the process had taken a full day and they had managed to sink the two corpses, one of them in pieces, only with the help of one crew member who knew they had paid Havlav for similar services. Of course, his price was steeper.

Franco spit over the railing.

Bastardo maledetto.

He had considered killing *that* one, too. Only the priest's entreaties had kept Franco from slitting the pig's throat.

"You can't kill everyone," Tranelli said.

Franco made a face.

Yes, I could.

But it all added to his foul mood.

For some reason, he started thinking of his father, Giovanni, and what had happened between them. It wasn't all that long ago in years and months, but it might as well have been decades. Franco had been a child, but even then his hand had wielded the glowing blade of the Vatican dagger with amazing sureness for one so young. His father's blood, corrupted by the lycanthropy sickness, had spilled out over him as he'd driven the blade home. The rest had been a nightmare from which he couldn't awaken, but only until he had started killing other werewolves, most of them Nazis.

Now, having killed the murderous Tomas, he felt little of the fire that had energized him at the start of the sea voyage. Perhaps, he thought, seeing an innocent such as Havlav slaughtered primarily as a taunt had simply tired him out. But then, he had been willing to use Havlav himself, hadn't he? Maybe his conscience was pricking his soul.

Even the ample charms of Caterina Cavalli, the wealthy passenger who had taken him to her bed and taught him so much about carnal pleasure, even she no longer held his attention after the murder. He had let her use his body, and she had certainly done so to her immense pleasure, but the spark that had occupied his brain before was gone, leaving behind a dark void he fell into willingly. After a brief but loud row, he had kept to himself and hadn't even seen Caterina for almost two days despite the proximity of her cabin and the ghost of her alluring scent in the corridor.

For his part, Father Tranelli had retreated into endless bottles of *slivovitz* and cheap wine, preferring to drink himself to sleep while Franco brooded through the latter portion of their journey. Now that landfall was at hand, the melancholy veil that had settled differently over both of them was lifting, and Franco sensed the possibility of a renewed sense of purpose—and urgency.

There would be contacts to make in order to attempt infiltrating the ratline, the escape route for Nazis—and specifically Nazi werewolves—that extended from the port of Genova right to Buenos Aires, and the larger nation of Argentina.

Tranelli had given Franco what intelligence Corrado and his network had shared with him before the unexpected journey. For instance, the fact that no less a personage than President Juan Perón had not only opened the borders to such immigrants, but also welcomed them openly. As, indeed, the table talk had indicated on that first night of the crossing.

"First we will cable Corrado that we have arrived," said Tranelli, now taking over. "Then we will eat some food that won't slide around on the table. I have heard they have steaks the size of platters here. I'm tired of cabbage and potatoes and beef fat passing for actual beef."

After the ship passed the long breakwater and tugs pushed her into the harbor proper, the hawsers and chains were uncoiled and the ship moored to one of the long piers. Rows of brick warehouses across the busy street were their first glimpse of the Argentine port, but the city's wide, flat sectors spread out from there and they could see several tall buildings, South America's first skyscrapers built in the American style.

Leaving their confiscated belongings behind, they were the first to descend the gangplank. The crew set about preparing to unload the ship's cargo.

Tranelli made the sign of the cross, knelt, and kissed the ground. He smiled at Franco's smirk. "There was no guarantee we would make it," he said. "Why not be grateful?"

The priest spoke passable Spanish, so as soon as they spotted a rough-looking dock worker they stopped and made inquiries. The gruff man's directions took them to La Boca, a waterfront district known for its large population of Genovese immigrants. Logic, said the priest, was that since the ratline went through the port of Genova their contacts—and their quarry—would be also be located here.

But where? That was the question they should put to a prisoner, Franco thought.

They found a busy cable office and Tranelli wrote out a flimsy in his spidery hand.

Franco was amazed at the Italian voices he heard on the crowded streets, speaking in the Genovese dialect his father had preferred. And the music that leaked from the doors of clubs and taverns. It was as if there had been no war at all.

And it was more so when they ate at a crowded *churrasquería*, where one diner's serving of steak would have equaled Franco's entire family's for two months. They further lightened the Germans' wallets and gorged themselves on beef, stew, bread, and a strong table wine—"Equal to the best I have ever had, including at the Vatican!" Tranelli proclaimed loudly, his chin covered with grease.

Stuffed, sated, full of plans for the coming mission—as they awaited Corrado's response and instructions—they made their way back to the ship.

The balmy afternoon air was darkening and most ships in port had lit up as their crews loaded and offloaded cargo. But when they reached their ship, there were no lights. And the ship's cranes were silent. No one was lifting pallets of crates from the ship's hold, and no bustling crew worked the cluttered deck. No one wielded the ubiquitous mops and brushes.

"Wait," Franco said as they stood on the gangplank. "Something's wrong." He drew the Beretta from under his coat, while Tranelli clutched his sheathed Vatican blade close.

"We have to go, Franco," said the priest. "We must see what's happened—and we have belongings to collect. The stones—they were sent back to Europe to fund the escape plans, I suspect. But we mustn't lose them!"

"There's more to worry about than the diamonds, old man!" Franco felt panic beginning to choke him. He started up the swinging gangplank at a run, followed much more slowly by the Jesuit.

When he reached the main deck entrance, Franco looked around and saw no one at first.

The priest reached him, breathing hard.

"Where is everyone?"

Franco shook his head slowly. "I don't know, but they should be here."

They made their way to the superstructure and to one of the main hatches, entering the quietly humming vessel's inner space. "Listen," said Franco. "The boilers are very low." The typical throb of the engines was missing.

The long corridor was vacant. Then they entered the crew's mess hall.

It was a slaughterhouse.

Blood covered the deck and had been splattered on the bulkheads seemingly by the bucketful.

But there were no bodies.

By now Franco was also holding his Vatican blade, for they knew what they faced.

"*Dio mio*," whispered the priest, making the sign of the cross.

"God won't help them now, father."

"We can pray."

"Later."

They stepped down the corridor, surprised at the lack of blood. But then the crew's quarters yielded what they sought.

A dozen of the crew had been butchered here, where there was both blood and human remains. Their bellies had been torn open, the entrails pulled out and left partially consumed in grotesque mounds. Their throats chewed open, their heads then ripped from their torsos. Ragged limbs with jagged bone protrusions littered the deck, which was awash with more blood.

Breathing hard, they climbed the metal ladder to the upper deck, where they found the officers' mess and quarters in the same shape. Here was their old table opponent Kamil, his body chewed to pieces. His pig-eyes shut for good. Others with whom they had become friendly. Tranelli stifled a sob. These men were hardy and companionable and hadn't deserved such butchery.

They steeled themselves and climbed one more ladder, cautiously and as quietly as possible, though their shoes clanged on the steel grating steps.

But there was no one alive on the bridge, either.

The officer Milos Havlik was dead, decapitated and his head mounted on the ship's wheel like an obscene ornament.

Captain Nepovim had fought them. His body was crumpled in a corner of the bridge, mostly intact, a severed hand still holding the Russian Tokarev pistol he had apparently emptied into his attackers. His head was missing, but they saw that it had been hoisted on the aerial outside the wheelhouse.

For the tenth time, Tranelli made the sign of the cross and muttered a prayer.

A useless prayer, Franco thought.

Then he froze as if he'd been struck by lightning.

Caterina!

He must have been sluggish from the food and wine, and then in shock by what they had found, for he hadn't thought of her until now.

Heedless of Tranelli's entreaties as he followed, Franco raced down the metal ladders, abandoning all attempts at stealth as he made for her cabin.

The door was ajar, blood splashed on it in a pattern that made it seem artful. Inside, more blood coated every surface, as in the crew's mess hall.

Franco shouted her name over and over, but there was no answer. Her adjoining cabin was similarly arrayed with recently-spilled blood, but no body or body parts were to be found.

Tranelli dragged the boy out into the corridor and slapped him hard on the cheek.

Immediately Franco's features hardened in rage. Tears came, but they were no longer a boy's tears of loss. They were tears of frustrated hate and anger.

"I swear right now I will get the bastard who did this." His fists were white with the intensity of his clenching the pistol and the dagger.

"That may be, my boy," said the priest, "but now we had better leave. This place will be swarming with police when someone realizes no cargo is moving. We don't want to be caught as murderers, or...perhaps caught by the murderer if he returns, or is still here."

Franco nodded. His reason was returning and what Tranelli said made sense.

They made haste of retrieving as much of their inherited stock of belongings as they could, then took one more quick detour. It was Franco's idea, and they climbed the decks back to the bridge.

Tranelli stood guard as Franco ransacked the storage lockers and map drawers, carefully avoiding the lumps of meat that had recently been human. But he stared at Havlik's head on the wheel and the officer's open, startled eyes, which seemed to follow him in his quest. Finding nothing except nautical items, he then searched the captain's body, checking under the thick seaman's coat. He took Nepovim's papers and passport, several full magazines for the Tokarev, as well as the money Franco had given him—apparently the captain had kept it on his person the entire trip. Then, grimacing, he pried the pistol itself from the captain's severed hand and pocketed it.

Tranelli was waving at him to hurry, but he didn't seem panicked.

Franco turned and spotted the door at the rear of the bridge—on a hunch he opened it and found the captain's cabin. It was masculine, Spartan, and well-kept, a paneled chamber with a small private head, a wider bunk than average, and a full wardrobe. But what caught Franco's attention was the desk. He pried the drawers open with a letter opener and caught his breath.

There was more money, both Argentine peso and American dollar banknotes, which he pocketed quickly. And there was a captain's log and a ledger. Plus, there was a sheaf of notes with columns of names and addresses.

"Hurry!" Tranelli called out into the bridge. "I see police lights."

Who had called the police?

Hurriedly he scooped up the cash, books, and documents, and raced out to where Tranelli was almost jumping out of his skin. They were still far away, but he saw blue flashing lights in the distance, getting closer. It would take them a little while to reach the ship on the crowded pier. They walked as fast as they dared down the open stairs, several decks, and then down the gangplank.

Before long they were losing themselves in a crowd of bustling workers.

Caterina, Franco thought. *Murdered.*

Or...murderer?

After taking rooms at a waterfront pensión, they set off to find the nearby addresses. As they expected, they were soon back in La Boca district, where the nightlife was vibrant and music from the storefront *cantinas* clashed with their grimness. The second on the list was a private dwelling, a narrow three-story limestone building sandwiched between two much larger tenements with colorful balconies.

Franco knew they had found at least one safehouse when they watched a man in a dark jacket with a hat pulled down low wait at the door as someone inside checked him out, then allowed him to enter.

Seething with rage, Franco promised they would pay that place a visit.

Father Tranelli countered, "It would be best if we first just follow anyone who leaves there and see where they go."

When the door opened some time later, while they watched from a dingy coffee shop, two people left—a man and a woman.

And though they were too far to see well, Franco thought the woman was Caterina Cavalli, wearing man's clothes and with her face hidden.

He rushed from the shop, furious.

Father Tranelli

Tranelli made the sign of the cross. He sensed there were forces swirling about them that neither understood. And he sensed that there were more Nazi werewolves here than they had expected.

He gripped the dagger in his pocket and set off after the reckless youth. The aura of danger threatened to smother him, and he prayed for guidance.

But none came.

A shadow moved in his wake.

Chapter Thirty-Three

Corrado

He let himself into the storage space office. It wasn't unusual for Ari to ask him to meet on short notice, but they'd never met here.

Inside the door, he stood in the near dark and surveyed the stacks of file boxes and the rows of file cabinets. He couldn't help remembering the many years of struggle. *Giovanni, Franco, Tranelli, Caterina…*names from the past.

He was melancholy.

He was careless.

At first he didn't notice the shape of a body lying near the rear of the unit, behind a small pyramid of cardboard banker's boxes piled behind the desk at which he and Lupo had sat. And then suddenly he did.

"Maledetto bastardo!" he uttered under his breath. "Ari?"

He couldn't see. One hand went to the pistol under his coat, the other went for the light switch.

"Ari?" he said again. His heart sank. He couldn't see any blood, but the shape's splayed out legs and arms told the story. If that was Ari, he was dead.

Corrado stepped forward. Suddenly the thought that he should force a change came to him, and he began his process.

But he had been distracted. He hadn't checked the shadows in the corners behind him.

The cold round shape of a gun barrel touched his neck and scorched him, and as he began whirling around the pistol barked once. Twice.

Corrado was flung toward the desk, the slugs burning like lightning bolts.

He fell across the surface, knocking off the blotter and stacks of folders as he rolled on his side and fell off. He slid down beside the gray metal and lay still.

One hand twitched, then stopped moving.

The door opened, then it closed.

DiSanto

He slid the key through the swipe-box and waited for the light to turn green. When it did he pushed it forward, jammed a suitcase in front of the door to keep it open, and kicked a gym bag inside while dragging a large case on rollers with him as he entered.

It was a Residence Inn right near the airport, tucked away just off of South Howell. There was a famous strip club across the busy street, a squat building with a garish, suggestive sign, and otherwise only airport-style industrial buildings, monster gas stations, and shut-down plant nurseries dotted the area.

He stood amongst the mess of his luggage around his feet and surveyed the space he would call home for the foreseeable future.

He sighed.

Even as much as he was already missing home and his kids, he burned with lust and a need as great as that of a drug addict.

Immediately he started to plan his trysts. Would he entertain Heather—and her *friend*—here?

Because nothing says "available" like a sparsely-decorated, generic crackerbox.

Featuring the stench of old cologne and illicit cigarettes, no less.

And bad food badly prepared in the kitchenette.

He sighed again.

Christ, what was he thinking? His wife would gut him in court. He'd never see his kids again. He'd be lucky if they didn't kick him off the force for one reason or another. All he had to do was screw up once, big time.

And Lupo would most certainly tear him a new one when he found out.

He sat on the edge of the lumpy bed and fought off tears.

Welcome to your new home.

Lupo

He climbed out of his Mustang, rather more tenderly than he liked, and was waiting for Barton when the DHS agent reached the car. It was a dented Buick Century in that champagne shade that made it practically invisible.

Barton was walking with his head down, but when he raised his head and saw Lupo standing there he stopped on the sidewalk. They faced each other silently for a few minutes.

Lupo said nothing. He was still hurting from his cuts, scrapes, and burns, but he felt like he had all day.

"Man, Detective, you look like shit," Barton said finally.

Lupo still said nothing, but his gaze was direct.

"So I guess you followed me?" Barton said, breaking the eye contact.

Backing down.

"Uh uh," said Lupo. "Didn't have to. Put a tracker on your car. You shouldn't use your unofficial cars more than once."

Barton squinted at him. "Have lots of experience with that, do you?"

Lupo chuckled. "I might."

"I heard you had a spot of trouble." He made a show of examining Lupo's face. "Apparently."

"Ah, nothing I couldn't deal with." *With lots of help.* Lupo changed the subject. "I assume you found the bus shooter. And he's no longer a threat."

"I hear that might be the case." Barton looked around nervously.

Lupo made a fake laugh noise. "So your task force is done? Mission accomplished. You'll be moving on?"

"Maybe. There's some cleaning up to do, or there will be after we're officially informed of the outcome."

"What about my dad's old friend, Corrado? What about him? Does he get pulled, too?"

"I'm afraid I don't—"

"Cut the crap, Barton. You know damn well who I mean. You and he have been like vultures hovering over me long enough. And there's somebody else, I think, but I haven't figured it out yet."

"Vultures?" Barton's eyes were slits. "You don't know the half of it. If anything we've been your guardian angels…"

"So now you suddenly know who he is."

Barton made a wave-off gesture. "Listen, if you knew the overall picture, if you had any idea of the stakes…"

"Then why keep me in the dark?" Lupo said with a growl that came from more than just him. The Creature was back, awake and alert, and more than able to come out and play. "Why not deal me in, if I'm close enough to the game to get burned?"

"It's not my call, Lupo. I wish it was. I'm just a soldier." He edged toward the car.

"So that's it? You take out the bus guy all Clint Eastwood-like and slink away?"

"Live to fight another day. Isn't that what you do?" Barton climbed into the Buick, ground the starter, and rolled down the window. "I were you, I'd get the fuck out of this area. You don't want to be around when the shit blows up."

"Tell me, what did the bus shooter have to do with me? Come on, Barton, give me something."

Barton looked through him for a second, as if he were surveying an open field in the distance.

Then he decided. "He wasn't directly involved in *this*, but Wolfpaw mercs killed his entire squad over there. He was the only survivor. We know they killed a shitload of natives, but there aren't so many instances of them murdering our troops. This was a bad one, and he could have helped prosecute, but of course it was…uh…wolves, wolf-related, however you wanna put it. Wouldn't have been easy. Plus it was too much trauma. The whole fucking thing drove him over the edge. Imagine the PTSD the poor bastard suffered."

"And you were here because…?"

Barton tapped his hand on the window frame, as if counting out time. "Look, I was supposed to hunt down this stone killer before he shot up another bus or a train or a mall, but face it, what could we do with him in court? He would have raved about werewolves everywhere. Statements would have been taken, reports filed, stories written. Nobody would have wanted him alive. They'd have killed him in custody."

"Yeah, this was definitely more humane." Lupo made a face. "A real show of justice."

"No different from you, Lupo. No different from anything you've done. At least I can face it honestly." He put the car in gear and roared away, leaving Lupo standing on the sidewalk looking at the taillights.

"He's got a point," Ghost Sam said from where he was standing a few feet away, on the curb.

"Shut up, Sam."

He headed for his car.

Barton was right.

But I don't have to fucking like it.

Epilogue

General Johnston

Alpha Bunker
Somewhere in...

The General didn't appreciate cooling his heels like this, sitting in a luxuriously-appointed waiting room meant to make him forget it was just that, a waiting room.

He didn't like the lack of respect. Didn't they realize that, now Lansing was dead, it was he, General Johnston, who headed the Wolfclaw group? The drone command facility had been moved at the last minute, so when those civilian idiots blew it up, it was already abandoned and the drone-grabbing software was already running on different systems. They were still able to commandeer DoD drone squadrons, but now the operation would be run from Alpha Bunker, a spectacular vertical cylinder dug deep into the ground where even a nuclear weapon detonated on its roof couldn't make more than a dent—a technology gift from the original Paperclip scientists before they'd been snatched away by the United States. Little had the damned Allies known how many of these supposedly meek scientists were also members of an elite group officially a part of the Werwolf Division, a group tasked with infiltrating

American and British walks of life at all levels. It had been a perfect little Trojan Horse, a final gift from the Third Reich. A preparation for the Fourth.

General Johnston muttered and thumped the fine leather armchair under his hands. This was getting ridiculous!

The sideboard held a raft of top-shelf bottles, so he mixed himself a solid gin and tonic and sipped it while he continued to wait.

He was eager to get Wolfclaw completely back on line, but it was the leadership in Alpha Bunker who held the purse-strings. Those investments many decades ago had multiplied exponentially and now the Wall Street barons who were more than what they appeared to be controlled a fortune that could bankrupt all but the largest economies, and the mercenary armies at their beck and call could keep it all together for the final conquest of unimaginable consequences for the human race.

Slaves, that was what they would become, slaves to toil for the glory of their betters. Slaves to feed their betters.

He swirled the alcohol and ice in his glass. Drank it down, then mixed himself a second.

Just like them, keeping him waiting. He muttered a curse. He needed to get back to their new quarters, where the rest of the Wolfclaw survivors waited for the go-ahead.

The door at one end of the long room opened quietly.

"Finally!" Johnston said, unable to help himself. He waited, but no one came out to greet him. He set the drink back on the sideboard and approached the open door.

Ah, this is more like it!

The Great Man himself was behind the vast desk, empty save for a computer monitor and low-rise keyboard.

"Welcome, Herr General, welcome. It is my distinct pleasure to have you here, to see for yourself the progress we have made and that which the newest generation will be handed." The Great Man smiled. The lycanthropy had indeed lengthened his life to an impossible age—over a hundred ten—yet he looked to be barely seventy. The gene had done well with him, and his offspring.

Where it hadn't done well was his eyes. The General looked into them now and it was like opening a spyhole into the depths of hell itself. When the Great Man opened his thin lips, it was even worse.

Suddenly the General felt his solid footing here slipping. A thin sheen of sweat began to tickle his brow and upper lip.

"It is my pleasure also to inform you of the next phase of our master plan." The Great Man's English had improved over the years, and even though it was still accented it was now eminently more understandable than the first time he had heard it. He had been a mere captain, then. Now he sat here, a full general, and instead of feeling a sense of pride he found that his stomach was beginning to flutter.

"Yes, I had hoped we would have some direction to take us forward," Johnston said tentatively. Despite the setbacks with the drones, Wolfclaw had done well. Hadn't they?

The Great Man wagged a thin finger. "Hmn, some direction would have been advisable earlier, no?"

"I'm not sure—"

"Some direction would have not resulted in the use of the drones for so unworthy a target. We nurtured the Wolfclaw group for future plans, not for, hmn, playing games."

The general was sweating profusely now. The Great Man was still smiling, however, so he tried to calm his breathing.

Damn that Lansing, he always was a hot-head. He had leap-frogged Wolfclaw too far, and now he wasn't around to take the heat. The general stiffened in his seat.

The Great Man continued smiling, and it was the most frightening thing he had ever seen.

"Why do you think the Wolfclaw group was undermined? And who do you think gave the order? Lansing became, hmn, a liability and he forced our hand much sooner than we had planned." He pushed a button on a keypad.

The door through which the general had come opened again silently and two burly attendants entered. They took up positions on either side of the general.

And a voice came from a hidden speaker: "Jawohl!"

To Johnston: "There are consequences." To the voice on the speaker: "Take General Johnston into the punishment room. We have already heard the evidence against him. This meeting is a formality. Verdict is guilty."

It took some seconds for the general to comprehend, and when understanding dawned, his face turned a pasty white.

"No, please! I was against it!" he shouted, wheedling. "It was Lansing, he forced us to follow him. He was crazy! We have been religious about following directives from your..."

The burly guards waited patiently until he rose of his own volition. Though he was reluctant, he had no doubt they would have dragged him. His breath came faster now, and the sheen on his brow returned.

"You are to go with them now," said the Great Man. "Perhaps you will learn something. You are, hmn, dismissed."

Johnston walked with them because he did not want their arms on his elbows, in case he decided to try and make a break for it. But surely there would be no need...? Surely, they had served their master well over the years? Surely that should count for something?

He clung to the hope that all could be resolved with a small punishment, perhaps a fine, or at worst a demotion.

But when the guards steered him into the other room, General Johnston's knees went weak, suddenly turning to rubber. The guards grasped him and held him steady with rock-solid arms. Now he understood why this was the punishment room, and he lost hope. Not only hope. *All is lost.*

What he saw shook even him: several werewolves were in the act of devouring the bodies of his fellow Wolfclaw members.

And some were still alive.

There on the slick floor dotted with drains was General LaPorte, his belly ripped open and entrails spilling out in grotesque chains. He whimpered as two slavering snouts dug into the cavity, shredding his still-living flesh and bone. And there, in the center was General Pedersen's head, kicked to the side like an unwanted soccer ball, his headless body nearby. Two wolves were lapping up the blood that had leaked from the stumps at both ends.

Then Johnston struggled against the grip in which he was held, but it was too late.

The last thing General Johnston knew was when a huge wolf landed on his shoulders and squashed his head between its massive jaws. He might have lived past the wolf's ripping and sawing, but he did not live past the moment his head was ripped off the rest of his torso. The wolf swallowed quickly to drink as much of the other werewolf's blood as he could, then he turned his attention to the torso's belly.

The feeding continued as the last of the punishments was meted out.

In the anteroom, the Great Man watched and listened on his personal channel. The sounds of gluttony continued at length.

Occasional punishments were just the ticket to relieve some of the boredom created by the bureaucratic shuffle of the new order's needs.

He licked his thin lips, then used them to smile.

Lupo

Jessie stepped out of the Mustang and again he marveled at how this earthy, outdoorsy woman who made his life bearable could look so much like a movie star when she chose to.

She was wearing a shimmering low-cut gown of aquamarine and heels a mile high, and she looked like she belonged on a red carpet anywhere in the world. The late winter was being kind, and she didn't need a coat—though he had one in the car for her—and she turned and smiled at him as he held the door. She wore her makeup expertly, eyelids matching the dress and a classic red on her lips, and he knew without looking that everyone nearby had turned to look at her as she walked into the central precinct on his arm.

She was smiling, happy for once, and he felt the electricity of her touch where their hands joined together.

He knew and she knew how close they had come to losing each other, and she had somehow forgiven him his little faux pas, not having informed her he was heading north. He had lied a little, saying it was a surprise and he was planning to clean up the cabin and take her there, but he knew she probably didn't believe him.

Nevertheless, they had celebrated their renewed love with a long session of intimate therapy.

And she hadn't once mentioned becoming a werewolf, relieving him of the pressure.

He remembered to limp a little, but some of this limp wasn't artificial at all. She walked slowly for him, and he put his hand on her back, wishing he could slide it lower but keeping it classy.

Tonight Ryeland was making good on his threat and presenting Sergeant Danni Colgrave with a commendation and, it was rumored, also a promotion.

As Lupo and Jessie reached the main doors and passed into the high marble foyer of the police headquarters building, Lupo noted that many officers and their families had already gathered. There was DiSanto, but he was alone. There was Barton — they nodded curtly. Ryeland was beaming, stepping from group to group and pressing the flesh for the photographers, with a chagrined Colgrave in tow.

She looked great, too. Not at all like a woman who had just shot a fuckin' helicopter out of the sky. She wore a long silver dress and her dark hair was piled on her head and she winked at him when they passed. Colgrave and Jessie touched hands — what signal there?

And then Lupo spotted Lieutenant Roman.

Roman was alone, of course, lurking on the edge of the crowd, staring at everyone. At Lupo and Jessie. At Colgrave. At Barton. At DiSanto...

Lupo knew that DiSanto had started doing some careful checking on Roman's past. Right this moment, Lupo hoped DiSanto hadn't raised a cloud of mud — and called attention to himself, because Roman was definitely giving him the creeps.

Then he spotted Marla Anders, and she was also smiling at him. Weirdly, he thought he glimpsed Ghost Sam at her side. Considering that he thought Sam's ghost was only in his mind, this was disconcerting at best.

A whispering voice out of the crowd intruded on Lupo's ear.

"I know what you are, and what you did, and I'm watching you."

Lupo whirled, careful not to let Jessie notice his distress, but there was no one there. Or maybe it was Roman, who was just disappearing among the uniforms as they formed into ranks, ready for the presentation.

Lupo gripped Jessie's hand harder, and she returned his squeeze. Her face was radiant.

But his thoughts had darkened.

Nothing's ever over.

Meet the Author

W.D. Gagliani is the author of the horror-thrillers *Wolf's Trap* (a finalist for the Bram Stoker Award in 2004), *Wolf's Gambit*, *Wolf's Bluff*, *Wolf's Edge*, *Wolf's Cut*, *Wolf's Blind*, and *Savage Nights*, plus the novellas *Wolf's Deal* and both the original "The Great Belzoni and the Gait of Anubis" and the upcoming Acheron Books version. He has published fiction and nonfiction in numerous anthologies and publications such as *Robert Bloch's Psychos*, *Fearful Fathoms*, *Undead Tales*, *More Monsters From Memphis*, *The Midnighters Club*, *Extremes 3: Terror On The High Seas*, *Extremes 4: Darkest Africa*, and others, and early e-zines such as *Wicked Karnival*, *Horrorfind*, *1000Delights*, *Dark Muse*, and *The Grimoire*. His fiction has garnered six Honorable Mentions in *The Year's Best Fantasy & Horror* (one of which, the story "Starbird," is also part of Amazon's Story Front program). His book reviews and nonfiction articles have been included in *The Milwaukee Journal Sentinel*, *Chizine*, *HorrorWorld*, *Cemetery Dance*, *CD Online*, *The Writer* magazine, *The Scream Factory*, *Science Fiction Chronicle*, *Flesh & Blood*, *BookPage*, *Hellnotes*, and many others, plus the books *Thrillers: The 100 Must Reads*, *They*

Bite, and *On Writing Horror*. He is a member of the Horror Writers Association (HWA), the International Thriller Writers (ITW), and the Authors Guild. Additionally, the creative team of **W.D. Gagliani & David Benton** has published fiction in anthologies such as *THE X-FILES: Trust No One, SNAFU: An Anthology of Military Horror, SNAFU: Wolves at the Door, Dark Passions: Hot Blood 13, Zippered Flesh 2, Malpractice, Masters of Unreality*, etc., online venues such as *The Horror Zine, DeadLines* and *SplatterpunkZine*, plus the Amazon Kindle Worlds *Vampire Diaries* tie-in "Voracious in Vegas." Some of their collaborations are available in the collection *Mysteries & Mayhem*.

Contact:

www.wdgagliani.com
www.facebook.com/wdgagliani
Twitter: @WDGagliani

Books and Novellas:

Wolf's Trap
Wolf's Gambit
Wolf's Bluff
Wolf's Edge
Wolf's Cut
Wolf's Blind
Wolf's Deal
Savage Nights
Shadowplays (Tarkus Press; story collection)
Mysteries & Mayhem (Tarkus Press; story collection, *with David Benton*)
I Was a Seventh Grade Monster Hunter (Tarkus Press; Middle Grade, *with David Benton*, as A.G. Kent)

"The Great Belzoni and the Gait of Anubis" (Tarkus Press; novella)
"Jack Daniels and Associates: Hair of the Dog" (Kindle Worlds Novella; A Jack Daniels / Nick Lupo Thriller)

Curious about other Crossroad Press books? Stop by our
website: http://crossroadpress.com
We offer quality writing
in digital, audio, and print formats.

Subscribe to our newsletter on the website homepage and
receive a free eBook.

www.ingramcontent.com/pod-product-compliance
Lightning Source LLC
Chambersburg PA
CBHW021447240626
47153CB00001B/339